SHIMMER CHINODYA was born in Gweru in 1957 and educated at the University of Zimbabwe, where he studied literature and education. He later atten... the famed Iowa Writers' Workshop, where h... in creative writing. *Dew in* ..., written when he was ninetee... went on to write *Farai's G...* ...nd *Harvest of Thorns* (1989). ...mmonwealth Writers' Prize for the Afri... ...0. His collection of short stories, *Can we ta...*, was shortlisted for the first Caine Prize for short-story writing in Africa.

Chinodya has worked extensively as a curriculum developer, materials designer, editor and screen writer. He has been awarded various fellowships abroad and from 1995 to 1997 was the Distinguished Visiting Professor in creative writing at St Lawrence University, New York. He lives with his wife and family in Harare.

SHIMMER CHINODYA

DEW IN THE MORNING

Heinemann

Heinemann Educational Publishers
Halley Court, Jordan Hill, Oxford OX2 8EJ
A Division of Reed Educational & Professional Publishing Ltd

Heinemann: A Division of Reed Publishing (USA) Inc.
361 Hanover Street, Portsmouth, NH 03801–3912, USA

Heinemann Publishers (Pty) Limited
PO Box 781940, Sandton 2146, Johannesburg, South Africa

OXFORD   MELBOURNE   AUCKLAND
JOHANNESBURG   BLANTYRE   GABORONE
IBADAN   PORTSMOUTH (NH) USA   CHICAGO

© Shimmer Chinodya 2001

First published by Mambo Press in 1982
This edition published by Heinemann Educational Publishers in 2001

British Library Cataloguing in Publication Data
A catalogue record for this book is available from the British Library.

Cover design by Touchpaper
Cover illustration by Anne Simone Hutton
Author photograph by Stella Nova

Phototypeset by SetSystems Ltd, Saffron Walden, Essex
Printed and bound in Great Britain by
Cox and Wyman Ltd, Reading, Berkshire

ISBN 0 435 91206 2

01 02 03 04 05 06 10 9 8 7 6 5 4 3 2 1

Introduction

Dew in the Morning was first published in 1982, less than two years after Zimbabwean independence. The cover note on the first edition promised readers 'Work and life and tales of the country . . . a breath of fresh country air', which encouraged us to read the book as a series of charming if inconsequential anecdotes. Several readers, however, saw the first edition as a more substantial achievement than the blurb implied. When Doris Lessing, one of the novel's most famous admirers, heard that it was being republished, she recalled the novel's 'fresh and lyrical writing by a man remembering a country childhood so strongly that you would believe you were there too'. But she added that 'village life has its dark side and Chinodya does not shrink from describing it. I read it nearly twenty years ago and have not forgotten it.' The dark side of village life and the 'breath of fresh country air' are difficult to reconcile, but these different responses can be partly explained by recalling the expectations in the early years of Independence of what Zimbabwean writing should affirm. The country was only two years away from the Liberation War, and any war simplifies the competing ideologies that inspire the warring sides. In an anti-colonial war, nationalism as an absolute good pits itself against imperialism as an absolute evil. The novels in English that an independent Zimbabwe celebrated were those such as Wilson Katiyo's *A Son of the Soil* (1973), which became an O level set-book, or Edmund Chipamaunga's *A Fighter for Freedom* (1983). Both belong to the familiar genre of decolonization narratives that erase divisions of ethnicity or class as the colonized people of the text discover a common will to overthrow the enemy. Such narratives have a value in providing the myth of unity without which the nation can never discover its larger self. At some point after Independence, however, any nation has to confront its own heterogeneity. If nationalism does not acknowledge and accommodate difference, it will invoke an invented, homogeneous culture to identify and punish whatever it designates as deviance.

The colonialists associated cities and settled-controlled space with progress and the rural areas with backwardness. Nationalism responded to this myth by locating the spirit of resistance among rural people, who were able to resist because they had remained true to tradition and all over the world nationalist writing valorizes rural people. In this respect at any rate, a casual reading makes *Dew in the Morning* a conventional nationalist text. Colonialism has made country and town sites of equal economic significance and the narrator, Godi Wamambo, accords them this equivalence: '[In town] Father spent the day on his feet, his workshirts slightly torn under the armpits, selling clothes . . . [while] Mother spent the day weeding, and pacing the fields in her tattered gumboots, defending her precious crops.' But the text does not extend that parallelism to allow town and country an equivalent human significance. Chinodya's prose gives the countryside a sensuous immediacy, through detailed descriptions that possess the authority of close observation. These details are most obviously present in the descriptions of crops, but they also make accessible to the reader the hostility of the countryside – the dead cow whose belly is torn open by a hyena, ghosts, witchcraft or the ceremony to smell out witches. By contrast, a minimalist prose describes the town, and a set of discrete, disconnected items makes it a place of alienation. The father sleeps alone in a double bed, his radio has no battery and newspapers take the place of the lively gossip of the village. If the mother and children grow into an organic relationship with their fields, the father relates to the town and his job intellectually. Only when he returns briefly to the village does he become a vital presence in the text as he cultivates the family's fields. The countryside may offer a fuller humanity to the family than the town is able to do, but the novel does not translate this into an authentic rural culture that opposes the corrupt syncretism of the city. This apparent failure to consolidate the nationalist project made *Dew in the Morning*'s early nationalist readers uneasy.

In fact, the novel records an important moment in the politics of Zimbabwean nationalism. Chinodya does not identify the area in which the novel is set – it could be any district in the northern Zimbabwean midlands. In the 1950s, as the population pressure on the southern reserves such as Chivi and Gutu became unsustainable, people were moved to places such as Silobela, Zhombe and finally the northern parts of Gokwe. This movement of people coincided with the Land Husbandry Act through which the settler government attempted to regulate the number of people on the land by instituting strict agricultural management. The Act required that local authorities rigorously demarcate areas for grazing, cropping and homesteads. Behind the Act was a more radical re-imagining of the place of blacks in Rhodesia. They were no longer to be temporary sojourners in the settler cities: some would constitute a black proletariat whose members had no claim on the land and who from now on would be people of the city. Over the years, the knowledge that in some rural area there was a place of refuge to which they could return when city life became intolerable helped to mitigate the multiple insecurities colonialism induced in the Zimbabwean people, especially those who lived in town. The Act denied whole populations this rural refuge. The areas from which people were moved and the new areas which they were colonizing became as an almost direct result the heart of the new nationalist politics. Because the city populations were involved in the consequences of crowded reserves, they had no difficulty in finding common cause with the rural areas.

At first reading in a novel set in Rhodesia, white settlers are an unexpected absence. In fact, the signs of both their presence and their power are ubiquitous, from the towns themselves to details of clothing and the parents' obsession with their children's education so that they have colonialism's tools to confront the colonial order. The novel mentions the colonial government, however, only when it arranges to bring in new settlers from the south, the so-called *derukas*. Equally noteworthy is the complete absence of confrontation with colonial rule. The *derukas* certainly oppose the plan to move them from their 'densely populated region' where the 'soil [is] old and overworked . . . into the remote virgin land in the north to give the denuded region a chance to become green again' but their opposition is short-lived. Even the impression of benevolence behind the movement from sterility to fecundity is immediately contradicted: 'eventually, after much persuasion, they agreed to destroy their homes, leave their deceased kin's graves and their fatherland and move into the new land'. The stridency of popular nationalist narrative is absent here but this is not writing that is politically unaware. Within this passage two phrases stand out: 'The government had observed the area with a wary eye' and 'it was decided to move people'. Colonialism is always a system of unequal power relations and power resides firmly with the wary, alert government. The casual passive voice suggests that there is no need to identify the final power that decides that the *derukas* should move. Persuasion and agreement are mere euphemisms for coercion. Chinodya's writing makes evident an unequal balance of power, but it also conveys an unequal balance of emotion. The government's surveillance is detached, and the *derukas*' lands are as remote from government as are the virgin lands remote from the *derukas*; the re-greening of the *derukas*' ancestral lands is mere chance, finally a matter of indifference to government. For the *derukas*, however, the move involves something akin to death: the destruction of houses, the desertion of ancestral graves – they are being uprooted from their very fatherland. Nuance has replaced the stridency of polemic.

The novel ends with the burial of Jairos, the former headman, and a bloody package associated with witchcraft lies on the grave. Whether this is for good or evil is not disclosed since it is something 'that no one dared to touch or describe'. Instead, the mourners move from the grave 'to go home to prepare for Christmas'. The silence, the withholding of explanation, is a typical trope within the novel. The unexplained package denies Jairos' burial the ritually satisfying restoration of a man to his ancestral soil, although Jairos is one of the few characters in the novel whose ancestors preceded him on this land. In the same way, we cannot read Christmas as an explicating closure, a Christian feast whose unambiguous meanings are set in comforting opposition to the arcane and fearful beliefs of the rural people. Christmas does not have a stable meaning any more than the soil does. In the early chapters, Christmas marks the passing of the years but it is a profoundly securalized Christmas, less significant than other rituals observed during the year. Godi notes when his father holds a Christmas service during the family's first Christmas that the people attend out of politeness, 'thinking that the Bible account of the birth of Jesus was a superb folk-story'. Shortly after that Christmas, a rain-maker is brought to the village and the ceremony during which she is possessed and her spirit diagnoses the causes of the drought touches the people's lives in a way that the Christmas story has not done. When the village observes her prescriptions, rain comes. On the second Christmas, the headman Jairos invents a tradition that newcomers should brew beer to thank the elders for welcoming them into the community. Although the Wamambos belong to a

Christian sect that allows neither drinking nor smoking, Masi-ziva's tact in dealing with her fellow villagers prevails. She gets women to brew beer on her behalf, and the beer rather than his preaching guarantees a large congregation for Mr Wamambo's service. On the third Christmas, Mr Wamambo writes that the burden of raising school fees makes it impossible for him to come to the rural homestead for the holidays. After this there are only casual mentions of the Christian feast until the last lines of the novel. As a holiday of the colonial order, Christmas loses its relevance beside the imperatives of the soil and the agricultural seasons. Christmas, however, is one signifier of the alternative temporal order over which colonialism presides. That time scheme generates alternative economic, legal and educational systems, a larger context of modernity within which the village finally subsists.

Jairos and the invented tradition that newcomers brew beer is only one of several signs that not only do cultures grow and change but also that an invented tradition can be invoked as a mode of control. Jairos does not preside over a benign rural order with the dignity invested by tradition in his office. When the newcomers fail to provide him with gin, he threatens to refuse to allocate them land and, when he does give the Sizivas more land, the fee is 'ten dollars and one hen and one bottle of gin'. Before his death at the end of the novel, his brother has taken over his duties and Jairos, who has been bewitched, wanders around the village, the butt of the children's jokes, scrounging food and messing people's toilets.

If one cannot read *Dew in the Morning* as a conventional nationalist novel, there is a temptation to read it as pastoral, a genre that in the western tradition idealizes the countryside at the expense of the city. At its most satisfying, pastoral alerts the socially complex to the fundamental assumptions of its own being which it has lost sight of. The movement in the novel, however, is a movement away from an urban life in which people are superficially involved in the new economy, towards an engagement initially with nature and then with a complex society which is absent in the town. At the beginning of the novel, the family are pioneers on the frontier of what the father calls 'virgin land' and it is the wilderness that he celebrates. Although he is a man of the town, he wants no more intricate authority than Jairos' headmanship provides. He is unexpectedly a romantic. 'It doesn't matter,' he tells his sons, 'if you are all going to be graduates and live in nice big town houses . . . You can never make a final break from the country.' It is in this spirit that he opposes a rural council raising taxes and even fencing the land. 'Councils will turn the village into a town,' he says. Later we are told of plans to create contour ridges, fence off grazing areas and create a system of careful land management – although these intentions are soon lost amidst both the habit of independence of the villagers and the knowledge they have of how best to use their land. Two different scientific concepts are opposed, for example when Masiziva sees the fenced vlei as nothing more than a breeding ground for mice that will destroy crops.

No concept of land management can accommodate the number of people who want to live on the land. By the end of the novel the wilderness has made way for the 'the reign of the axe and the goats; the axe which opened the forests to the ravishing plough, and the goats, which mushroomed in number and were rarely killed for meat, but served only to create hatred between neighbours'. This is very different from the community Jairos believed that the newcomers would help to create: a paradise of endless beer parties. After ten years of a steady flow of people from the south, there is a 'strain on the land'. The people rather than the government are 'fencing off their compound areas'. More significantly for the fear of landlessness that still haunts

Zimbabwe, farmers are 'already putting pressure on Simon', Jairos' brother, 'to guarantee the availability of land for their teenage sons'.

The naivety of Godi is important to the novel's structure. He registers more than he understands. What he records with neutrality, we experience as deeply unnerving, and this involves both aspects of coercion in the rural culture as well as attempts by the powerless to use illicit spiritual power in order to assume some control over their lives. One of the tropes of silence, of absence, in the novel concerns the death of Masiziva's father. On his deathbed, he asks Masiziva to remove a speck from his eye. If she finds it, he promises her prosperity. She looks for it but cannot find it and as she is looking her father dies. The narrative recalls the incident at several points, most strikingly when the village invites Chikanga the witchfinder to cleanse it of those who are witches or merely dabble in witchcraft. Chikanga knows the story about the speck without being told it and explains that Masiziva, who relies on her own wisdom rather than medicine to protect herself from neighbourly malice, is in fact protected by her father's spirit. Once again, the syncretism of the incident insists on the complexity of contemporary Zimbabwe. The speck recalls Matthew's gospel where Christ admonishes us to look for the beam in our own eye rather than the mote in our neighbour's eye. But Chikanga immediately disavows that Christian reading. 'No one is safe from witchcraft and medicine,' he admonishes Masiziva. 'You may go to church but you must never forsake your deceased father.' Is the Christian reference affirmed only to be immediately displaced? Is the beam in her eye the certainty of her Christian faith which means that she looks with scepticism at the beliefs of rural Zimbabwe? Is Chikanga right in his confident assertion that it is not the Christian god but her father who protects her? Whatever reading or combination of readings we choose, Masiziva is safe and relatively prosperous and yet she never found the speck and her father assured her of his protection only if she found it.

The multiple meanings in this episode introduce the multiple discourses within the witchfinding ceremony itself. Throughout the novel, Mai Mapanga is known as a witch. While the village is small, her malice is contained and her powers are disabled. Witchcraft threatens the village only as it grows and prospers with the hardworking *derukas*. The evil within the community, the 'hatred between neighbours', is a direct consequence, therefore, of colonial land policies. In hunting for signs of witchcraft, Chikanga is not addressing the real evil: the land which the settler authorities have designated as land for exclusive black occupation cannot accommodate the number of people who want to live on it. The ills of the village which manifest themselves in witchcraft are rooted in the insecurities of a rural economy. A woman is childless because she refused to assume the mantle of witch that her grandmother had in life. To be childless in an economy where the family is the unit of production is to be poor. A man who is lazy is accused of drawing the greenness from his neighbours' crops into his own unworked fields and another finally confesses to having bewitched Jairos: 'He gave my field to a newcomer,' is sufficient explanation. Only Mai Mapanga is the classical witch who loves evil for its own sake, who eats human flesh. 'People like her don't die,' says Chikanga. Any discourse is a site of contestation, and the people in this penultimate chapter are potential victims of evil spirits hostile to humanity as much as they are part of a vulnerable peasantry trying to extract a living from overworked land. They could also be the dupes of Chikanga, confidence trickster, who knows how to play on their fears. Chikanga with his Combi and suit, accompanied by pretty young girls, is a product of colonial modernity, not someone whose work is authorized from a pristine tradition. The witch hunt refuses disclosure in the penultimate chapter as much as does Jairos' burial in the final chapter.

Chinodya began this novel during Zimbabwe's Liberation War. It is tempting to recover the text for nationalism by arguing that the unspoken disclosure, the final absence of the novel, exists in fact, in history, outside the novel: the war with its certain enemy and its successful conclusion removed ideological ambiguity from the lives of the Zimbabwean peasantry. Such a reading does not accommodate the carefully sustained ambivalence within the text and indeed within the title. The morning dew suggests a freshness that one can only recall: it is an image of lost innocence and the appropriate title for a novel about childhood. The novel reminds us, however, that dew is the product of the night and is tainted by the night. If morning dew assures nothing else, it assures that night is over. But night and the dews of night will come again. The novel refuses to allow Zimbabwe's past, present or future to resolve its multiple meanings.

Land is an important site on which a romantic nationalism constructs a Zimbabwean identity. A modern economy, however, makes different and competing claims for the land. In two decades the virgin soil of the north has become as crowded as are the lands of the south. The land is unable to continue as a source of both economic and spiritual well-being. The novel shows the discourses of both postcolonial modernity and nationalist tradition unsettling each other, and in that instability our only certainty is that identities and traditions shift constantly as they adjust to new realities.

Anthony Chennells
Associate Professor of English at the University of Zimbabwe

The author has made minor cuts to the text since the first edition.

1

We arrived just before sunset, and by the time we had finished unpacking the lorry it had grown dark and the dew was already falling on the grass. That night the moonlight fell on the village huts and the metal of the lorry gleamed. Everything that had been taken off it lay in a confused heap on the ground.

I could hear my father talking in low tones to the village headman and somewhere an owl hooted. At last we went to sleep. We simply threw mattresses and blankets on the earth and lay down, the big yellow moon above us.

We woke up to a fine blue morning; the doves were cooing and birds heralded the morning:

'*Alu – Alu*
Oro Wani
Alu
Oro Wani
Alu'

Very soon we were running about, finding pleasure in the forest and hacking away at the undergrowth like wood-starved animals with our shiny little axes.

We finally managed to make a rough wooden sledge, on which we took turns to sit and push each other over the sand. Then, needing water to drink, we asked a small boy to direct us to the village pump. He touched his rubber catapult and fingered his fine long bark whip and stared at us.

'We want some water,' said Yona. 'Where is the village pump?'

'You left it behind you,' said the boy in a dialect slightly different from ours.

'Is it far away?' asked Jo.

'No,' said the boy, cracking his whip loudly on the sand. 'You can come with me if you want water.'

We followed him across the clearing towards the closest of three squat huts. Inside a young woman sat dozing in the heat. Thick dark knots of plaited hair covered her head. She had taken off her blouse. A little baby boy nestled in her arms, barely shielding his mother's breasts. The hut was small, and black with the smoke of a thousand fires. The roof was low, black like the walls, and from it dangled axes, cooking sticks, strips of oxhide and other strange objects. The smell of cowdung rose from the newly polished mud-floor, where a three-legged pot lay on its side, cakes of dry sadza on its insides. There were a few dirty plates in disorder on top of a built-in earth shelf, a wooden mortar and a grinding stone. The boy handed us water in a gourd and, while we were drinking, the baby pushed his head into his mother's belly and butted her like a calf. She protested, pushing her nipple into his mouth. He did not suck but plucked his mouth away from her and yelled, leaving a ring of moisture round her nipple.

'Ah! Ah!' she protested again, slapping the boy on the tummy. Then, turning to us, she said, 'Hello. Are you the new family?'

'Yes,' replied Yona. 'How do you do?'

'Thank you for the water,' I said, as we stood to go.

'No need to thank me,' laughed the woman, her white teeth flashing. 'Now, what can you eat? Give them some *mazhanje* from under the granary, Tani.'

'Thank you,' said Yona, 'but we have to go.'

'What! You won't have *mazhanje*? Perhaps you people from towns don't eat fruit. Why? Why? Perhaps your mother does not want you to eat in people's houses. All right then.'

2

I would have liked to eat some fruit, but Yona had already declined, so we had to go. The dwarf hut with its smoke-blackened walls, warm smoky smell and half-dressed occupants gave me a strange sense of freedom. When we were outside Jo started talking to the boy and asked him for his whip.

'But do you have cattle?' asked the boy, giving him the whip.

'We don't herd cattle in town.'

'So you live in town?'

'Yes. We come here only during school holidays.'

'You go to school,' he grimaced. 'Teachers beat people.'

'Not if you do your best.'

'I think they would break my body.'

'Are you going after your cattle now?'

'Yes. I might lose them and they might go off and eat some-body's mealies and then I'd be in trouble.'

'Have you ever lost them?'

'Only once. They ate an old man's crops. He was hiding in a bush. He caught me and whipped me.'

'Oh.'

'Hyenas might also eat cattle.'

'Do hyenas eat people?'

'Only drunk old men with too much mucus in their noses. Hyenas love mucus.'

◆

Before he left for town father found a man to build our huts and instructed the village headman to give us a temporary piece of land to farm.

After four days the huts were finished and we moved into them. We helped mother build a long bench of beaten clay round the inside of one of them and an earthen shelf for the pots and plates. We cleared a square patch round the huts and planted

3

flowers in neat rows. Village women frequently stopped to admire our garden on their way to the water pump.

Jairos, the village headman, came frequently to see us. He was a thin man in his fifties. His head was small and bald, his only hair was his small twisted moustache. He wore khaki clothes normally worn by people in the Civil Service and these were brown with too little washing. He spoke so avidly that whoever listened to him had to steer clear of the globules of saliva that spattered from his mouth. When he smiled, he exposed a fine set of teeth stained grey with four decades of tobacco. He had been introduced to money and gin early on, and would do anything to obtain them. He possessed a sense of dreamy optimism, a belief that things would turn out well no matter how bad they got. He also seemed quite lazy: he would have a little boy to scratch his arm for him if he could. Only a few days after our arrival he had asked me to build a framework for his fowl-run for the small fee of a coin. Mother had laughingly stopped me from displaying any of my expertise.

Jairos was very fond of tea and sugar, bread and margarine. Unfortunately, he could not afford these provisions regularly, so he made himself our guest at mealtimes. He would put as many as twelve spoons of sugar in one cup of tea and when sadza and meat were placed in front of him, he always ate the meat first. Eventually he grew bold enough to serve himself from the pot. One day he brought a young girl with him. He proceeded to occupy an empty chair and rolled himself a cigarette while the girl sat cross-legged on the floor.

'Masiziva,' he said to my mother, 'I have promised so often to show you my daughter. Unfortunately, her mother has been keeping her busy but my conscience has been nagging me, so I decided to bring her over today. Here she is.'

'What is your name, girl?' mother asked with a smile as she put some food in front of Jairos.

4

'Her name is Lucia,' Jairos announced. 'You can call her Lulu.'

Lulu declined to eat. It was bad manners to eat in strangers' homes on the first visit.

'But I thought your oldest girl was married,' said mother, puzzled.

'My oldest girl with my first wife – yes,' explained Jairos, munching away at a bone. 'My first wife died long back, of pneumonia, if you want to know.'

'Does Lulu go to school?'

'Not yet. She will go as soon as I get the money.'

'But when will that be? The years will not be waiting. How old is she?'

'Let's see,' said Jairos, putting down his spoon to ponder. Then, after a pause, 'How old are you, Lulu? What! You don't know how old you are? Come on, tell Masiziva your age.'

'But you don't know yourself, Headman Jairos,' teased mother, 'perhaps she is not your daughter.'

'Oh yes, she is,' Jairos protested. 'Can't you see that she is so much like me? All her features came from me. Only her toes came from her mother. I don't have toes like that!'

'But you still haven't told us when she was born,' persisted mother.

'Oh yes. I remember. She was born when the road from town reached this village. The mealies were tasselling . . .' he said, throwing his bone down in mock exasperation.

My mother answered with a quizzical nod.

Jairos finished eating and I held up a dish of water for him to wash his hands. But when he saw me collecting the dishes to wash outside he looked alarmed.

'What, Masiziva! You make your boys wash dishes?'

'What can I do, Headman Jairos? My girls are still too young.'

'Well, then get a girl to do the washing up. Come on, Lulu, my girl. Help Godi wash Masiziva's dishes.'

In the end Lulu helped me. We worked quietly outside the kitchen, until Jairos took her away.

I met Lulu again at the pump a few days later and she agreed to go picking *mazhanje* with me.

'The forest is dangerous,' sang Jo, when I ran back home to fetch an empty flour bag.

'A man got lost there for a week,' sang Yona.

'We won't get lost, mother. Lulu knows the forest like her mother's hut.'

'All right, just bring us back some fruit,' said my mother.

Just outside the village the fruit lay thickly under the *mazhanje* trees, like brown eggs waiting to be collected, and it pained me to think that a lot of it would rot on the ground. Lulu knew the delicious trees and we filled our containers from them. Eventually we came to a clear stream where I could see small fish darting about.

Lulu took off her dress and waded in for a swim. I followed slowly. I couldn't swim, so I gulped and choked as I paddled madly like a dog, while she laughed at my antics. Afterwards we lay on the grass drying in the sun and soon fell asleep. When I woke up Lulu was dressing. The sun was low in the sky and the birds were flying to their roosts. I put on my clothes as well. Then we picked up our fruit and hurried home.

◆

As soon as Jairos found us a small plot of land we started planting our crops. Matudu, the man who built our huts, came to plough our field with his fine pair of oxen. We followed behind the plough, dropping seeds into neat brown furrows and savouring the smell of oxen and newly turned earth. The seedlings soon germinated, small and tender in the dew.

We rose early in the blue-grey dawn to the shouts of the

ploughboys and the bustle of yoking up the oxen. We walked across the glistening green, dew-laden grass to the fields. While the sun ascended in the sky, we sweated in the fields. Our backs ached, hot sand burnt our feet, and the hoe-handles drew blisters. We drank *maheu*, worked again, then went home for a late breakfast at noon, when we usually met the herd boys bringing the cows home to be milked.

Usually we returned to the fields late in the afternoon, when it was cool, to put in a few more hours of work. Then after supper we read for an hour or two in the lamplight before going to bed. The nights were short it seemed. Dawn came soon with mother, hoe in hand, rapping on our door.

To break our regular routine, we decided to go fishing on Thursdays and Sundays. Then we sat on the bank of the stream pushing worms onto our hooks before we threw the lines into the water. For hours we sat watching our corks for promising ripples. But the fish did not bite. By sunset, we had still caught nothing. The frogs started croaking from the reeds.

'Go –
Go –
Go –
Go home.
Go home.
You've – caught – no – fish
No – fish – '

We collected our things and hurried home, sunset upon us. There was no moon on that occasion and darkness fell quickly, so that we strained our eyes to see the path. We found mother waiting for us anxiously at the village pump.

'What are you doing at the stream after sunset? Don't you know you can drown? And walking in the darkness too – don't you know there are snakes and hyenas here? I'll have to stop you from going to the river if you do this again. How much have you caught anyway?'

Twice more we failed to catch any fish. Each time we went to the river in high spirits, mother having convinced us that it was the best weather for fishing. All day we sat quietly, watching the water and hoping. A dirty old man in rags often fished beside us. We watched him enviously while he hooked fish after fish from the stream. In the end we felt that the stream was favouring the old man because he was old and poor. Eventually he asked us to show him one of our lines. He took it between his long, uncut fingernails, adjusted the cork and gave me back the line.

Feverishly, I pushed a fresh worm onto the hook and threw the line into the water. Almost immediately, the cork darted forward.

'Pull,' said the old man.

I felt the weight on the hook and whipped the line out of the water. The fish broke out of the stream and flew towards me, its silver skin shining in the sun. It was only a small fish, but big enough to make us wild with joy. Jo rushed to where it flapped on the grass. He lifted it between his finger and thumb and danced with joy, while the old man's face broke into a toothless smile.

Yona and Jo had their hooks adjusted too and we went home carrying a tin heavy with fish and were heroes that evening. Mother thought that the old man must have given them to us.

◆

Our mother had warned us about snakes and hyenas, and we soon understood why, when she spotted a huge black mamba while she was clearing a patch of ground for sweet potatoes. She screamed, threw down her hoe and ran, stumbling in her gumboots.

8

A man passing by heard her scream and came hurriedly towards us. After a rapid glance, he gave a low whistle. Then he cursed the snake as if to disarm it, and picked up a thick stick. As he inched forward, I felt my whole body shaking. I wanted to hide my fingers. The snake was a cool glimmering black. Thick as a child's leg, it had yellow beady eyes that seemed too small for its body.

I was beginning to hope it was dead, when it made a slight movement as if readying itself to strike. But the man was too quick for it. His stick came down again and again with a sound like wood hitting rubber till at last, squeaking like a giant mouse, the snake rolled into a bloodless death.

That same morning, when we had scarcely recovered from the shock, Lulu came breathlessly to tell us that hyenas had attacked and killed one of her father's cows which was about to calve.

The attack had occurred deep in the forest, under the great, shadowy trees. We saw the mutilated remains of the cow. Its huge belly had been torn open and was almost empty. The intestines and liver had been eaten and its ribs jutted out like a frame. Its big eyes were open, its pink nose half buried in the earth. I tried to imagine how its belly was pierced and the liquid calf torn out of its womb by sharp carnivorous teeth. Jairos and his family chopped the remains of the animal into sizeable chunks and threw them into the cart, hides and all. Chattering frivolously, they seemed to see the meat as a bonus.

'Half a cartload of meat,' Jairos explained to my mother. 'You can have some of it. We don't charge anything for meat like that.'

Mother shook her head quietly.

◆

Mother was packing our trunks, but had to stop to make Jairos a cup of tea.

'So who will look after your crops while you are away in town, Masiziva?'

'I am only taking the boys to school. I will be back in a week.'

'Bring me some old newspapers for my tobacco and tell your husband to buy me two bottles of gin,' he said.

On the morning of our departure, everything took its normal course, as if we were a negligible part of the village. But somehow the trees seemed taller and greener, the dew glossier on the grass, and I knew nostalgia was descending on us even before we had left.

Lulu came with us to the bus stop, admiring our clothes. I did not think I looked my best. My trousers swept the ground and my white shirt blew into a balloon behind my back. I wanted to tell Lulu that my best clothes had been left in town.

We reached the terminus and eventually a battered old yellow bus arrived. In the flurry of carrying things and the crisis of finding a seat, I forgot to wave goodbye to Lulu.

◆

'It's virgin land,' father kept explaining to the many townsfolk who came to ask about our new country home. 'It's a young land with lots of wide-open space and good soil.'

'I hear there are donkeys and no cattle in your home area,' taunted the boy next door, licking an ice-cream.

'That's not true,' I said, 'there are cattle, sheep and goats as well.'

'*And* tsetse flies!'

'Not any more. The tsetse teams pushed the insects down to the Valley.'

'But it's quite a bushy place, isn't it, with no roads and only a few scruffy huts?'

'There is still a lot of bush of course, but . . .'

'And you have to walk miles to get your water.'

'Not at all. The village pump is only two hundred paces from our compound.'

'That's still far if one wants to have a decent bath. What are your houses like?'

'They are not exactly houses. They are huts, made of poles and grass.'

'And those accounts of the snake and the hyenas the teacher read to us from your composition. Are they true?'

'Yes.'

'And the villagers collected the remains of the cow and ate them?'

'Yes.'

'And you ate the meat too?'

'No, only the headman and his family ate the meat.'

'I don't believe you. There are no butcheries there and you couldn't afford to leave it alone. You probably ate it too.'

He didn't finish the sentence. I hit him hard on the mouth and he threw the ice-cream away, howling loudly and fingering his swelling lips. I felt my anger subsiding quickly into remorse and fear. Eventually his mother came to take him away. Exaggerating the degree of his injury, I felt like a murderer. Of course, when he recovered, we became friends again and I wondered how I could have felt any remorse after his insults.

2

April holidays in the country are fun. There is a sense of ripeness everywhere. The grass is fully grown. The trees seem to dance in its wavy, brown sea. The village paths are littered with dry maize leaves, nut-shells and sticks of sugar-cane. In the fields, the sweat of December bears fruit. The mealies are tall and ripe, the fields strewn with round yellow pumpkins and greenish-blue watermelons. It is hard to believe that such crops were planted by men. From the window of the bus, the golden brown sea of grass threatens to spill over the road. A village occasionally spins past and the crouching huts appear threatened by the green mealies surrounding them, like so many soldiers, tasselled and plumed.

We arrived at noon, when everyone was in the fields. We took off our shoes, dropped our things in a heap near the kitchen and set off. The girls saw us first and ran up to meet us. Mother simply laughed and raised her arms in joy.

'We were expecting you tomorrow,' said mother, putting aside some groundnuts and shaking the soil from her bosom. She had gained weight. Her arms were a little broader, the sun had given her skin a darker hue.

'You should all put on weight,' she said, giving us boiled pumpkins, 'you worked hard last summer.'

The girls went off to fetch green cobs and very soon they were sputtering on the fire. We ate our fill, capping our repast with sweet melons, digging into their soft red flesh with our fingers.

We worked till sunset, picking nuts and talking. Then we returned home, feeling happy and needing rest. Presently the moon came out and the night burst into light while mother read the letter from father and opened the parcels.

We went out to play in the moonlight and while we were there Lulu came to join us. I decided to accompany her home afterwards. It was not far. The leaves gleamed in the blue light, as if a coat of oil had been rubbed onto each leaf. Her family were fast asleep in her compound. I left her on the border of the clearing, and turned back along the path feeling unafraid and happy. I felt like sleeping outside in the moonlight but I knew it would be very cold at midnight and the dew would soak me.

On the way home, I noticed that part of the forest on one side of our compound had been destroyed. The trees had been felled; the great trunks sprawled on the ground, dry brown leaves clinging to the withered twigs and branches, yellow chips littering the perimeter of the tree-stumps. Only one huge tree remained in the middle of the scene – the sole survivor of the axe.

'There are people who want to come and live here,' mother explained. 'A retired policeman and his family.'

'A retired policeman?'

'Yes, so you had better behave yourselves, because he still has his handcuffs.'

'When are they building the huts?'

'In June.'

'But did they have to chop the trees down now?'

'Yes. So that they can burn them before the beginning of the rainy season.'

'Have you seen the family, mother?'

'Only the father. His name is Pendi. He came to talk to Headman Jairos.'

'What is he like? Is he the kind of person who will give us trouble.'

'No, Godi, you worry for nothing. It will be nice to have neighbours, newcomers too.'

13

I did not think so. I wanted the forest all to ourselves.

As soon as he caught wind of our arrival Jairos turned up to collect his old newspapers.

'Where is the gin?' he demanded.

'Father could not afford it,' said Yona.

'Not afford one small bottle of gin for his headman. Jairos is disappointed and he might not get the big field I promised him.'

He rolled himself a cigarette, crouched at the fire to light it, and sat back at the table blowing horizontal mushrooms of smoke into the hut.

'The chief tells me I can accommodate more *derukas*, more newcomers,' he told my mother. 'Very soon you will be having the Pendis as your neighbours. Pendi will be coming to build his huts in June. He's a real man. A fine man. Last time he came he brought me two crates of bottled beer and two bottles of gin. Now that's a man I wouldn't mind taking into my village. I want this village to be full of people like Pendi so that we can have beer parties every night. I want this to be a big, happy village. There is plenty of land for everyone.'

I did not like the sound of Pendi.

◆

By May, after the harvesting work is over, the grass has achieved its maximum growth. There are acres and acres of it – golden elephant grass. In the morning it is loaded with shiny beads of dew, and walking through it, a man is soaked to the waist. Village women begin cutting it. They work with sickles, cutting the blades at the roots and laying them out in bundles. The sun grows warm and the women remove their blouses. The grass tickles them. They return home just before noon, carrying thick bundles of grass on their heads. The bundles are carefully stored away for later use. In the fields the working season is over. The

14

maize stalks have been stripped of their cobs and stand lamely in the field, bent by the wind or broken by the hooves of cattle. The weeds grow without disturbance, threatening to obliterate the dry maize stalks.

The fields have become grazing areas. The cattle are no longer looked after, they spend weeks browsing in the fields and eating the delicious dry maize stalks. The herdboys are on holiday for about five months. Their only work is to assemble their herds once every three weeks to take them to the dip. The dip tank is about eight miles away. The boys wake up in the chilly dawn to open the kraal. The journey to the dip is a long hot run through the forest along cattle tracks clouded by swirling dust, the discordant tinkling of cattle bells, the stink of cattle and the warm damp steaming cakes of cowdung. The boys are pouring with sweat and the cattle trotting quietly by the time they reach the dip tank.

The dip tank is not a big place. It stands in the middle of an open space denuded of its vegetation by cattle hooves. It is covered by a low roof of zinc tiles, and tailed by a narrow wooden passage through which the reluctant cattle are driven into heavy, grey, metallic dip water.

The dip man, a middle-aged person in khaki, ticks off the cattle on the brown tickets. While the cattle are taking their turns to plunge into the dip, the boys compete – cracking their whips to see who can make the loudest noise. Some of the boys play paper-football, eat salted groundnuts, chatter, laugh and quarrel. They are all rather reluctant to go home when the dipping is over.

May gives way to June and the weather becomes cooler. The days are short and the crisp air numbs fingers in the morning. The nights are long and the trees grunt and croak in the wind, complaining. Because the nights are long people don't go to bed early. They sit round the fire, pushing time in talk, telling stories and roasting groundnuts. There are more beer parties and more drums. The drums beat louder and the singing is more energetic. This is also the time for courtships. The shy-eyed girls stand under the afternoon shade of the trees, unconsciously chewing grass stalks and twigs while the sweet-tongued young men pour out their hearts to them. These are long, lazy months.

September brings higher temperatures. Veld fires soil the blue skies with their smoke and there is a smell of burning in the air. The tall elephant grass is burnt down to the roots and the tree trunks are charred and blackened. The once flourishing plains of golden grass are reduced to a flat black landscape.

October, the hottest month of the year, brings a metallic sun that pours its hot rays onto the earth. The sand becomes impossibly hot to naked feet. Rivers run low. The land aches for rain.

Rain comes in early November, washing the soot off the trees, soaking the black plains and bathing the land. But rain does not come every year.

◆

That year the rain did not come. The ground remained black from the burning in October. The tree-trunks stood grey with soot. The cattle roamed the plains and untilled fields, nibbling the meagre green-black shoots battling to come out of the ground. Day after day the villagers looked at the unpromising sky, shielding their eyes from the hot sun with their hands. It was the same story throughout the country – drought; no rains with Christmas only a week away. The rain was two months overdue.

Even in the towns people noticed the drought. The small vegetable gardens started wilting behind the houses. People sweated and drank iced drinks. At night the heat made them sweat in their beds. The streets were dirty and dusty with the dirt of months, stained with half-dried pools of oil and dog's urine. Black smoke oozed persistently out of the factory chimneys, defying the brazen bright-blue sky. There was no rain to wash away all the carbon and soot.

In the countryside it was a long hot holiday for us. We sat in the shade, waiting for the rain. Instead of the rain, fat black edible *madora* arrived. Caterpillars about ten centimetres long, dark green and segmented, with little hairy legs. They are full of a green juice which squirts out when they are squeezed. When boiled with salt and sun-dried they make a crisp, tasty relish.

The *madora* don't come every year but when they do, they come in monstrous numbers. They are not as destructive as locusts because they only eat green tree foliage and their spell only lasts a week or two. Nobody is sure where they come from or what they really are. A villager may chance to see two or three of them on a leaf but three days later there will be thousands, millions of them in the trees and the bushes. That year they came like raindrops. They massed on the ground, flowed into the trees and attacked the foliage, gobbling up the leaves till one tree in ten stood winter-naked, and the ground under the denuded trees went black with their droppings.

The *madora* had been sent to relieve the effects of the oncoming drought, people said. Women went into the forest in long files, balancing buckets on their heads, pushing torn blouses into place, babies strapped to their backs. Sometimes a few men went with them, carrying axes to fell the trees in which the *madora* lodged.

We loved *madora* but mother was afraid of the forest. She only allowed us to go after Lulu had promised to come with us. Lulu's mother was in the party. She was short, slim and light-skinned and walked briskly in front. We went past the crouching huts and thin howling puppies, past the scorched fields, which should have already been tilled. We crossed the river in which

Lulu and I had bathed the year before, and climbed into the forest. Here the trees grew closely together, the sun filtered through the leafy canopy and danced on the grass.

We spread out over the pathless forest. The *madora* hung heavily on the branches. Everywhere the leaves had been eaten. The creatures hung virtually motionless from the twigs like thick shreds of black string. Occasionally they had fallen to the ground: a looping trail of fat caterpillars

Picking *madora* is like picking loose threads from a cloth. They come cleanly off the branches and we plucked them into our buckets till our fingers ran green with their juice. The sun rose and we felt thirsty. We ate some berries and picked *madora* till our buckets were full. Then we sat down to wait for the others who had gone further afield. Presently, Lulu's mother emerged from the bush, put her bucket down, groaning from its weight, and threw herself onto the grass near Lulu and her cousin.

There was no hurry so we sat in the shade for about an hour, till Lulu's mother said worriedly, 'Lifi has perhaps taken another direction home.'

Lifi was an energetic old woman whose daughter was mentally retarded.

'She will find herself in Mbumbuzi Forest before she knows where she is,' remarked Lulu jokingly. Mbumbuzi was the most remote part of the forest, south of the village. Few people ever went there.

We eventually went home without Lifi. The other women had returned but Lifi had not come. Jairos came to tell us that he was organising a search party to find her. For three tense days the people in our village talked about Lifi. For three successive days the search party made excursions into the forest to search for her, beating their loud drums, only to return at sunset with the hopeless news that Lifi had not been found.

When Lifi finally appeared, accompanied by two strangers,

18

people were reluctantly beginning to believe that she would never be found, so there was much rejoicing in the village.

◆

The forest was on a gently rolling slope with no hills, boulders or crests to indicate direction. Lifi thought the sun was strangely out of place. Nothing seemed familiar. In the latter part of the afternoon, in desperation, Lifi started walking towards the setting sun. Little did she know what this mistake would cost her. Had she remained where she was for a little longer, she would have heard the drums of the party that had gone to look for her.

She was still walking when the sun set. The forest showed no sign of thinning out. No familiar stream appeared. She sat against the trunk of a big tree and felt hungry for the first time that day.

She ate some half-ripe fleshy brown berries. They had a sweet, sickly taste but she wanted the water in them. By the time she had finished her meagre supper the darkness had descended. She pulled her cloth over her head and tried to sleep.

Sleep did not come quickly. Where was her daughter? Perhaps no one would find her and she would sleep in the bushes and catch a cold from the dew. A snake might strike her. Lifi shivered at the thought of snakes. She gathered her cloth round her. The crickets cried and the bats flapped among the trees and far away an owl hooted. Not a frog croaked. Eventually she fell into a deep dreamless sleep.

The birds were chirping and the sun shining when she woke up. The sun was warm and cheerful and she felt happy. She let the dew dry. Her *madora* were still alive in the bucket after the night and she started squeezing them.

After the dew dried she started walking again, this time towards the east. Had the other women gone home, she wondered, or had they got lost too? Why didn't someone come to look for her? Or didn't anyone care? She ululated. Her voice rang through the forest and died away. She walked on – and on.

That night she slept under a tree again, feeling very hungry. She was sitting with her head bent over her chest in contemplation when she sensed a movement close to her in the moonlight. She lifted her head in alarm and the curious buck galloped away, crashing through the bushes in fright. She dreamt that the search party was passing a short distance ahead of her. She hailed them and ran to meet them. She tripped, fell, rose and fell again, shouting. The party did not seem to hear her. They disappeared into the forest, beating their drums.

At last morning came and Lifi woke up. She had been crying. She ate green berries and started walking. She felt an urge to walk, she knew that if she remained in one place hunger and thirst and despair would drive her mad. It would be better to die where human beings could find her before the vultures and hyenas came to finish her off. She limped on, tired, hot and constantly thirsty.

Towards sunset, the forest started thinning out. Lifi suddenly found herself entering a vast grass plain. Right before her two boys sat weaving cattle whips out of strips of bark.

Her mouth opened but no sound came out. She stumbled towards the boys holding out her hand as if to prevent the scene from melting away. Her bucket fell from her head and clanked noisily onto a log. The green *madora* scattered everywhere. She hurried on.

The two boys raised their heads at the noise and looked with a mixture of surprise and dread at the unexpected woman. Lifi asked for milk. Her voice was cracked and dry. For two days she had not talked to anyone. The two boys gave her milk and took her to their home. The people there gave her a proper meal and listened in amazed sympathy to her story. Old as she was, she had walked forty miles from her village with only the berries to eat, narrowly escaping the hyenas that roam the forests at night. After resting for two days, Lifi was accompanied by two men back to her village.

3

We did not collect *madora* again after Lifi's ordeal. Instead, we started making preparations for Christmas.

The huts needed a fresh coating of red mud. We dug a circular hole; surprisingly the earth was quite soft and stoneless until we reached the fine, red, virgin sandy clay four feet down. We watered the red clay into a thin paste and smeared it over the walls with our hands. Soon the huts were looking neat and pretty in their new coat of ochre.

We weeded and swept the compound, raising clouds of dust that made us cough. There was firewood to be chopped and brought home in the wheelbarrow; cupboards, tables and chairs to be polished; pots, plates and pans to be thoroughly scrubbed with Vim; and bread and cakes to be baked over the sand in the three-legged pot.

Tired, we fell asleep early, and much later stirred awake to find father standing at the doorway, smiling at us. He threw a giant packet of sweets onto the blankets and said festively, 'Merry Christmas'. It was a merry Christmas, though very different from the colourful celebrations we were used to in town. We wondered aloud if the cats and dogs knew it was Christmas at all.

Father sent us to call the village elders for a Christmas service under a tree. I went to Simon's compound. Simon was the brother of Jairos, but he drank far less and worked hard to feed his family. The path I took was well trodden and flanked with thorny bushes. I ran swiftly and broke into the clearing of Simon's homestead with its two small huts. Three dogs glanced indifferently at me as I walked across the clearing. Two huge drums of beer stood under the eaves of the huts. I crouched beside the doorway of the hut and said, 'Good morning.'

Simon's strong bass voice called me in. The ground smelled of dirty water and urine. I went into the hut, bowing my head, and sat on the hard earthen bench near the door. Simon's wife sat near the fire, cutting up a chicken. Simon himself sat on the bench two feet away, skinning what looked like a hare. His small boy helped him by holding the animal for him to cut. His daughter sat cross-legged near the fire, watching the chicken with interest.

I greeted them slowly, and then quickly told them why I had come. Simon puffed at his strong-smelling, home-made cigarette and continued cutting up the hare. There was no hurry. His wife unaffectedly brushed her faded blue dress, closing it round her legs, scratched her cracked foot and loaded the chicken into the pot, pressing it down with the lid.

'Did your father bring us gin and cigarettes for Christmas?' asked Simon, grinning to show a cracked grey tooth.

'My father doesn't smoke or drink,' I smiled, 'but he brought many things to eat.'

'Where is the service?' asked Simon's wife, a short dark-skinned woman with surprisingly small limbs.

I told them.

'We will come,' said Simon ceremoniously, and then address-ing his wife jokingly, 'You leave your chicken for a while, mother of my daughter, and come to the service.'

'You go,' she said, unmoved by his humour. 'I can't leave the pot alone.'

'Your mother is very fond of chicken, my son,' Simon said, winking at me. 'Never mind. I will come. When does your father want us?'

'He wants you now,' I said as politely as I could.

Simon laid the gleaming naked pink hare on its dark brown skin, wiped his fingers with a cloth and came with me. His small boy accompanied us, doggedly running in front.

There was quite a small gathering under the tree by the time we arrived. The women sat on the mats chattering, my mother among them. A few blank-eyed men sat on the logs. Father sat on a chair in the middle of the group checking his Bible-reading one last time.

We started off with a Christmas song, the girls singing the first part, mother humming the alto, we boys singing in tenor and father chiming in with the bass. Father read the lesson and then gave an elaborate sermon. The congregation listened with loose attention. Women chatted freely, casually greeting each other, laughing. Jairos stumbled in late and took his position on a log and sat down to listen to the sermon, nevertheless coughing and smoking freely to assert his importance.

The congregation watched father, nodding slightly, understanding very little and evidently thinking that the Bible account of the birth of Jesus was a superb folk-story. At last the service was over and everybody rose to go, the women yawning and stretching their arms, obviously happy that it was over. Half the congregation came to our compound for breakfast, either upon my father's lavish invitation or at their own. Bread and cakes and biscuits were brought out, and tea made in a bucket. There were not enough cups to go round so the children had to wait. Eventually we had our turn and a score or so of other children joined us in gulping down mountains of bread and oceans of tea.

It was a heavy breakfast. Afterwards we fooled around eating sweets, kicking balloons and waiting for lunch.

Lunch was hot rice and chicken and there were only two elderly guests, the rest of the morning guests having flocked off to the nearby township to spend the day there. The night was dark and moonless, but the beer parties continued. Everywhere we could hear people singing drunkenly in the darkness, paying no heed to the barking dogs or the dark night.

On Boxing Day we set about repairing the barbed-wire fence around our home. We replaced two worn poles with fresh ones, sweating and panting as we planted and pulled the wire into place. My father sometimes believed in work for its own sake, and he wanted to go back to town feeling he had done some work over the short holiday, even if this meant uprooting a thick pole and planting it half an inch further to the right. Consequently, late that night, in spite of the pressing darkness and our fatigue, we were levelling the slope of our clearing by shovelling earth from the higher end to the lower one, while feeling sure that a heavy storm would dislodge it.

The next day father left for town, taking with him a liberal package of sun-dried and salted *madora*. We accompanied him to the bus stop and left him once he was on the crowded bus. We trudged home to another hot afternoon. The rain had still not come.

◆

The sky remained blue, and the earth cracked with the heat. Everywhere, people talked about the lateness of the rain and the growing prospects of drought. The same story came from other parts of the country.

Then, one hot afternoon, it was reported that the rain-maker had arrived. We were lying in the shade to avoid the afternoon

24

heat, and saw people moving along the path to Jairos's compound. Jairos himself came to tell us that we must attend the rain-making ceremony.

We went rather reluctantly, not believing it would work. There was quite a large gathering in front of Jairos's homestead. Groups of women and children crowded under the eaves of the two small huts for shade; the men sat with their knees up to their chins in the hot sun, sweating, holding slim knobkerries and axes and walking sticks.

In the corner of the gathering sat the rain-maker. She was dressed in black from head to toe: an elaborate headpiece of black feathers on her head, black cloths binding her chest, abdomen and legs, black bangles – she even sat on a black mat. She was light-skinned, tall and slim, a thin-faced woman in her early thirties, alert eyes glancing easily and authoritatively over the gathering, hands folded humbly in her lap.

Jairos rose from among the men and stumbled towards the rain-maker. He stood above her, bowing his head as he bent down to say something to her. Simon shouted from the crowd, angrily advising Jairos to revise his manners and crouch as he talked to her. There was silence. Jairos looked around him dubiously, then hunkered down on his heels. He brought out his tin of tobacco and began to make himself his usual wet cigarette. The rain-maker spoke to Jairos in subdued tones, unaffected by his bad manners. Then Jairos rose to say briefly that everybody was to go to the tree of the ancestors.

The crowd got up, muttering about why they should be moved, and formed a rough line. The rain-maker rose elaborately, taking her time. Somebody started singing and the crowd joined in, clapping to the rhythm. Then the rain-maker led the procession, Jairos close behind her. Women ululated, children sang praises and men grunted as the procession reached the tree of the ancestors and formed a ring.

The tree was in the forest some distance from the headman's compound. It was a tall *muhacha* tree, towering above the other ones. Its trunk was wide, its branches small and numerous, forming a leafy crown. The ground around the tree was grassy, without any bushes, showing that the area had been trodden on before, but not for a long time.

Close to the tree, on either side of it, were two graves. One was that of Jairos's grandfather and the other of Jairos's father, who had been the previous headman. The two graves were now mere frames of wood enclosing the half-moon-shaped mounds of earth. The wooden frameworks had almost collapsed, the slim poles were rotten and eaten by ants. The heaps of sand had subsided with the passage of years and now the weeds grew thickly on them. The crowd ringed the area in between the two graves. The singing continued for an hour, oxhide drums beating out the rhythm of the tunes. Expert dancers rose to sketch their steps, turning their feet jerkily over the grass.

Suddenly, the rain-maker's head shot forwards, burying her headpiece of feathers in the dust. Her body shook, jerked and shivered as if she was battling with death. Froth foamed and bubbled from her mouth. For a split second the singing stopped and all eyes were glued on her. Then the singing started again, slowly climbing to a climax.

Jairos and Simon grabbed the rain-maker by the arms and held her down. She kicked and her body writhed like a worm, her legs pedalling the air, head tossing from side to side, her arms pulling powerfully away from her whole body which contorted into impossible angles. She gasped heavily through her frothing mouth, her belly heaved.

The black cloth around her abdomen broke free with the force of her movement and fell on to the grass, exposing her chest and stomach. Her breasts were full and brown like a girl's, her long black nipples were upturned to the sky.

26

Jairos and Simon struggled with her and gradually calmed her. The singing stopped. She spoke in a thin voice, gasping like a drowning person. She spoke a strange language, her voice thin and loud, and meaningless to us. The men held her closely and let her speak till she finished and fell on her side, dragging her nipples in the sand. She lay as if in sleep and they covered her with the black cloth. Eventually the rain-maker awoke from her trance and told them what needed to be done.

There were two strange birds to be caught and destroyed, and a dead woman's hut to be burnt. The two birds lodged within the trunk of a tree on the borders of our homestead. Simon went to fetch them and returned within half an hour, carrying an eagle-like bird in each hand. Jairos cut the birds up and burnt them over the blazing logs. The fat hissed and everywhere there was the sweet smell of burning meat. A hungry dog unadvisedly pounced on one of the fleshy fragments. Jairos saw it, cursed violently and hurled a blazing splinter at the dog. The scalding splinter caught the dog on the belly and it scuttled away, whimpering.

The hut to be destroyed stood alone on a cleared patch in the middle of the forest. It was an old deserted hut with rotten poles, which crumbled at the touch of a finger. Green shoots were budding in some of the younger poles. The old grass roof was broken and half the grass had fallen into the hut. The hut's former occupant, an old woman with no known relative, had died from a lightning strike.

Towards sunset, they set fire to the hut. The old grass caught fire quickly and the rotten poles blazed into ash. The thick black smoke rose up to the yellowing sky.

The rain came that night.

I woke to the sound of it.

Lightning flashed through the darkness. Through the slit in the doorway I saw slanting white rain and the pools of water forming on the sand.

It poured steadily. Drops of rain trickled through the grass roof and dropped onto our blankets. I suddenly felt cold and a fear of the darkness and the lightning.

The rain continued for the next two days. It poured down from the grey sky without a break, till the ground lay covered under inches of water. Droplets trickled through the roof and fell on our damp, dull fire, giving rise to more smoke. Frogs croaked.

Then on the third day the rain stopped. The sun broke suddenly through the grey clouds. The leaves in the trees moved freely again and the birds sang.

For three thanksgiving days the people were forbidden to do any work in the fields.

Then ploughing started. At four in the morning people woke up to harness the oxen where they stamped and clanked their bells in the muddy kraals. The morning was full of the shouts of the boys driving the cattle, the splitting cracks of cattle whips slashing bare oxhide and the squeak of the plough wheels in the grass.

Matudu came to till our new plot of land. His fine pair of oxen worked from dawn to noon turning our field into one stretch of brown earth.

Everywhere, the black burnt fields gave way to rich brown soil and later to green shoots. The weeds sprouted with the crops again – demanding the labour of the hoe and the free flow of sweat over black flesh in the strong blazing sunlight.

The rain came again and again and the crops grew. We had only half finished the weeding when the holidays ended but when we came back in April we were to return to the biggest harvest ever known.

4

Elsewhere in the country it had not been such a good farming year. The rain had come in two lean spells lasting a few days each, insufficient for the proper germination of seeds. In the southern regions of the country, the drought had been acute. People had taken refuge from the sun on the verandahs of white brick houses. It was a seemingly prosperous land of well-built houses, flourishing supermarkets and district councils. But people could not eat brick houses and supermarkets and council buildings. Although people there used tractors and fertilisers, and took advice from local agricultural demonstrators, farming was bad. Because it was a densely populated region, fields were small and the soil old and overworked. Most of the trees had been cut down for wood and the land lay in aching nakedness, raped by the plough and the axe.

For seven successive years the weather had been harsh in this region. The government had observed the area with a wary eye, resenting the erosion, land wastage and the diminished contribution to the economy. At last it was decided to move people into the remote virgin land in the north to give the denuded region a chance to become green again. At first there was opposition to this plan by the villagers but eventually, after much persuasion, they agreed to destroy their homes, leave their deceased kin's graves and their fatherland and move into the new land.

Others simply decided to move north on their own. Some of these people were misfits – alleged practitioners of witchcraft, crop thieves or just bad neighbours who moved to exchange their identity for a new one. The third group of newcomers were people like us, city dwellers who had decided to re-establish their links with the countryside: seasonal migrants who moved between town and country.

Towards the end of July, during the middle of the cold dry season, when roads were negotiable, the movement from the south started. Families came in convoys of closely packed government lorries, taking two or three days to complete the journey, so that passengers frequently camped out for the night.

The first, the bigger train of lorries, passed our village and rumbled on into the remote forests where some people still only wore pieces of cloth between their legs and girls went around bare-breasted. The newcomers were received with curiosity, reserve and suspicion. Closer to our own village, a trickle of newcomers like us had prepared the local people for the invasions. In the end, however, we had relatively few newcomers, only about half a lorry-load of passengers descended to settle in our village. They were not an unusual lot, four or five families who spoke with the lazy southerly accent. Jairos was interested in them of course, and at once gave them generous grants of land.

The newcomers were called *derukas*, and they brought with them a distinctive *deruka* life-style based on shrewd hard work. The ambition of every *deruka* family was to build a good brick and zinc house. Building was done in the dry winter. All aspiring house-owners became builders at this time. Everywhere the earth was torn open into little quarries and men dug down in search of soft brown clay. Boys were seen pumping water into drums and then rolling them to the quarries where the clay was mixed, bricks were moulded and laid out in neat rows to dry in the sun. Few builders fired their bricks. Scarcity of rocks in this area of deep aeolian sand, the cost of bringing material from the town and the shortage of building experts were other reasons why an alarming proportion of the newly built houses began to crack only months after completion.

The *derukas* were generally great farmers. They cleared huge fields and grew maize and groundnuts. A few started to grow sunflowers and cotton to sell to the Grain Marketing Board. They kept many cattle, grew vegetables, dug fish-ponds by the river and raised chickens. Some of them sold vegetables, milk and eggs. In contrast, the local people seemed to live from one day to the next, eating sadza, drinking beer and raising children. They built their huts with grass and poles, seldom bothering to plaster the walls with mud so at night firelight peeped through the gaps between the poles.

At that time there were about twenty homesteads in Jairos's village. Before the Pendis arrived the compound nearest to ours was Jairos's, with nothing to distinguish its owner beyond one small granary that held no more than four bags of grain and a few small chickens.

Further on was a larger compound which had seven or eight huts built dangerously close together – a single fire could burn them all down. It belonged to a polygamist, the only one in the village. His name was Ndoga and he had three wives. He was short and ugly, with dirty black woolly hair in which there were always grass seeds and strands of blanket wool. He had bulging eyes and wore khakis which were greased with the sweat of years. But beneath his appearance, he was a hard-working man. His granaries were always full and his sons brought buckets of white milk from the kraals at midday. For a polygamist, he kept his wives happy. He had thirteen industrious children and five lean hounds that accompanied him on buck-hunting trips. Further up the slope were two compounds close together. The first of these was that of Jairos's brother, Simon. The other belonged to an old bachelor who lived alone in a single hut. He was a tough, drinking man with a coarse voice. His main pastime was drinking, and when he drank, he sang even more loudly.

Among the women was Lifi, the old woman who had lost her way in the forest while picking *madora*.

'My husband was a tractor driver and foreman on a farm,' she would recall slowly. 'I used to have everything I wanted. When the owner of the farm killed a bull for the workers it was I who shared out the meat. I always had the liver and the tongue to myself. But then my husband died of a strange disease. Perhaps some of the jealous workers he supervised killed him. That was when I fell from comfort. Would you believe I was once an important person? No! You look at these rags, and you do not believe me.'

A tear trickled down her cheek. At her age, crying seemed a natural thing to do.

'Old age is a worm that eats youth away, Masiziva. But you have got many years ahead of you and lots of healthy, happy children. You will live to a ripe old age like me. But you will be wealthy and happy.'

'Won't you eat before you go?' my mother would plead with her. 'The girls are putting the pot on the fire.'

'I shall eat some day before I die. I have to follow my daughter now.'

Lifi's retarded daughter spent most of her time delivering firewood. Villagers took her in and gave her food when she appeared. So it was that one night we went to our hut and found the woman lying half asleep. Mother wrapped her up in a blanket and took her to her own hut where she stayed until Lifi came to fetch her in the morning.

◆

'They are great people I am bringing in,' said Jairos with gleaming eyes. 'Rich people with great totem names. I want this village to be filled up by *derukas*. I want beer parties every night in this village. I want all these thick forests to be chopped down to provide fields. I want my people to be happy and prosperous.'

He looked very happy with himself.

'Have you got a fire burning?' he asked, and hissed with pleasure on seeing the fire. 'My people, locals and *derukas* alike, love me very much,' he said happily, emptying his bulging pockets out of which came four small dry fish, three eggs, a piece of onion and a shred of biltong. These all went onto the table, each item being given a brief explanation as to its source: the fishes were given to him by friendly boys at the river, the eggs by a generous housewife, the meat and the onion bulb were saved from the cooking pot.

We gathered around him, laughing, as he surveyed his small treasures. He tossed the shred of biltong into the fire, where it smoked in the heat. Then he snatched it out again with his fingers and threw it onto the table.

'Salt!' he cried, making swallowing movements. Shuvai got him the salt. He heaped two teaspoons onto the meat and disposed of it in two quick bites.

'Water,' he cried next, munching. 'Put it on the fire. Yes, in the kettle. Not too much! Bring it here.' He put the eggs very carefully into the kettle and put it on the fire. Just over a minute later, he jumped from his chair to look into the kettle.

Half a minute of frantic blowing at the fire and he said the eggs were ready. I watched mother trying to stop herself from laughing as Jairos half ate, half drank them straight from their shells.

He licked his fingers dry, whisked the fishes back into his pocket and rose to go, momentarily forgetting the onion.

'Oh,' he remembered suddenly. 'Plant this onion for me. Keep it well watered, you hear.'

It was only a small bulb, one that wouldn't grow much.

'Oh yes,' he remembered again. 'You boys must go and repair my wooden fence. You know where my garden is, in the vlei.'

'No.'

'Well, you can ask, it's the big one near the stream, the one with a big tree. You can't miss it. The goats broke down part of the fence. All you have to do is put in a few logs. It shouldn't take you thirty minutes.'

'He is going too far now,' protested my mother, after Jairos had left. 'Doesn't he know we have a great deal of our own work to do? Just because he is the village headman he thinks he can make us slave for him. The regional chief himself has no right to give such orders.'

In the end, mother decided that we would have to go and repair Jairos's garden, otherwise we might seem to be disobedient children.

When we went to the vlei to have a look, however, we found nothing growing in the garden.

Only one end of the plot was fenced and this was poorly done; fragile stakes had been piled into a rough wall that would collapse with a slight push. We returned home depressed.

Fortunately we were spared the effort of working on Jairos's fence. A mouse-hunting party was held in the vlei. Boys burnt the grass, so that the mice scuttled into the open, where they could be beaten to death, sliced open and roasted over the fire. The fire ran out of control, burning half the vlei black. Jairos, fuming with anger, came to tell us about it.

'They dare to burn the vlei without my permission! They destroyed my garden, the headman's garden! Jairos's. It's Makepesi's boys who did it.'

'Who is Makepesi?' asked mother.

'You don't know him? He is the snake in this village.'

'Is he the one who lived in the city?'

'Yes. He thinks he is clever. Everybody in the village fears him, except me. They think he is a gangster. His father was a renowned medicine man and people think Makepesi got his pretty young wife with a charm. That's nonsense which only fools believe. His charms will not work on me. This very morning I am going to order him to pay a fine of a goat. His boys can't be allowed to fool around like that. I don't care what people have been saying about him. He threatened to kill me last December when I talked about giving part of his field to Charamba. Why am I not dead? Why didn't his charms finish me off? And why shouldn't I give his field away? He hasn't paid his taxes, and has committed many crimes against honest people of this village.'

'Perhaps it was an accident, Headman Jairos.'

'An accident, Masiziva! You don't know Makepesi. He is a real shrew, that man. He did it deliberately to spite me. I am not letting him get away with it this time. Not only am I fining him a goat, but I am going to give his field away to Charamba who needs it.'

'But Makepesi is a dangerous man, Headman Jairos.'

'Not at all. He wouldn't hurt a finger of mine.'

5

Although the Pendis had not made a second appearance for many months, Matudu had been building their huts.

One hot afternoon we were playing at Matudu's claypit, filing toy bricks out of hardened clay, when a battered Zephyr faltered to a halt not far from us. A man opened the door of the car with a flourish and jumped out. He walked with a sprightly step towards the semi-finished huts where Matudu and his sons were fixing the roofs. He was a tall slim man, light-skinned, with alert eyes and a forked moustache. He made his way carefully round the claypit as if it were some infernal hole. He looked down in a superior way at us, mud-splattered. He nodded vaguely and grunted.

Then a woman eased herself slowly out of the car. We could see that she had the comfortable features of a city woman – a vibrant well-oiled skin lightened by Ponds Vanishing Cream, stockinged legs, a shiny dark wig. We even caught whiffs of her perfume as she walked past us, followed by her children.

Mr Pendi was now talking to Matudu about the huts. The woman inspected them critically, taking care not to ladder her stockings against the walls. She spoke quickly, sharply, to her husband; even from a distance we could tell that she was not satisfied.

Mr Pendi continued talking to Matudu, unaffected by his wife's criticism. We took this opportunity to slip away quietly. Mother stood in the doorway of the kitchen, watching the visitors unobserved, brushing her dress in preparation for going over to make their acquaintance.

Then she went round to shake hands with the visitors. There was the customary long talk between Mrs Pendi and mother, in the middle of which the latter called us over to introduce us to the new family. I sensed a change in Mrs Pendi's attitude when she realised who we were – she smiled constantly and her voice sounded buttery.

That night a strong sweet oily smell of frying meat drifted from our neighbour's huts and we could hear frequent laughter above the music of the gramophone. The noise went on into the night, long after we had gone to sleep.

As we lay in the darkness of our huts, I caught the smell of tobacco and heard the muffled sound of sandals on the sand. Later I heard Jairos's familiar laugh. He was already paying his fourth visit to the Pendis.

Their huts were completed within two days. Mrs Pendi took off her stockings, stiletto shoes and wig, and set to work giving the mud walls a tan of red and black, and sweeping the clearing to make it habitable. Mother went over to help her. They worked together like old acquaintances.

Not all the family possessions had been brought on the Zephyr, so the next day Mr Pendi went back to town, by bus, to fetch the rest of their property. He came back three days later, in a hired lorry.

They unpacked the vehicle at once, and we helped them. There were sofas, coffee tables, wardrobes, trunks, boxes, plates and pots – all sorts of household goods. Mrs Pendi explained the history of each item, fingering them possessively while complaining of the scratch marks they had sustained on the lorry.

The Pendis had four children, the oldest being a girl of seven. The children came to play with us and were soon sharing half of our meals, and mother didn't mind. But the visits continued with such precision that we began to fear playing host to four more little Jairoses. At last when they arrived for the umpteenth time mother told them to go and fetch cups and plates from their mother's kitchen since we did not have enough to go around. The kids raced home eagerly but their mother intercepted their return, obviously sensing the trick behind it all – which was not obvious to me. For a while mealtime visits decreased in number.

One evening I was bathing on the lawn just before supper. I splashed myself quickly, eager to move back to the warmth of the kitchen, when suddenly I sensed a shadow standing close beside me. I was startled for a moment, and hurriedly rubbed my eyes. It was five-year-old Sam Pendi, paying us his evening visit. He gloated over me, naked and soapy in the zinc bath, waiting for me to finish so that we could go into the hut together. I was slightly irritated by the presence of the boy. Then an unmistakable jet of urine splashed over my back. I smelt it and felt its warmth. I turned and it splashed into my face. I thought I heard Sam giggling as he propelled the jet.

Blinded by anger, I jumped out of the bath, overturning it and cutting my leg on its edge as I did so, but I didn't feel the pain. I gave him a clean hard slap that sent him to the ground. He stumbled to his feet crying loudly, boldly, deliberately. A wave of guilt swept over me as I dried myself and snatched up my clothes. Mother caught me hesitating at the door outside the kitchen.

'What happened?' she asked sternly. 'Why is Sam crying?'

'I don't know,' I croaked.

'Yes, you know. Why is he crying?'

The smoke stung my eyes. Mother went outside to talk to Sam, who was still crying. I saw orange tongues of light from Mrs Pendi's lamp as she came out of her hut. Eventually Sam stopped crying and went away with his mother. Moments later mother returned, looking very serious, and I felt like a brute.

'You beat the boy.'

I kept quiet.

'You know I have always told you to be good to our neighbours.'

'He urinated into my face, mother.'

'Did he do that? Urinate in your face? But then you should not have beaten him.'

'I was angry.'

'But he is only a young boy,' said Yona, Sam's best friend.

'Perhaps it was an accident.'

'It wasn't an accident!' I shouted angrily. 'He did it on purpose.'

'You shouldn't have beaten him all the same,' said mother and added, 'Go and apologise.'

I felt guilty and afraid of the dark. But there was no evading mother's orders so I crept out of the hut.

The moon was rising over the horizon, a big orange ball clothing everything with its yellow light. The sand gleamed faintly. I felt less afraid in the moonlight, closed the steel gate behind me and walked quietly. There was still no fence round the Pendis' homestead, so I went straight to the huts across the clearing.

In the moonlight the two huts were clearly outlined, the big four-cornered hut with the slanting roof dwarfing the smaller round hut. I made for the smaller hut. It faced away from me, so that I could only see a small trapezium of red light coming from the doorway. I hesitated near the door, plucked up my courage and slipped into the hut.

They were having their supper. Mr and Mrs Pendi sat at the table and Mrs Pendi suckled the infant as she ate. The man's fierce face was lit by the oil lamp, so the shadows of his moustache looked like two huge barbs. He attacked a bony chunk of meat, fat dripping from his fingers. Sam and his sisters sat on the floor eating.

'Good evening,' I muttered, as I had not been noticed.

Mrs Pendi ducked her breast into the blouse when she saw me, plucking it out of the infant's mouth.

'Have some sadza,' said Mr and Mrs Pendi together from the table.

'Thank you very much,' I said tensely, 'I have eaten.'

'Then eat some more,' said Mr Pendi, grinning at me.

'I came to apologise. I beat Sam.'

'It's all right,' said Mrs Pendi, smiling. 'Sam is a very naughty boy.'

They didn't want to know why I had beaten him, I supposed.

'Have some sadza,' said Mrs Pendi again, forcibly, as if I would be committing a crime if I went away without eating.

'I have to go now,' I said, rising. In a moment I was out in the moonlight, hurrying home and feeling much better. Apologising had been easier than I had anticipated.

◆

The Pendis aspired to being progressive. Their children were clever. Sam was the second child, the first was a girl called Emma who was sometimes vulgar and spoilt. On one occasion when we were playing with them she had invited Jo to be her hide-and-seek partner, and he, obviously misunderstanding the invitation, had behaved in a priggish manner by refusing and calling Emma names. She would complain when her mother told her to wash the dishes or fetch water. Many times her mother beat her but she was a fast runner and would try to get away. But Mrs Pendi was a runner too. She would simply gather up her dress and pursue Emma like a bolt of lightning.

In spite of the childbeating and the noise the Pendis were not bad neighbours. And occasionally Emma could be a surprisingly good child, washing her infant sister's napkins and voluntarily going to fetch water. Mrs Pendi railed endlessly about her children, her husband, her huts and fields, but she had warmth and was sociable and generous. She confided in my mother about her aspirations, hopes and fears.

One day she came to our field to help us pick nuts. We sat in the shade eating boiled mealies and she talked. She told us how she had gone to a boarding school and excelled in English and athletics; how she had always wanted to go to a sewing school but failed because of her family's poverty; how she had married Robson Pendi because he was smart and intelligent; how she had suffered on delivering her first child, Emma; how Sam's birth had been worse, almost fatal; and so on. She explained how the operations she had had when delivering her first two children had left her a fragile woman and the housework was rather too heavy for someone in her condition so she got girls to help her.

The first of these girls was a tall dark strong southerner with powerful arms and limbs. She took long, strong strides but when the baby cried she rocked her to sleep, singing. She never complained when Mrs Pendi scolded her though perhaps her heart cried out. None the less she did not stay long but was soon dismissed and replaced by Mary, an easy-going beauty. When Mrs Pendi scolded her she smiled and answered back.

At that time the Pendis were building a brick and zinc house. An expert from the south had come to do the building, and Mr Jacobi's boy, Thomas, was to help the builder. He was a strong boy who laughed and sang. One of his favourite tunes had the refrain: 'Help! Get me some help!' He sang with so much emotion that you felt sure he genuinely needed help.

Mary had taken a fancy to Thomas and we often heard them talking. 'I love you, Thomas,' she would say very loudly as she straightened her back and put down the pot she was scrubbing. 'I love you like a banana.'

'If you love me like a banana, then eat me,' Thomas would say.

'Truly, Thomas, I love you. I can't sleep nights because of you.'

Thomas would burst out laughing, and the builder would join in. Sometimes he sang love songs, and she stopped to listen to them, but he always laughed in the end. This extravagant flirting would go on till Mrs Pendi stopped it by calling Mary in to do something.

41

Mr Pendi could be a violent man. He was a hardened drinker, often going out to drink and coming home late in the evening, singing his way home through the darkness. At beer parties he could be seen sitting on a chair in his dignified suit, while everybody else sat on the ground, but because he spent his money freely on beer he had a huge following of friends.

He had a gun, and sometimes he went out at night to hunt, so that we saw the bright beam of his powerful torch flashing boldly among the trees. We never heard the bark of his gun, but he almost always brought back a buck. Sometimes he gave us some of the meat, which was lean because, mother said, the animal fed poorly.

He could be hard on his wife. We often heard them scolding each other, far into the night. Her voice was loud and sharp, half pleading and half protesting; his, deep and firm and decisive.

In his wife's presence Mr Pendi was loud and hard on Mary, their housegirl. But when he was alone, he talked softly to her.

'Warm the water for me, Mary, my girl. I want it real warm today. Soap and towel, Mary.'

'Yes, sir.'

'Make sure the water is warm, Mary.'

'It is.'

'Good girl. Now take the water to the bathroom.'

Mary carried the water to the bathroom, a rectangular wall of grass open at the top.

'Mary,' called Mrs Pendi. Silence.

'Mary!' she called again, more loudly.

There was a moment of silence, and then Mary's voice came from the bathroom.

'Mary. Where have you been? I called you two times and you did not answer. Where were you?'

'What is wrong?' said Mary.

'Stop asking me questions. I do the asking and you do the answering. I demand an answer. Where were you?'

Mary shook at the pointedness of her questions.

'You are a stupid girl, Mary,' said Mrs Pendi, her voice rising. 'I will tell you where you were. You were in the bathroom with my husband. You want to take my place, don't you? Tonight I will teach you to leave men to their proper women.'

Something violent must have happened for we heard Mary running away crying, her voice receding, between sobs saying that she was sick and tired of it all and was going home; that she was sick of the bullying and slave-driving; that she was going away, never to come back again, never to this troublesome place; she was going home to her mother.

If it was acting, it was excellent. Mr Pendi calmly finished his bath.

'What is all this noise?' he demanded. 'Why is Mary crying? Why has she gone away?'

'Don't ask me,' replied Mrs Pendi edgily. 'You should know.'

That pressed the red button.

'What's wrong?'

'What's wrong indeed! You think you can cheat me and get away with it! You think you can fool around with any dirty savage girl and get away with it? I am not blind, am I?'

'What!' he exclaimed, surprised that she was so explicit.

'What were you doing out there in the bathroom with Mary?'

He laughed angrily.

'I said, what were you doing out there in the dark with Mary?' she continued relentlessly. 'You think it's decent for a married man to behave as you did. With a woman – a girl – a housemaid, a dirty ignorant girl from two compounds away. And right in the bathroom ten paces from me and the children?'

There were tears in her voice. Her trampled heart was crying out but her indignation was like a rubber stick hitting iron.

'You are a troublesome woman,' he said, evasively. 'Do you think I will stand for your empty accusations? You treat me like your own son, your own little boy. What would I do with a girl from two compounds away?'

'What did you do with Mary?'

'Just because she took my water to the bathroom, you think I was having fun with her?'

'What else could you be doing?'

'Watch out!' he shouted. He must have made a movement to strike her, for she lowered her voice immediately.

'I will leave you to marry your Claras and your Marys and see what good housewives they will make you.'

'You can leave tonight, if you want to.'

'All you care about is your beer,' she said.

Things were getting dangerous.

'You don't care for me or for the children. You don't love us. You always come home late, and then I can't say one civil word to you. How do you expect me to react if you make passes at every girl with a bust in this village? How can I stand it?'

'You have a very wild kind of jealousy. Why are you not going away? I said you could pack and leave tonight. Why are you not packing?'

'You have no feelings. You treat me as if I am just one of your Claras, your Petulas, your Marys.'

She was crying loudly now and the children cried with her. He let her cry for a while and then muttered her into silence. But the quarrel had not ended. We woke up to it. It must have been midnight. I woke up with a start to the sound of rapping on mother's bedroom door and a girl crying.

I jumped up and peeped through the doorway. The moon was bright outside.

Emma was crouched down at mother's door, crying. She was naked.

'What's wrong?' mother asked quickly.

'He is beating her,' she cried.

'What?'

'Father is beating mother. He will kill her if you do not come to stop the fight. He has been drinking. Please come and stop it. Please! Please!'

From the Pendis' hut we could hear thudding sounds, as if a man was throwing logs onto the floor, and muffled screams.

'Please!' cried Emma, as the thudding sounds came faster. Emma had sometimes been a naughty and disobedient child but I admired her that night.

Mother stood on in confusion while the ruthless wife-beating went on.

'Go, mother,' urged Yona timidly.

'I can't go,' said mother mildly. 'I am also another man's wife. I cannot intervene. I am not a man.'

She could not go then, even if she heard him beating her to death. He wouldn't kill her. He would come to his senses before he killed her.

It could not go on. It stopped with a final thud and a crack. I thought bones had been smashed to fragments on the floor.

'Go back to bed, boys,' said mother. She took Emma's hand and led her away to the fence. Emma held the two strands of wire apart and stepped across. Mother stood at the fence for some minutes, listening. The handle of the lamp clinked on the glass and the yellow flame fluttered in the wind. There was a smell of paraffin in the silent night. Slowly mother came away from the fence. The wind tugged at her petticoat and threatened to blow out the lamp.

We went to sleep.

We woke up to a quiet morning. Mr Pendi was up and about, but we did not see his wife. Eventually he went away with his gun and while he was away mother went to see Mrs Pendi. Mr

Pendi returned an hour or two later, with a dead buck on his shoulders.

There was the smell of roasting meat in the air, and a buck skin hung drying on the line. There was no talking and laughing yet. But Mr Pendi had apologised.

6

We had never wanted housegirls, being a close-knit family, and somehow the incident at the Pendis' household had made us more hostile to the idea of them. Many of the *deruka* families who employed local girls did nothing but complain about them. It was alleged that either their affairs interfered with their work or endangered their employer's reputation, or that the girls had to be dismissed after stealing this or that, or that they simply absconded from work claiming they were being mistreated.

When mother was advised by the doctor not to do any heavy work after she suffered from severe pains in her legs, we had little option but to get a housegirl to do the cooking and the housework. The prospect of living for the first time with an outsider in our home naturally made us anxious.

The news of our wanting a girl spread quickly around the village. Soon we found a woman waiting for us with her daughter when we returned from the fields. The girl was dark with long hair and good white teeth. Her eyes were large and wide apart, giving her face a serene look. She was fourteen or fifteen but already a young woman, sitting in cross-legged silence even after her mother had left.

'I want you to feel at home here, Cheru,' mother said. 'I want to treat you as my own child and I want you to regard me as your mother. My boys will treat you like their sister. I want us to live nicely together. I won't drive you like a slave because you are only a girl and will be helping me. But you will work well, right?'

Cheru's large black eyes remained fixed on the floor.

'Your work,' explained mother, 'will be to cook, wash the dishes and clothes and help in the fields whenever you can. I will show you how to do your work.'

Cheru washed the dishes with the girls, Shuvai explaining to her in her calm dignified way the use of Vim and dishcloths. Mother prepared supper, explaining elaborately how much salt she wanted in the meat, how she wanted water to simmer on the fire before mealie-meal was added and how she wanted the cooking sticks and pots to be washed immediately afterwards to discourage flies.

In the morning we went with Cheru to harvest the mealies. We worked quietly for a while. Her dress was torn under her armpits, showing her thick damp curly hair. She evidently wore nothing under her thin blouse, as her nipples stuck out like marbles. She stood knee-deep in the grass, softly plucking the mealie-cobs from the stalks. There were grass seeds in her hair. She had strong slim arms but her nails needed cutting.

A locust jumped out of the grass and fluttered desperately away, landing near her feet. She crouched down quickly. Her cupped hand snatched the insect from the grass. In a second she had pulled off its legs.

'Put it in your pocket.' She gave the locust to Yona.

'Can you eat it?' asked Yona, and Cheru nodded.

'Don't you eat locusts?' she asked. Her lips were dry, but her pink tongue glistened wet behind her white teeth.

'We only eat certain kinds,' explained Yona.

47

'People say that if you eat this sort you will have bad eyes,' said Jo.

'Gossip,' said Cheru, smiling. 'My mother and I have been eating these since I was a toddler but we can still see well. We used to catch enough locusts to fill a small pot.'

'We caught *madora*,' I said, not to be outdone.

'We did too,' she said. 'Buckets of the creatures, and then we would have relish for months. Sometimes my father came with us. He brought an axe to chop the trees, so we could pick them easily from the branches.'

Talking, she was free and bright.

'My father was a violent man. He used to fight with my mother, and my sister and I ran out to sleep in the bushes. He chased her around with a spear. He had the spirit of a dead man inside him and no one could drive it out. Wherever the drums were beating, he was there. If there were no drums beating in the neighbourhood, then he walked miles at night to find drums. Everybody knew him. His spirit made him drink like a bull and quarrel with people. But he worked hard in the fields and we cried very much when he died.'

'Your father died?'

'He died in a fight with another man. I was like Tendai when he died, but I still remember him. He had been drinking heavily with his friends when they started quarrelling. They stabbed him with a knife. There was dry blood all around his body when we discovered him the next morning. He had bled like a slaughtered ox.'

'Did the police find his murderers?'

'No. No one called the police. We just buried him. My father had been wronged but he got his revenge. Two weeks after we buried him the man who stabbed him died of a strange disease.'

'Your dead father had the power to kill his living enemy?'

'You don't know my father. He was the strongest medicine

man in our village. At that time we lived about two days' walk from here. Many people came to my father with their problems, while he was living, and he cured them. He knew the medicines to keep ghosts and witches away from the compound. We never saw any near our compound.'

'Have you ever seen a ghost?'

'Only once. I will never forget it. I was coming from my uncle's compound with my mother at night. The path went between two graves and an old homestead that had been abandoned. We first smelt a strange smell, a smell like rotten sacks. Suddenly, we saw it. It was right in front of us. It was very tall and very dark and had its head in the sky. We fell down in fear and closed our eyes. I couldn't speak. It went away into the trees.'

'A tall dark ghost! But people say that ghosts are like fires, and that they shine like lamps.'

'Yes, there are all types of ghosts. There are tall dark ones that are really the spirits of dead people. They appear at graves, usually near abandoned homes. The ghosts that shine like fires can be seen anywhere at night, especially by those people with medicines to keep them away. There are also the ghosts kept by witches. They are like very small men and they have very small feet. You can tell that the little men have been in your compound if you see the small footprints. The witches send them to beat people. Sometimes they will even beat a man to death.'

'How do the witches get their little men?'

'If you find a stickhole spun into the mound of a grave only two days after the burial, then you will know that the witches have raised the spirit of the dead person and turned it into one of their little men.'

Perhaps her smiling eyes were only telling established untruths.

'You said you were living in another village. Why did you leave it?'

'It turned into a bad place. People were dying like ants. Every night before we went to bed we emptied our water buckets and threw away any food left from the supper. We feared poisoning. There were too many graves and too many corpse-eaters in the village. Many of the graves were dug up and the bodies removed. A child once reported that his mother stored children's hands and legs in a big three-legged pot. My sister died and my mother decided to leave the village.'

'Is there anybody living in the village now?'

'No. Everybody left. Few people go there now, especially at night. They are afraid of seeing the strange fires.'

The sun had gone down. Winter was on its way and darkness fell quickly.

As we walked among the shadowy trees, going home, I saw an imaginary tall dark giant striding across the path ahead of us, dragging with him his chilly atmosphere of death and rottenness. The fireflies suddenly chilled me as they flashed in the grass.

Perhaps the spirit of Cheru's dead father protected us, for we got home safely.

Cheru's mother was at home when we arrived. She was very much like her daughter, with a large wide face and a smooth dark complexion. But instead of being white and well placed, her teeth were small and brown from drinking too much. Her face had many razor slashes where the medicine man had cut her to put herbs in her bloodstream. Her dress was torn, exposing her gleaming black shoulders.

Cheru gave her mother a short greeting and sat cross-legged near the door of the hut.

The woman talked about the weather, the rain, the scarcity of relish and about *madora*.

'Please keep a keen eye on Cheru,' she said after a while. 'Don't let her play with boys. I don't want her coming home with twins in her belly. But I don't mind if she plays with your

50

sons. They are all too young to harm her, and besides they are good boys, are they not?'

'She will be all right,' laughed mother. 'She is old enough to realise the dangers of being free with boys. As for my sons, you can rest assured they will treat her as their own sisters.'

'You are a good woman, Masiziva. You are better than all the newcomers. You are kind. Some new families wouldn't give poor people like us a grain of salt, even if we asked for it.'

'Perhaps you want some salt.' Mother took the hint. She said to Tendai, 'Give her a cup of salt and a bucket of nuts for peanut butter, boys.'

Cheru's mother clapped her hands in gratitude.

'Oh thank you, Masiziva. You know the trouble of your fellow villagers. Now I will have enough peanut butter for months. You are very kind.'

'I was thinking,' continued mother, 'of sewing a few clothes for Cheru. A working girl should wear good clothes to show that she is working.'

'You are a good woman, Masiziva. Even if you don't give my daughter her pay for two months, I won't worry because I know she is safe in your care. Be good, Cheru.'

She put the bucket of nuts on her head and took the cup of salt carefully in her free hand. She went home in the darkness, the gate tinkling shut behind her.

◆

Cheru was a willing worker but a little childish. She was only fourteen.

She loved little Rita, and when she cried she took her into the bushes on her back, and sang her to sleep.

'Keep quiet Ri Ri Ri Rita.
Hush Rita, baby of the mother.'

51

When she met her friends at the pump, she talked for hours, sometimes only hurrying home at sunset to wash the afternoon dishes just in time for supper; and there were lumps of mealie-meal in her sadza.

But mother was invariably patient with her. We loved Cheru when she talked but felt uneasy when she spent hours at the pump and burnt the meat. She was a free girl. Once I found her singing and dancing alone behind the hut, wheeling her hips. She stopped uneasily when she saw me.

Her best friend was Mary, the girl who worked for the Pendis. She was about sixteen and even more flirtatious than Cheru. Their friends sometimes came to see them and they played till the young moon threw long shadows – singing, dancing and giggling. Once or twice we went to join them. But on most occasions we stayed in the hut like a pack of prudes, lending a half-deaf ear to their girlish screams as we pretended to be reading.

One day we went to the river to fish and at about midday a group of girls came down to swim. There were about eight of them all talking and laughing as they approached the water. Cheru was with them.

When they saw us they came to a dead stop.

'There are boys fishing here,' said one of the girls, needlessly.

'No use swimming then,' said another girl, and they turned away, their skirts dancing above our heads.

When we arrived home just after dark, we met Cheru at the gate on her way to the pump.

'No wonder she is always late preparing supper, she plays the whole day,' muttered Yona. When we went in with the fish, mother was holding the basin of sugar, saying, 'This basin was full of sugar after breakfast.' We understood the implication.

Shrugging her shoulders, mother took the fish away to scrape, when Cheru suddenly arrived, a bucket of water on her head.

She loomed in the doorway like a woman of the night, with droplets of water on her eyelids.

She wasn't afraid of the dark. She wasn't afraid.

◆

After about three weeks Cheru fell ill. She could not move, and spent the whole day lying lethargically on a blanket near the fire.

'What's wrong with you?' mother asked.

'Nothing.'

'Do you feel any pains?'

'Nothing.'

'Perhaps we ought to take you to the clinic?'

'No. I will be all right.'

'Has this happened to you before? I suppose your mother ought to know.'

Her mother came and took her home but returned that evening to explain.

'It's nothing, Maziziva,' she said, 'she will be all right.'

'But don't you think you ought to take her to the clinic?'

'They wouldn't be able to help her.'

'And you have no idea what her problem is?'

'It's nothing to worry about, Maziziva.'

'It's just that she seemed such a healthy girl and then yesterday morning she couldn't move. Naturally I'd be worried . . .'

'There is no need to worry. Of course it's not your fault! I know you too well even to suspect . . .'

'But please, Mai Cheru, just to relieve my anxiety . . .'

'Well, if you are *so* worried,' said Mai Cheru with a sigh, looking sadly into the fire. 'It's like this . . . Cheru has been suffering from a strange illness. Actually, it's not an illness. It's the spirit of her dead aunt who wants to possess her. It affects her mind and body. That is why she is so quiet. I was quite reluctant to let her work for you, but she insisted.'

'Is that what makes her ill?'

'Yes.'

'You are sure, Mai Cheru?'

'Of course. Other things have happened in our family since Cheru's father died and we have paid many visits to spirit mediums. Every time we have been told that it's Cheru's aunt who has been causing these happenings because she has something to say to us.'

'And unless you allow this aunt to possess her, Cheru will not be well?'

'No, she won't. Unless we brew some beer and meet her wishes there can be no rest.'

'Poor Cheru. Such a young girl, and so quiet too.'

'It's nothing to be frightened about,' laughed Mai Cheru, her eyes sparkling in the firelight as she crossed one leg over the other. 'It's not an evil spirit. It's just that Cheru's aunt wants to get in touch with us, to say that she is looking after our problems and let us know what she thinks. You know people in the world of the dead see things better than we do. She wants to help us but she can only do so if she gets somebody to act as her mouthpiece.'

'And Cheru is to be that mouthpiece?'

'Yes.'

'And is she going to remain her normal self?'

'Why, yes, of course, except when the spirit possesses her, and that happens not too often, maybe once or twice a year.'

'I suppose, if that will help her to get better, you had better do it.'

'Yes, Masiziva. What can we do? We people with a black skin cannot escape from our customs. We have actually started brewing beer today, and we will have the possession ceremony

54

this Saturday. There will be many people, and lots of food. Meat, stamped mealies, beer, *maheu*, dancing and drums. You can let your boys come to see how it is done, so that they can know of it and write about it in their books at school.'

'Well . . .'

'Perhaps your church does not allow you to take part in such festivities?'

'Not quite . . .'

'Or perhaps your husband?'

'To tell you the truth, Mai Cheru, my husband and I know very little about these customs. Not that we hold them in contempt, but because we have lived in town for a long time.'

'And you never hold beer parties to honour your dead?'

'Not as far as I remember. I know my people did various things. But generally we believed that the dead should be allowed to rest in peace.'

'You probably have good ancestors, Masiziva. Your ancestors are lying still in their graves and don't believe in causing any inconvenience. But they are looking after you very well, Masiziva, or you wouldn't be alive.'

'What would eat me?'

'It's such an evil world, Masiziva, that someone has to watch each step you make. This dark night holds every kind of evil. You have been living with us for quite a few years now, but have you buried any of your children? Yet you hear of a death here, a death there, every day. Not ordinary deaths caused by ordinary diseases, but most unusual ones. We have seen people die of a swollen stomach, a swollen toe, or from lightning descending from a clear winter sky. And you don't believe there is evil? You don't believe that you have strong ancestors looking after you?'

'You are very right, Mai Cheru. Our deceased parents do look after us. It's only that we don't speak enough to them. You wouldn't believe what my father said to me on his deathbed.'

'What did he say?'

'He asked me to remove a speck in his eye. I couldn't find that speck, but he promised me a good life.'

'You see now, Masiziva. The dead are alive. A person just doesn't die and vanish. The human soul is too strong for that.'

'Yes.'

'Well, I have to go now, Masiziva. I am sorry Cheru had to leave so suddenly.'

'No, it's all right. I can see it's urgent.'

'We will have to work fast. The worst we can do is disappoint the dead.'

She stood up to go and then mother said, 'If there is anything you need . . . Oh yes, Cheru hasn't had her pay this month.'

'But it's only half way through the month, Masiziva.'

'It's all right. It isn't her fault that she has had to leave work.'

'Oh thank you. It's so nice of you.'

'She can always come back to work if she gets better and feels like doing so.'

'I will tell her that. Now I have to go or I wouldn't stop thanking you. Good night.'

'Goodnight and good luck.'

'Do you believe in ancestral spirits, mother?' we asked quietly after Cheru's mother had gone.

'Everybody does.'

'Then why is it that you don't pay much attention to them?'

'Perhaps we don't need to. Unless they show themselves first.'

'What about ghosts and witchdoctors and things like that?'

'That's another thing,' she laughed.

'Some people believe in planting odd things around their homes to keep evil away.'

'Yes. But one doesn't have to touch a herb unless one has to.'

'And you think there are evil people in this village, mother?'

'That's anybody's guess. As Mai Cheru said, every man is

capable of evil. But I would say this is a safe village, compared to others I have known.'

'What happened there?'

'You had better stop asking too many questions, or you will be afraid to go to your hut in the dark!'

◆

On that Sunday, the drums boomed all night in Mai Cheru's compound. In the middle of the night, when the half moon was climbing to the zenith, we heard Cheru's voice screaming at a very high pitch as the mysterious spirit possessed her body. She raced into the forest, gasping indistinguishable totem sounds among the excited and gratified shouts of the crowd who ran after her, listening to the messages from the world of the dead. When we saw Cheru again she was fetching water at the village pump. She looked very normal, and greeted us. But she did not come back to our home.

It was only then that I realised that Cheru, with her chilling night stories, quiet dark eyes and flowering womanhood, held a mysterious promise.

7

'Not another chicken stolen!' exclaimed Jairos on hearing of the theft. 'And another batch of eggs gone!'

By then we owned about a hundred healthy chickens. They laid scores of eggs every morning in the bushes, on rooftops, in cardboard boxes. Admiring our chickens, Jairos had proposed to bring three of his hens to our coop, ostensibly so that they could adopt our breed of chickens. But soon after he brought his hens over, our stock started diminishing.

Naturally, on learning of the disappearing eggs, Jairos got worried, since his own hens were in danger. He brought over some roots one day and mixed them with chicken droppings, setting fire to the mixture.

'The thief will confess that he stole the eggs,' he said laughingly as he performed his small ritual. 'The stolen eggs will cackle in his stomach till his health and conscience inevitably drive him to confess.'

I imagined that Jairos had brought the nearest roots he could find and had improvised the ritual. If it worked at all it was not impossible that Jairos himself would suffer the inconvenience of chickens cackling in his stomach.

'Oh yes,' said Jairos again, brushing ash and bits of herb off his hands. 'The thief will come and beg forgiveness.'

And a few moments later: 'Masiziva, here we have a simple custom that I haven't explained to you yet, which is that every *deruka* family should brew beer for the village on at least one Christmas. We call it thanksgiving beer. Just to show the elders you are thankful that they accepted you into the community. You haven't brewed that beer yet, so I don't see why it shouldn't happen this Christmas.'

'But I can't brew beer,' said mother anxiously.

'You will have to get someone to do it for you, Masiziva. I know you are disappointed that someone has been stealing your chickens and eggs but that's to be expected in any village, and shouldn't stop you from showing gratitude towards the elders.'

'It will be a noisy Christmas,' complained Yona, after Jairos had gone. 'People will be making an open beerhall of our homestead.'

'And urinating behind the huts,' remarked Jo.

'I doubt if it is the custom of this village to make newcomers brew beer,' laughed mother. 'I don't really trust him. But I will have to find someone to brew the beer for me.'

That person was Simon's wife, Mampofu. She brought two huge drums and we went to fetch wood for the fire.

Soon a big fire was blazing and Mampofu stirred mealie-meal into the drum of boiling water. Late that night the thin porridge was still bubbling, even after she had removed the fire and covered the drum with zinc sheets. The brewing continued for the next four days. *Mumera* was added to the porridge, which was boiled again, diluted and left to ferment.

The day before Christmas, three women came to help Mampofu sieve the beer. They squeezed the thick brew with their hands, talking, gesticulating, turning to blow their noses and rubbing their slimy fingers on the sleeves of their old dresses.

Villagers trickled in to taste the brew. They sat near the grain hut chattering, arguing over the small white mug, and demanding more beer while Mampofu, the brewer, authoritatively refused to refill the mug. It was good beer, very good beer, they said.

After supper we left for the bus stop to meet father. The night was dark and in the starlight we groped our way along the narrow path. Already the dew was falling. We could feel it on the grass, soaking our tennis shoes.

We went down into the valley and the night chill hit us, numbing our mouths and fingers. Even in the starlight we could see the faint yellow grass and the greenish black of the tall reeds. The frogs croaked in the murk and the fireflies flicked their lights on and off like little torches. We left the valley and its orchestra of frogs and went up the bank into the safe, warm darkness of the trees.

Our path ran into a big compound. Two huts suddenly loomed in front of us, the warm homely smell of smoke and sadza drifting out of the glowing doorways. We could hear the chink of crockery inside and knew the inhabitants had finished supper and the girls were washing the plates. We went on past the kraals. We saw the dark forms of cattle, their shiny black eyes gleaming in a darkness full of the smell of cowdung. We broke out of the wood onto the dust road which ran like a long dark groove between the two flanks of trees, huge and desolate.

Then we sat under a tree in the silent night and waited. Silent, holy night, I remembered, and the shepherds waiting. But all was not calm and bright. Dark clouds were rolling over the horizon. The sky swelled. The wind swept in from the south, dusting our faces and pulling at our clothes. Overhead the clouds scrambled, scattered and crashed.

Then the wind stopped suddenly and the rain came down. We crouched against the tree-trunks, away from the rain. A whip of lightning and thunder cracked overhead, the earth trembled as the echoes shook the rain-sodden forests. The rain drove round against us and for some minutes we were exposed to it. It left us soaking. The spent clouds rolled down towards the horizon, exposing a crisp half moon. We shivered.

We heard the bus miles before it appeared, chugging and rumbling through the forests. Its headlights cut the damp night sky. The beams hit us before we saw it going down into the valley. As it drew nearer we smelt its heat and its petrol. It stopped right beside us and the conductor jumped out and ran up the steps to the roof. Two men followed him, a tall man in a hat and overcoat, and another short and fat, wearing a thick coat. We turned excitedly towards the tall man.

'Haa! Hello, boys. You came in the darkness and rain to meet me and it rained enough to sweep away a hut. You are all as wet as fish. I didn't expect you here at all. But then you are grown-up now and no longer afraid of the dark.'

Their luggage was lifted down from the roof of the bus. Then the conductor jumped back inside and the bus plunged away into the darkness, leaving us standing in the cool crisp moonlight.

'This is Mr Jacobi,' said father, introducing the short, plump man. He shook our hands and his hand was huge and fat and soft. He had only brought a crate of beer and an oil lamp for Christmas.

Yona and I took up the two heavy boxes and Mr Jacobi lifted his crate determinedly onto his shoulders, having refused to let Jo help him.

'I will light my lamp so that we can see our way,' he said, stopping.

'But it's all right,' protested father. 'There is enough moonlight.'

Mr Jacobi lit his lamp. The flame flickered and threw its yellow light on the wet grass. We set off again.

'Mr Jacobi lives up on the slope,' father explained. 'He has built himself a good brick and zinc house, the first one in the village.'

'You know Petros?' said Mr Jacobi briefly.

'The tall boy with big gumboots . . .' said Yona.

'The one who shoots birds with a gun?' I added.

'Yes,' replied Mr Jacobi. 'That's my son.'

'I see,' we said.

'Have you finished the weeding?' asked father.

'Not yet.'

'The rain disturbed you?'

'Not very much, the virgin soil is very hard to weed.'

'Oh, yes, very hard. But it is a good soil. It drains easily. You can go weeding immediately after a storm, don't you agree, Mr Jacobi?'

'A very good soil,' nodded Mr Jacobi.

'Good soil and good land,' said father.

'I like this village because people brew beer,' said Mr Jacobi. 'Has your wife brewed beer for Christmas?'

'I don't know,' said father. 'The boys know better.'

'Jairos asked mother to brew the thanksgiving beer for the village,' Yona explained. 'The beer was strained today.'

'He insisted!' exclaimed father, bemused.

'Is it good beer?' pursued Mr Jacobi.

'Everybody who has tasted it says it is good beer,' said Jo.

We went into the forest and passed the huts we had seen earlier. They were more distinct in the moonlight. A dog bayed weakly from under the grain bin.

'I have never seen such stupid villagers,' said Mr Jacobi. 'Do you see what this is?'

'What?'

'This earth mound. It is an old grave. Three paces from the path and five from the hut. How can people live so near a grave?'

We had not noticed the grave on our way to the bus stop.

'These people like to live with ghosts,' continued Mr Jacobi. 'Why otherwise would they have their graves so close to their huts? In the south where I come from graves are placed away from our homes.'

'But this is not the south,' said father. 'The people here are not as superstitious.'

'You think so? I don't think so. I think they are stupid not to send their children to school. Look at the way they build their huts – a confusion of grass and poles – and their huts are built so close together that one little fire will burn down a whole compound. And the way they grow their crops – weeds and plants and bushes compete for the soil.'

'They still have a lot to learn.'

'And there is that headman, Jairos.' He was laughing now, loud fat laughter which I thought must be heard for miles around. 'That imbecile, Jairos. He has not one little idea of administration in his head. Giving people's fields away for money is all he cares about – and, of course, asking for tobacco and gin. They should set up a council to run things properly. Jairos! My son would run this village better than he does.'

'No,' protested father. 'Councils are bad. They force people to do things they do not want. They make you work on stupid projects and pay money to build beerhalls. They force cattle into paddocks and people to get licences to cut grass or timber. No! Councils will turn the village into a town.'

We crossed the stream among the frogs and fireflies. It wasn't exciting any more, not with Mr Jacobi railing about the village, while the bold yellow light of his lamp eclipsed the fireflies.

At the pump Mr Jacobi left us to take another path, and we continued home. Mother came sleepily out of the hut, her face puffy with sleep, so that her head fell sideways when father rather too excitedly tried to kiss her. But we had to wait until we got to our sleeping hut before we could laugh about it.

◆

It turned out to be a very noisy Christmas as Yona had predicted. Very early that morning the beer drinkers assembled to drink our excellent brew. They sat in a ring, men and women alike, while the white mug was passed round so that everyone could take a swig.

The attendance at father's Christmas service was bigger than it had been the previous year, and afterwards we had many guests for tea, although the beer party dispelled some of them.

After breakfast we left the noise of our compound to attend a wedding ceremony a mile away. There was already a huge gathering when we arrived. The wedding pair sat in an artificial sackcloth shade. The bridegroom, newly barbered, was sweating slightly in his uncomfortable brown suit. The bride was a light-skinned beauty, cool in her spotless wedding dress. They were southerners.

The crowd stood round them singing and clapping their hands. Now gifts were being given and a balding old man climbed onto a drum to announce the presents, shouting vigorously. Pots, pans, mats, chickens, goats, money and even cattle were given to start the pair off in their life together. The wedding was conducted in town fashion and the local villagers were impressed by the grandeur of the occasion.

A few metres away a bull was being skinned for meat. The sweet oily smell of roasting meat hung in the air. Women sweated over the roaring fires, cooking the food in huge black drums. Jairos could be seen actively helping himself from the pots. There were large dishes of mealie rice, almost drowning in pools of fatty yellow soup and chunks of meat. There was rice and chicken for the special guests. The children dashed for the meat, although there was enough of it to cause toothache afterwards. There was Mazoe, Coke and *maheu*, and, of course, beer. Buckets and buckets of thick, khaki-coloured beer.

After eating, the singing and dancing was resumed with renewed vigour, with drums and gramophones and human voices mingling their noises uproariously. Jairos rose, drunk to his nose, to give a speech on little other than money and beer and meat. He sounded patronising but no one minded. In the end the bridegroom himself rose to jive to the gramophone, throwing off his coat and kicking his shoes away. The sun was setting when we left the wedding.

'Let us go to the field,' said father. I could see he was in one of his happy, extravagant moods. He had been to see the field in the morning, but he wanted to go again.

We plodded along the sandy path in our Christmas trousers and shoes, but before long we had taken our shoes off and were walking barefoot on the warm sand.

We broke into the green expanse of the field. Here the work of the hoe, the labour of hands, the ache of the back, the salty taste of sweat and burning thirst had been transformed into living green plants. The mealies stood erect and tall. The lush, thick-stemmed groundnuts were flowering, pumpkins and melon tendrils meandered in the green. You felt like standing there for hours, admiring the very colour of it, as if you could actually see the plants growing and hear the infiltration of their roots.

Down in the vlei the fireflies were burning and the chilly air absorbed us. It was time to go. We turned back along the path, among the tall trees and crouching bushes where the birds roosted secretly, past the tree-stumps where the buck had galloped away.

The beer party was still going on in our compound. Men and women sat in broken half rings, chattering at the top of their voices. Father went round telling the party to disperse. Eventually people clapped their hands in thanksgiving and left in staggering pairs and trios. Matudu came forward hiccupping to say that my father was the kindest, wisest, richest and the everythingest man to tell the party to disperse. I expected the beer to spill out of him at any minute.

As I stood in the doorway of the kitchen, watching the last drunkards staggering home, I heard little voices and turned to look round at the back of the hut.

A female figure was sitting across a man's legs and even in the darkness I saw the movements and heard the gasping noises – I had walked into them suddenly, without realising what I was doing. The movements and the voices did not stop. I went back quietly into the hut.

'Mrs Simon is an expert brewer,' mother was saying over the pots of rice and chicken.

I wondered who they were out there doing it just behind our hut. They were probably very drunk and might stay all night. But when I went out to check an hour later there was no sign of them.

◆

Boxing Day was not an anti-climax. Father's buoyant mood kept us happy. Early in the morning he sent us to call Headman Jairos. We found him already drinking off last night's hangover. He came with us at once, first shutting his beer away. He ploughed the path with his car-tyre sandals, wetting his trousers to the knee in the dew. We found father in the field, chopping down a tree.

'Good morning,' he greeted Jairos. 'How are you?'

'Hangover!' complained Jairos, making himself a cigarette.

'How was your night?'

'We did not sleep. We spent the night drinking.'

'You drank more after the wedding and all those beer parties?'

'Yes, Munyu brought a pot of delicious beer from Goto village and we drank till the second cock crowed.'

'You enjoyed yourself. How is your wife and your girl?'

'They are all right.'

'And your crops?'

'Oh, they are well too, the mealies are tasselling now.'

The crops were not well. In fact there were no crops in Jairos's field because he had not ploughed a single furrow since the rains began.

'I called you, Headman Jairos,' said father eventually, 'because there is a piece of land I want to add to my field to make it straight.'

'Yes.'

'You see this edge here. The person who chopped down the trees left too many bushes close to the edge. These will harm the crops.'

'Yes,' said Jairos pacing nearby. 'I can see the corner is not straight.'

'I need to grow more crops to sell,' explained father. 'My family is growing.'

'Go ahead and chop down the trees,' said Jairos, laughing. 'But you will give me ten dollars.'

'Ten dollars!' smiled father.

'Yes. Ten dollars is not too much to pay the headman for moving him in the morning dew on Boxing Day. You will give me ten dollars and one hen and one bottle of gin.'

8

Exactly a year later, a few days before Christmas, father wrote to say that he would not be coming home.

'He says he can't afford to come,' mother explained soberly, folding his long letter. 'He has more than enough expenses as it is – your school fees.'

'Won't he come at all?' asked Tendai, touching the letter as if she could read.

'I don't think he will come at all,' said mother gloomily. 'He isn't sending us anything for Christmas either. No meat, no beans, no flour. We will just have to do the best we can on our own.' She laughed bitterly, holding the letter out. 'You can read it if you want to.'

Yona took the letter, read it quickly and passed it on to me. It was an elaborate one, written in father's clear bold galloping handwriting. He began by asking after everybody's health, the weather and the crops. Then followed a detailed account of all the school fees to be paid, the rent, the water charges and so on. He had compiled a neat list of our school uniforms and all the school materials needed. I knew it had taken him hours to compile and check the list to make sure it was accurate to a cent.

The total sum was formidable. Then followed a long paragraph explaining why he could not come home or send anything for Christmas. My eyes hovered questioningly over the last paragraph.

On Christmas Eve Mr Pendi came to say that he had seen father in town. There was no letter, no parcel. Christmas came. The Pendis invited us to breakfast. There was a bucket of coffee and a dish of bread, scones, biscuits and cakes. We reciprocated by inviting the Pendis to lunch.

After midday it rained. The torrent poured down from the black sky. Rivulets of water cut the sandy surfaces of our compound, dragging the fine sand to the edge of the forest. After an hour the sun came out.

'Go out,' mother chided us. 'You stay-at-homes. You never go out as boys of your age do. Do you want to spend the whole day indoors watching the turn of my cooking sticks?'

It was enough to make us put on our raincoats and go out. The wet sand was swollen. The rain had wiped away all the footprints. Raindrops hung glistening on the leaves and the grass.

We passed a compound by the side of the road where a beer party was in full swing, with drums and a gramophone playing simultaneously. A woman greeted us.

'Hello girls.'

Yona replied in a thin girlish voice and we ran away laughing. It was our raincoats that had made us look like girls.

We met a man we knew and said, 'Christmas Box!'

'Kisimisi, my children,' he said, giving us a coin each.

In the township the two stores were packed with boys and girls jiving to the gramophone. Girls with torn stockings and broken shoes stitched together for Christmas, barely concealing their cracked feet and heavily oiled legs; boys with heads newly barbered and combed, boys with clean white shirts, balloon trousers and shining shoes, sweating in their thin ties borrowed from brothers and fathers for Christmas. We saw Cheru in the crowd, wearing a bright-red dress and pointed high-heel shoes. She was spinning her arms and swinging her hips. She stopped dancing when she saw us, her lips barely forming an indistinct greeting. Then she started dancing again, very slowly, inching into the crowd, out of view. We stood in the doorway, and then the rain came down and we had to go in. The noise slashed the tin roof, drowning out the sound of the music. The roof was leaking in a corner and girls pushed away from the dripping roof, laughing and stumbling.

We decided to go back home before another storm built up. Already wild grey clouds were racing overhead. Thunder grumbled. The storm broke when we were half way home and closed in on us. We arrived after sunset, soaked to the skin and stood round the fire enjoying the warmth.

'Did you come by the field to check for stray cattle?' asked mother. We had forgotten to do so. We could not have done it in the rain, anyway. But by now stray cattle might be in our field, eating our mealies.

'We forgot.'

'Then I will have to go myself. It's no use sitting here round the warm fire while the cattle eat my crop.' She put on her raincoat and gumboots and went out.

We couldn't leave her to go alone, though we were soaked to the skin and cold. We left the warmth of the fire and trotted after her. It was getting dark and the rain was slackening. The grass was heavy with raindrops. My head hit a branch and water showered all over me. I looked up angrily.

On the other side of the path the open fields gazed at us, their low crops eclipsed by the darkness. We heard the sound of raindrops falling from the leaves and the sound of croaking frogs. We stood at the edge of our field scanning the dark for movement. 'I can smell them,' said mother. 'They were here a minute ago. Either they are still here somewhere in the field, or they have just left. There is nothing left in this field, I tell you. Nothing.'

I was afraid of her voice alone. It was loud in the dark. She splashed into the flooded furrows and we followed her. A firefly jumped up in front of us, clicking its light on. Jo gripped my waist fearfully with both hands. I was frightened and angry.

'Let go of me, you coward!' I shouted.

He let go quietly, and overtook me.

Mother strode on ahead. The great instinct of a farmer urged her on, driving her to defend her crops from animals even in the darkness and the rain. She came to a dead stop in the middle of the field.

'They have eaten everything here too. Good God in heavens, they have eaten every shoot.'

We looked down in the darkness and saw nothing. We turned back and went home. I was surprised. My mother's strange mood touched me lightly. It was the old and responsible who suffered most from such calamities.

In broad daylight, we saw the scale of the disaster. In every quarter of the field, the cattle had eaten the mealies. Almost every plant had been nibbled. The leaves had been ripped off, leaving only the stems.

There were hoofprints everywhere and many plants had been trampled into the ground. The greatest damage had been done in the centre of the field where the mealies had been the tallest. Here the shoots had been chewed down to the roots. The cattle had converged on the centre from every corner.

'This is what comes of worshipping Christmas,' said mother in a strange new voice. 'This is how people pay for staying at home and drinking tea while their crops are prey to roaming cattle. This is the result of my labour. Just look at this! My God! There was a whole kraal of them here. I leave my town with its

lights and its sofas and come to the country to work, and this is
what I get for my sweat. I do not work for the bellies of my
children. I grow crops to fatten other people's cattle for the
market . . .'

A woman came towards us from a path in the forest. Her
dress was wet with the rain and dew.

'Good morning, Masiziva,' she said, pausing.

'A bad morning, Mai Mashoko. Look at this! Surely these
people want something from me. Do you think anyone could be
so careless with their cattle? There was a whole herd here.'

'I saw the cattle yesterday afternoon,' said Mai Mashoko.

'Whose cattle were they?'

'Marufu's. You know him. He is a *deruka* who lives in
Headman Matuvi's line. He has a big herd, a very big herd. I
saw them in your field and drove them to his homestead. Before
I hurried home to attend to my sick child, I said to Marufu's
boys, "Why do you let your cattle eat Masiziva's mealies?" The
boys said they had been looking for the cattle, so I went to
Marufu and said, "Your cattle ate Masiziva's mealies!" And do
you know what he said? He said, "Did the cattle eat *your*
mealies, Mai Mashoko?" I said, "No," and he told me to go.'

'He said that, Mai Mashoko?'

'Just so. Every word with his own mouth.'

'If he thinks my field is a grazing area for his cattle. I will give
him a piece of my mind.'

'It won't have any effect on Marufu, Masiziva. He will shut
his door in your face and set his dogs on you. That man is a
devil. You say there is Satan, but Satan is nothing compared to
Marufu. Do you know what he did when his neighbour Gonai's
son broke the leg of his goat by accident? Although Gonai, that
blessed man of peace, made up by giving him not only a living
goat, but a much bigger one, Marufu killed the injured goat and

71

ate the meat with his family. He is not a man, Masiziva. He is a devil! If I were you I would not go to him.'

'Then what do you think I should do, Mai Mashoko? I can't just keep quiet about it.'

'Do anything, Masiziva, but don't go to Marufu. He cares more for the life of a goat than for the life of a boy. He will beat you up. Go and see Headman Jairos.'

'You think Jairos will help?'

'He is the right man to approach. Put a fence of barbed wire round your field, Masiziva.'

'Eh . . . Eh, Mai Mashoko, barbed wire costs money. And with this army of ours going to school there is no hope of buying barbed wire.'

'But you are a clever woman, Masiziva. You grow groundnuts. You sew clothes. Sell your groundnuts and your clothes and buy wire.'

'It was kind of you to drive the cattle out, Mai Mashoko. Thank you for your sympathy and advice.'

'I couldn't leave the cattle in your field, Masiziva, unless I was a devil. Not everyone in this village is a good person. I advise you because you are a good person. Not one day have I heard you open your mouth to slander anyone. But beware of devils like Marufu. Whatever you do, don't go to Marufu, Masiziva.'

◆

'The law of this land,' said Jairos emphatically that night, 'is that no man's animal should go into a person's field and eat his crops. No herdboy should ever lose sight of his cattle. Crops are vital to the life of every villager. All men know this.'

Jairos sat at the table, looking down on mother.

'That is the law of this land, Masiziva, and ever since I became headman thirteen years ago this law has been observed. The day

72

the first rains fall and people put their ploughs to use, the herdboys gather their cattle and graze them in Mbumbuzi forest. Only after harvesting can the cattle be allowed anywhere near the fields. You have been wronged, Masiziva. But there is one question I want to ask you. Whose cattle have eaten your mealies?'

'Marufu's,' answered mother, unnecessarily.

'Now what is Marufu?'

'What do you mean?' asked mother puzzled.

'I mean, is Marufu a local or a *deruka*?'

'He is a *deruka*.'

'Now you see the situation. Marufu is a *deruka* and you are a *deruka*. Now a *deruka* man's cattle went to a *deruka* woman's field and ate her mealies.'

'What are you getting at?'

'You don't see my point, Masiziva. The *derukas* are my guests and I don't aim to promote any quarrel between two of my guests.'

'But this is not a quarrel, Headman Jairos.'

'How do you expect me to react, Masiziva? It is not Marufu who ate your mealies. Marufu's cattle ate your crops. Now do cattle think and reason like people?'

'No.'

'No. They don't. Cattle will eat anything, regardless of whom it belongs to. Marufu's own cattle could go to Marufu's fields and eat Marufu's mealies . . .'

'Quite right.'

'Your mealies were eaten by accident, of course. Do you agree?'

'Well . . . yes.'

'Therefore we can't lay any charges on Marufu because it was an accident. One day you will own cattle too, Masiziva, and

73

your cattle will eat Marufu's crops. How would you like him to lay charges against you?'

'I see your point, Headman Jairos. My point in reporting this to you is so that you warn people to take greater care of their cattle . . .'

'That I will do, Masiziva. That I will do. I have always emphasised the importance of crops.' He finished eating and went away, and I knew he would never gather enough courage to speak to Marufu. He would break his promise, as he had broken numerous others.

Here was a headman who spoke of prosperity, peace and progress, and yet made not one positive effort to achieve these standards. He spoke of good houses when his own compound consisted of only two huts, two unplastered huts with old grey roofs. He spoke of cotton, groundnuts and sunflowers when his own fields were reverting to bush. He spoke extravagantly of paddocks, irrigation schemes and booming townships when he neither had the strength nor the determination to dig a single little ditch. He spoke of honesty and decency when he stole eggs and failed to hand in the taxes to the district office. The shocking state of his household spoke against him. Every three or four months he sold an ox, but he spent all the money on beer. He had even sold the oxen that drew the plough, and his family were all disappointed. He had never stopped long enough to think what he would use during the next ploughing season. His family had been so opposed to his selling the oxen that even young Kaya had refused to drive the oxen to the market. Eventually Jairos had driven the oxen to the market himself, swearing and cursing and driving with as much vigour as if the world might come to a stop before he could spend any of the money. He did not come home for three days after the sale of the oxen; then he came home ragged and hungry to beg. Rumour spread round that he had spent the money on beer and gambling and buying a very expensive herb that was supposed to make him the most prosperous village headman in the country.

'You will just have to forgive and forget, Masiziva,' he said.

Mother forgave and January showers fell, perhaps with a healing effect, because our nibbled mealies started budding again. But she never forgot and after the disaster which had occurred that Christmas, we never left our crops to the fate of roaming cattle.

I was sitting reading in the shade one afternoon when I heard the grunting and sneezing of goats. The leader of the group, a huge he-goat with twisted horns and dirty grey skin, stepped into the field, neatly uprooted two mealies and munched them. He looked at me with his bulging black eyes and I caught the stink of his body.

I picked up a thick piece of root and flung it at him in anger. The root caught his hind leg with a snap. The goats jumped and scattered into the bush, the he-goat limping frantically behind them. I followed them, whipping them with a stick till my arm ached and the stick broke into pieces.

I saw a group of herdboys standing in the bushes watching me. They were all youngsters of eight or nine, and held their whips in their hands. I threw my stick down and softly went up to them.

'Whose goats ate my mealies?' I demanded.

'We don't know,' said two of the boys.

I grabbed a whip from one of them. The youngsters jumped and ran, crying even before I hit them. I lashed furiously at their legs. The last boy to run away was too slow. I grabbed his hand. He embraced me in fear. His face looked up at me, making little expectant crying noises. I pulled his arms away and pushed him off. Up went the whip and I cut him on his neck, shoulders, arms and legs. He cried silently, twisting the flesh of his face. He made no attempt to run away. I gave his legs one final slash and let him go. I watched him go away slowly. I was filled with satisfaction and a strange fear.

'A woman was here with her small boy just now,' mother said to me gravely when I got home at sunset. 'The mother said you beat him.'

'Yes, I beat him. His goats ate the mealies. The goats come every day.'

'You shouldn't have beaten him in the face. His face and shoulders were all ridged up with the whip marks. His eyes were red and bulging. Beat them on the legs next time. His mother was complaining that you beat only her boy when there was a group of boys. She says you chose her boy.'

'But I beat all the boys.'

'You beat him too much. Beat them on the legs next time. The mother threatened to leave her boy here to see what you would do with him.'

'She trusts her witchcraft,' said Jo, blankly.

'Watch your words, Jo,' said mother severely.

After that incident the herdboys were afraid of me and kept their animals well clear of our field. The mealies grew again undisturbed.

◆

We left with heavy hearts at the end of the holiday, knowing that there would be only mother to guard the crops. Every single day of the week, every week of the month, for two months she and the girls would go to the fields to guard the mealies.

We arrived in town late in the evening. The bus had been late. The trunk clanked on the bricks. I knocked on the door. We stood like policemen, waiting for the door to be opened. The streets were quiet now, insects whirled round the glowing yellow street lamps.

A shuffle inside and the door opened. Father stood there, tall and muscular and hairy without his shirt. His face was half swollen with sleep, but he was smiling.

'Hello boys.' He held out his hands.

He was smiling, and we smiled back weakly, tired from the journey.

'You came alone?'

'Yes.'

'Come in. Come in.'

He carried the trunk in. 'Heavy with books,' he said.

He had moved the sofas and the small library. There were six new Reader's Digest magazines on the shelf. In the spare room the table was laid thick with books and papers. He had been doing the church accounts before he went to bed.

'I was getting tired of staying here alone,' he smiled, scratching his head. 'How were mother and the girls?'

'They were well and asked us to send greetings.'

'The bus was very late. When did you leave the station?'

'Five o'clock.'

'With school children coming back to town, you can't expect easy travelling.'

'About five full buses passed us without stopping. We were thinking of going back home and postponing the journey. The last bus came and picked us up just in time.'

'It's a booming countryside. You can tell from the way people crowd the buses.'

He scratched his armpits and hugged himself, looking blankly at the electric bulb, his smile disappearing.

'Why did mother not come with you?'

'She couldn't come because of the cattle. Hardly a day passes without them coming to eat the mealies. Marufu's cattle ate every stick of maize at Christmas.'

77

'Yes, I remember. You wrote and told me. After that I suppose there was nothing in the fields.'

'But you wouldn't believe the mealies had been eaten, if you saw them now. They are green and some of them tasselling already.'

'Don't tell me,' he said as if refusing to believe it. 'I thought there would be nothing left. It's all Jairos's fault. He gave us a good field, but it is in the wrong place. No field can thrive a few paces away from the vlei where cattle are grazed. Jairos should have given us a field up in the west, away from the grazing fields.'

'But if we had a fence, father, everything would be all right. The soil is very good, especially in that area around the thorn trees where the old graves and the old cattle pens were. The mealies are very tall there. All we need is a fence.'

'You are quite right but fences cost money. And with your school bills shooting up I can't spare a cent for a fence. That is the problem of having two homes, boys. I can't come home every weekend, let alone with rolls of wire. Your education gets top priority, boys, and that's why I think the fence must wait. That is why we can't buy cattle yet, and why we can't build ourselves a nice brick and zinc house. Wire, cattle and houses can wait but your education can't.'

Yes, our education could not wait. But could our country home wait? We had put too much into it, to bring it to a sudden standstill. Yes, our education was expensive, but mother would have to guard the field every morning, even if it was raining. She would act as a human fence to keep the animals away from the crops. I felt sad to see father going alone into the bedroom. He would be alone again when we left for our boarding schools. He would go to work every day and come back to an empty house and eat his meals alone. His sole companion would be the radio, but he could not even afford a new battery. That was why he had looked blankly at the electric bulb and asked why mother had not come. At least mother had the girls to talk to. Perhaps mother should have come with us. Or was father simply out of touch? Twenty years in town is a long time. That was the trouble with two homes – they kept the family apart.

9

Later during the school term as I lay snugly in my bed in the school dormitory I thought of mother standing in the darkness and rain, saying in a tearful voice, 'They have eaten everything here too. Good God in the heavens, they have eaten every shoot.' I thought of father sitting under the single yellow light and asking sadly why mother was not with us.

And I remembered my mother's heroic resilience. It all began with a story she told us when we were children:

Once upon a time a man had two dogs, a black one and a white one. One day he went hunting without them and a hungry lion forced him up a tree. The sun was setting and he was far from his home. But the lion sat motionless under the tree, waiting for the man to come down. Then the frightened hunter started singing to his dogs.

'*Machena my white dog*
Come and fight for me
Come and fight for me
And you Matema, my black dog,

> *Come and fight for me*
> *Come and fight for me.'*

The faithful dogs heard him and ran all the way to protect him. They killed the lion, and the tired hunter came down safely from the tree.

Whenever mother told us this story I looked uneasily into the darkness and moved nearer to the fire. There was something ominous about its atmosphere – the setting sun, the night gathering over the vast uninhabited forest, and the solitary hunter clinging precariously to the thin branches of a tree, looking down fearfully at the lion below. I could almost hear the sad echoes of his voice singing through the forest before his faithful dogs came to his rescue.

There were other stories too – the girl who drowned in a well and was captured by the river maidens, unknown to the people who drew water from the well, and whose efforts to find her were in vain. Somehow I found a similarity between mother and some of the protagonists in her stories. It was as if she shared with them a life of pathos and resilience.

A photograph of my mother at thirteen revealed a girl in a simple brown dress and a scout belt. She was already a young woman with a budding chest and legs that a man would turn to look at. She had been born on a farm and her father was the farm foreman: a farmer, who grew potatoes and kept cows. Traders came from far to buy his potatoes and his rich milk. He was a young man, smart, with trim hair and a dark moustache. His wife was also a farmer – growing peanuts and raising chickens. She was a smart woman who could not bear black specks in the milk or cracks in the walls of her huts.

My grandfather had died at an early age, when my mother

was still only nine or ten years old. The last months of his life were those of illness and coma. Hospitals had failed to cure him. He had asked to be taken to his village to die. His wife did not give up hope. Medicine men were invited from far away to cure him but they failed. On the day he died, his wife and children had gone down to the river with a *n'anga* to perform the rites that were supposed to drive away the spirits that were vying for his life. Only mother had been left behind to look after the sick man. The darkness started creeping over him in the afternoon. He asked for porridge but could not eat.

'Look into my eye, daughter,' he said to my mother. 'There is a mote which I want you to remove.'

My mother held the two thin eyelids apart and searched for the mote. She saw nothing.

'Remove the mote and I will give you all the wealth and wisdom you want. I will protect your homestead. You will not bury any of your children. Your crops will do well and your cows will give birth to females. Your chickens will hatch all their eggs. Your enemies will not harm you. Find that mote, my daughter, and I will give you everything you want in life.'

Again and again she scanned his eyeball and the thin cornea but she saw nothing. Then his eyelids froze beneath her fingers. He died so peacefully that the young woman thought he had gone to sleep. The family buried him the following morning on an antheap, and framed his grave with four blocks of granite. He left a family of five children. The first was a girl of marrying age, the second and third were young men, my mother was fourth and the last was a boy of nine. Shortly afterwards the eldest girl got married and went to live with her husband. The two young men packed their bags and went to seek their fortunes in the towns.

The family dispersed but the homestead did not crumble.

Under the stern hand of my grandmother, the remaining herd of cattle grew steadily and the fields were tilled. There were potatoes, milk and vegetables at all times of the year. A lorry came every May to take her maize to the market.

My mother and her brother went to school. My unenthusiastic young uncle soon left and followed his brothers to town. My mother was a bright pupil and in her eighth year at school she was made head girl. She was reserved and in her spare time she would shut herself up in her room to knit and sew. In the planting season she worked hard, yoking the oxen and holding the plough while her mother dropped seeds into the furrows.

She had few friends. The only time she had gone to the village concert was one dark spring night. She went with her two friends. The concert ended very late. On their way home they passed a deserted homestead and as they did so lights flared in each of the ruined huts, as if they were on fire. But the huts did not burn. When the girls saw the lights, they ran, losing their shoes in the dark and cutting their feet on the stony ground.

After that, my mother was nervous of the darkness.

But at night their crops were in danger from the wild pigs that came to eat the green mealies. They could destroy a whole field in a night. So during the crucial month before harvesting my mother and grandmother would go out in the darkness to chase away the pigs. I can almost see their two figures moving about, the wind playing with their clothes and ruffling their skirts as they passed the sleeping compounds where an occasional cock would crow. They were determined farmers.

Soon enough young men began to look twice at my mother. Sweet-tongued young gallants tried their luck, snatching short snippets of conversation with her at the pump or on her way to the fields.

She was not rude to them, but she was a girl who was cautious with words. Only one man seemed to have captured her interest:

a tall man, perhaps eight or nine years older than she. He dressed formally in the fashion of the time – black balloon trousers ironed to the finest crease, crisp white cotton shirts, stringy black ties and black shoes. He worked in town and came every Sunday to see her. Together they would go to church. He held the umbrella and she carried the bibles and the books.

He was a well-behaved man. He scorned beer, smoking and dicing. He was not afraid of his mother-in-law, as was customary with lover-boys of the time. To hide behind a bush, gesticulating and calling to his girl, was not his idea of decent behaviour. He was straightforward and went to his prospective mother-in-law to tell her that he loved her daughter and planned to marry her.

Before the courtship was completed my mother's people decided to emigrate. There was a small farewell party with rice and chicken. *Lobola* was requested and quickly paid. The day of departure came. The emigrants went off on a battered yellow bus. My mother cried as the vehicle departed. But she had decided to remain behind with her husband and she did.

He took her first to his mother in the country. She worked hard, going to the well, cooking, washing and weeding. She was a strong energetic girl and the old woman was very impressed.

Three months later her new husband came and fetched her. They lived together in town in a small neat house with four rooms, a wood stove, electric lights, a Marylin radio and a little garden with flower beds and choumoulier. They lived happily together but soon the children and the problems they brought with them were on their way.

10

Yona was not to come home with us in April. 'But father, just for the weekend, please.'

No. He would stay behind and try to find a vacation job in a factory. He would also keep father company.

We went home without Yona. He came with us to the bus, however, to help carry our things. He hated cooking and washing and I wondered if he would enjoy the holiday. Perhaps he would get a job.

'Why didn't Yona come?' said mother. It was her second question. 'Oh my son. When will I see him?'

'Let him work,' said Tendai, 'so that he can buy us sweets and dresses.'

'You guarded the mealies very well, mother,' I said, looking around the field. Her gumboots were torn and her toes were showing. She had grass in her hair.

'We've just finished doing the nuts,' she explained, 'there weren't many this year.'

'How many bags?'

'Not many. The mice attacked the crop in February. We only harvested seventeen bags in the end.'

I had thought it would be worse.

The girls came running towards us with a watermelon.

'Give the melon to the boys,' said mother.

'Boys from town don't know melons,' said Tendai.

We roasted mealies and went home. In the evening Mrs Pendi came to see us and brought her children. Emma was twelve and growing up. Sam was still too short for his age.

'Why didn't my friend Yona come?' he asked.

We talked and laughed into the night. Then we sang two verses of an old hymn. Mrs Pendi sang the alto. She had a rich voice. Afterwards she gave a long, elaborate prayer and we went to bed feeling happy. The dew was heavy on the grass in the morning and we spent the early part of the day sitting round the fire, so that our eyes blurred when we went out into the sun.

Jairos was coming along the path.

His appearance shocked me. Even from a distance he looked shrunken. His legs were as thin as stamping sticks. He had lost weight. His step was stiff, as if he were dragging painful joints. His head was rigid, as if his eyes were glued to something in the distance. His mouth moved slightly, as if he was talking to himself.

He stopped at the Pendis' gate and threw it open with a loud clank. He went past Mrs Pendi's kitchen and straight towards the lavatory. He came out a minute later, adjusting his wet, falling trousers, blew his nose with his fingers and wiped them on his coat. His nose blew like a horn and the sound attracted Mrs Pendi. She stood ominously before him but he took no notice and walked straight towards the gate.

'Hey you, Jairos,' she shouted. 'Didn't my husband tell you not to come and mess up my toilet?'

He hardly listened but waved his hand vaguely in the air, perhaps not at her.

She charged him with more words, putting the baby down to gesticulate.

'You come here every day and mess up my toilet. Why don't you build your own? You always come when my husband is away, because he wouldn't let you through the gate. Hey, Jairos . . .!'

She took a step forward but he was already through her gate, which he did not shut. He turned into our yard, his eyes fixed on the ground, mouth moving, fingers twisting.

'Your mo . . . mo . . . mother . . . is she in?' he stammered.

'No,' said Shuvai mechanically. 'She has gone to the fields.'

'Aaah!' exclaimed Jairos disapprovingly, refusing to believe it. His lips opened to show a grey tongue. Then he saw mother at the fire and sat down on the chair.

'Good morning, Headman Jairos,' said mother.

He looked into the fire and did not reply. His skull bones knuckled under his pale brown skin, his buttonless shirt open. I could count his ribs as easily as a plucked bird's. His feet, strapped up in black sandals, were cracked, thin and dusty. His mouth emitted little hissing noises.

He suddenly broke his long blank stare and looked up.

'Let me have *maheu*,' he said, in a bewildered way. Having drunk it at a gulp, he sat chewing the grains, raking his cheeks with his tongue, and spitting into the fire.

Then he rose to go without a word.

The kids in the next compound saw him coming and a small boy shouted.

'Go away, Jairos!'

Jairos fumbled to unfasten the gate.

'It's locked, Jairos,' said the boy, insolently. 'Go away.'

'Open!' shouted Jairos. 'You son of a whore!'

The kids laughed and went into the house.

Jairos gave up and left. I asked mother what was wrong with him.

'Didn't I tell you?' exclaimed mother, surprised. 'Jairos was ill for a long time after you left. Something seems to have gone wrong with his mind. People think he is mad.'

◆

We learnt from mother that when it started, Jairos had come home one evening and stood outside his compound looking at his huts. The light of the young sharp-horned moon was dim. Blueish smoke drifted into the night sky.

'I am Headman Jairos,' he burst out. 'I stand here just outside my own homestead. I see grey smoke coming from my huts. I don't want to go home. I see monsters. I don't want to go home because I see monsters in my hut.'

His voice rose to a pitch with a strange new note of fear.

'Ernest! Ernest! Ernest! Come and take me, Ernest. They want to take me, Ernest! Help me!'

His voice echoed in the darkness and there was silence in the village. 'Help me, Ernest!' he shouted again desperately. Suddenly, he was surrounded by people and Simon's voice was heard among the agitated voices of women.

'Come on, brother Jairos. Let's go home.'

'I won't!' he shouted, breaking loose.

'There is trouble in my family,' wailed Lulu's mother.

'He will be all right,' said Simon. 'Hold his hand.'

Then suddenly he quietened down like a mute child and they led him home. But next morning he wasn't there. For two weeks no one knew where he was. Then he returned very thin and looking twenty years older. For five whole minutes he wouldn't blink. He crouched near the fire staring into the flames with sunken red eyes. He refused to eat porridge. His wife wept for a very long time and Lulu ran away from home.

◆

Now, Simon was the acting headman.

He came to our compound one morning and sat on a stool in the sunshine. He wore a yellowing white shirt and grey balloon trousers which failed to disguise his small limbs.

'Wamambo,' he said in salutation, clapping his hands.

'Good morning, Mpofu,' said mother from the kitchen.

I brought a chair but Simon declined it, saying he was all right on the stool.

'Did you sleep well, Wamambo?' he asked us.

'Yes, we did,' we replied. 'How did you sleep?'

'My wife did not sleep at all. She is suffering from backache. She was in bed all afternoon. I told my daughter to make porridge for her but it didn't help. I went to Chiutsi and he gave me a herb. If that doesn't work, I will take her to the hospital and let the doctors cut her open to see what is wrong.'

'What a pity,' said mother, coming out with a mat. 'Her backache still troubles her. Maybe you should take her to the hospital right away. Doctors do help.'

'Hospitals are good, Masiziva, very good. But they want money and that I don't have. It's only people like you with husbands working in towns who can afford to pay doctors.'

'We are no better, Mpofu,' laughed mother. 'This army of ours drains every cent from us. You wouldn't believe how much we pay for their education. My only consolation is that here in the country, I can spend a week without parting with a coin. I pity my husband in town who parts not with coins, but with bank notes, every day.'

'Money is a problem, Masiziva,' said Simon, picking his nose. 'Have your sons nearly finished school?'

'Far from it,' laughed mother. 'It will be another six or seven years before Yona finishes.'

'Six years, Masiziva!' exclaimed Simon, genuinely alarmed. 'Your sons will grow old while they are at school. Let them find work now. They can read and write. They finished their grades long ago, didn't they? They have enough education. One of them can even teach in our village school. The others can work as office clerks in the District Commissioner's office.'

'No, Mpofu. We want them to have a good education. We don't care if it takes years to do that. Life will be very hard in the future and we might as well suffer now trying to make things better for them.'

'You are lucky your sons are doing well, Masiziva. My brother's daughter Lulu was intelligent. She could read and write anything but after her father fell ill she could not go to school any more.'

'A pity,' said mother.

Secondary school and university were beyond Simon's imagination. Education ended at writing and reading letters.

'The purpose of my coming, Masiziva,' said Simon eventually, 'is to let you know of the changes that will be taking place here. You probably heard that the administration of the village will soon be handed over to local councils. The council will control five villages – ours, Matuvi's, Mponda's, Rushwaya's and Joachim's. The council will collect the cattle taxes and give out dip tickets. Any man who wants to have his field extended or to have a new plot will have to see the council. They will decide everything. They plan to build new townships to encourage businesses, maize mills and stores. Eventually they will build a dam for the cattle in the dry season. People will be able to fish in the dam as well.'

He picked at his short beard and continued: 'Last week all village headmen were called to a meeting at the chief's kraal. The chief explained everything to us. From now on all fields will be ten acres each. Those on the steep slopes will have contour ridges to stop the soil from washing down to the river. Those on the more gentle slopes will have grass strips. The agricultural demonstrators have told us that the cattle are slowly destroying the stream by stamping on its banks. From now onwards all the cattle will go to graze in Mbumbuzi Forest. In the dry season, the vlei area immediately around the stream will be fenced off to protect the gardens. The demonstrators will be coming soon to peg the fields. Tell your boys to sharpen sticks for the peggers. . . .'

The peggers came a week later, to lay out the grass strips. They were two ordinary-looking men with short trousers and farmer's shoes. One man criss-crossed the field with a painted pole, while the other man viewed the field surface through a kind of plain-table, and measured the depressions against the marked, painted pole. The man with the table knocked the pegs into the ground to mark the grass strip areas.

'Who made such crude sticks?' he asked contemptuously. He was huge and hairy and he munched salted nuts continuously.

'What a waste of land,' exclaimed mother, surveying the wide grass strips.

'The strips will conserve the soil, lady,' explained the peggers laconically.

'Wait till you see the mice which will breed in the grass,' smiled mother. 'They will destroy all the crops.'

The peggers quietly folded up their instruments and went off to peg more fields. We were fortunate in not having to have contour ridges. Everywhere other people had picks and shovels, and were chopping the earth into neat trenches and ridges of soft brown sand. People complained about the new council. The construction of contour ridges and grass strips went ahead but the fencing off of the stream never happened. Perhaps Headman Simon forgot about it.

◆

Back in town, Yona had been working for three weeks in a factory. 'What do you do?' I asked hesitantly, fearing that he worked with picks and shovels, sweating over hot furnaces.

'I do a clerical job,' he explained. 'I help in the welfare

department, keeping records of the overalls, gloves and boots given out to the workers, for instance.'

'Is it exciting?' said Shuvai.

'Yes. People can be very interesting, especially Mr Rufoyo, the chief clerk. He lives in Zata Street – you should know him. He has been loafing recently because he has had me to do his work for him. He can be away from his office for hours at a time going to the time-office, toilet or even to town.'

'What is the time-office?'

'That's where people line up to have their work cards punched when they go into and come out of the factory. Mr Rufoyo will be very sad when I leave tomorrow. He has the shortest memory you can imagine. He keeps forgetting whether my name is Yona Wamambo or John Mbona. And right now he isn't sure if I am doing Form Five or Form Two! He seems to have a hangover every morning – he even brings beer to work!'

'It must be exciting,' said Shuvai, 'but where is that bag of sweets you promised us?'

Yona laughed guiltily. He looked so grown-up in his black coat and blue tie. But his hair was somewhat dishevelled after a day of headscratching. He went into the sitting room and pulled the string to the lightbulb, put the radio on and twisted the knob quickly to a shortwave station.

'Elton John's new record "Daniel",' he told us.

'You tune in to LM a lot?'

'Sometimes it doesn't catch the waves and the music fades out.'

'Headman Jairos has gone mad, did you hear?' said Jo. He couldn't wait.

'What?'

'Yes, he went mad,' I explained. 'One evening he came home shouting all sorts of things. Then he disappeared for two weeks

91

and returned looking very ill. People said he had been chopping down trees in Mbumbuzi Forest for no reason at all.'

'That's unbelievable.'

'He spends days walking up and down the village asking for food. He refuses the food his wife cooks for him.'

Yona opened a plastic packet and fished out a handful of nuts.

'How many bags this year?' he asked, munching.

'Thirty-one,' said Shuvai. 'We have already sold the bags.'

Yona munched away, tapping his feet to the radio. He loved music. Dirty plates were heaped on the stove. Shuvai pointed at the stove and Yona laughed.

'I didn't have time to wash the dishes this morning,' he explained. 'I was almost late for work. Now that you have come things will be easier.'

'We did a lot of work this holiday,' said Jo. 'The peggers came last week. The council is now going to run everything.'

Father leant his bicycle against the wall outside. He came in with a big black trunk. Jo had damaged his old one. His schoolmates would call this new one a coffin.

Father put the trunk down in surprise and smiled.

'We were thinking you would be late for school,' he said. 'You did well to come today so that you can get ready for your trains. How is everyone at home?'

In the spare room the table was strewn with envelopes, writing pads and various papers. He had been budgeting.

He went into the sitting room, tuned the radio for the news and slumped onto the sofa. Shuvai started washing the dishes. Jo and I went in to give father the money from the sale of our nuts.

11

The dark night was pregnant with the promise of a storm. There was a warm stillness in the air, and not a cricket could be heard. The dust road ran like a groove between the pressing flanks of trees. The bus had clattered away.

Jo and I lifted the heavy black trunk and Shuvai carried the blankets. The path was dark. Leaves brushed our legs. Perhaps it was two in the morning.

We moved quickly through the darkness. The tin trunk creaked and cut our fingers. We kept stopping to change sides. How much easier it would have been if Yona had come with us. The forest thinned out and the vlei came into view like a grey carpet. The grass was still. The reeds growing beside the stream were aglow with fireflies. The path widened, the sand deepened and gleamed in the darkness. I knew this was where the herdboys played, weaving their cattle whips, rolling on their backs in the sand and catching locusts, while the cattle grazed in the vlei.

But now there was not a sound. Even the frogs were quiet. If the fireflies could utter, we might have heard faint murmurings. At the bottom of the vlei, a cold blast of air hit us. The soft damp ground trembled under our feet.

We searched for the stepping stones and Shuvai went ahead. A bolt of lightning streaked across the sky, revealing bewildered purple clouds and momentarily clothing everything in artificial white light. I saw our images in the water. Jo slipped, lost his grip, and the trunk clanked as it hit a stone.

'You . . .' I turned on him fiercely. Somewhere in the reeds a frog attempted to croak but the other frogs did not join in and it shut up. We left the chilly grey vlei and walked up towards the warm dark trees.

The white walls of the mission primary school glimmered through the black trees. A dog bayed weakly at us. New huts had been built. We marched past the kraals where the cattle stamped and a cowbell chimed. There was a strong sharp smell of cowdung, of dust and human refuse. At night these smells seem to sink into the grass.

We almost ran into the water pump, but a pool of water round it warned us off. Here the grass was soft and green where women washed their clothes and puff-adders lay waiting in the grass.

Our three huts loomed ahead and the sand threw off a pale grey light. A dog barked sharply, the sound cutting through the night. I fumbled with the chain of the gate. The dog moved forward, growling. Even in the dark I could make out his huge shape. I suddenly remembered that mother had told us about him in a letter.

'Simba! Simba! Hello Simba! Come Simba!'

He stopped barking and rushed towards us, squealing with delight. The bedroom door chinked open and mother came out with a light.

'Oh, my children!'

She was leaner. Vimbai, Tendai and Rita lay on the floor. I went to Rita and shook her. She turned, opening her eyes, and uttered an exclamation of surprise. Her little body was warm as I took her from the blankets.

'You walked all the way from the station!' mother exclaimed, looking at her watch. 'It's three o'clock now. Were you not afraid of the dark?'

'Shuvai was,' said Jo.

'What about you? You dropped the trunk when lightning flashed and Godi scolded you.'

'I don't like the vlei at night,' I said.

'I know it's scary with the fireflies and the frogs,' said mother. 'So my Yona is not coming again.'

'He is starting work tomorrow at the factory.'

'Oh, my son. Anyway, let him work. He must help his father.'

'I smell the rain,' said Shuvai.

'It rained yesterday, but it was very hot today.'

The door of the hut opened and a boy came out and crouched at the door.

'Come here, Boyce,' said mother.

I had almost forgotten his name. Boyce was a tall boy, a young man in fact. He was slim and strong-limbed. His hair was long and kempt, although there were blanket threads in it. His face was swollen with sleep but I could make out his sharp features, his fine set of teeth and his light-brown complexion. He had pimples on the sides of his face and I knew he was about two years older than me. He wore a white shirt and green shorts.

'These are all my children, Boyce,' said mother. 'Would you believe it?'

Boyce laughed politely and shook hands with us.

'Boyce came to live with us and help us,' explained mother. 'He has been here since October. He comes from Matuvi's line. I don't think you have met him before.'

His face looked to me strangely familiar.

'His mother is Masibanda, the tall lady who usually passes along singing and stops to ask if I have any *mhunga* to sell.'

One April night there had been a beer party in the Pendis' compound. Masibanda, drunk, had sung exceedingly loudly. The grass near the kraals had caught fire and the flames had roared towards the Pendis' house. Men had raced to put the fire out. But Boyce's mother had protested, shouting, 'Let the fire burn and come to the house. I want to warm myself. I say let the fire burn . . .'

'Shut up,' the men had told her, but she wouldn't.

Boyce was tall and slim like his mother.

'Boyce is an expert with oxen. You will see how he handles them and makes them run with the plough.'

'Whose oxen, mother?'

'Didn't I tell you? I bought two oxen from Matudu.'

'You are wonderful, mother, you are wonderful. I never thought you could do that. I thought you were joking.'

'But I didn't see any kraal outside.'

'The cattle still stay at Matudu's kraal. You can go and see them first thing tomorrow morning before Matudu's boys take them out to the pastures.'

The lightning flashed. Boyce put his head out of the hut and announced that the rain was coming.

'You had better go off to sleep or you will get wet,' said mother. 'Boyce is a nice young man and I am sure you will live happily together. See you tomorrow.'

We went out. It was so dark that Jo almost ran into the wall of our hut. The storm was peeling confidently towards us. The air was very still and I could smell the rain. In the dark Simba grunted and curled up under the grain hut. Boyce lit the lamp. The hut was very warm. I suppose the walls had been heating up all day. The floor was newly swept and polished with cowdung. Boyce's mats and blankets were on the floor. He had tied a rope across the hut and his clothes hung from the rope – two pairs of shorts, a faded blue T-shirt and a brown shirt. He did not have a suitcase. We spread our blankets beside his and went to sleep. Boyce let the lamp burn for a few minutes and then blew it out. I could see his smile and his handsome teeth as he pulled the lamp to his mouth to extinguish it. The moment it went out the rain fell.

It washed down steadily, soaking everything. The ground

trembled to the thunder. I caught the wet smell of the grass and the sand but I knew we were safe.

It was nice to come home.

Perhaps I slept for five hours. When I woke up the sun was shining through the slit in the doorway. I could see the raindrops glistening on the grass. Boyce was out and Jo was jumping into his clothes.

'What's the hurry?' I asked.

'I am going to see the cattle.'

'Do you think they will run away? Take your time.'

He went out and a minute later I could hear him playing with Simba and greeting Mrs Pendi. I lay for another half hour, enjoying the warmth and the sounds of the morning. When I went out the sun was high. The sky was clear. I saw several rooftops through the trees. A blueish haze was rising gently out of the damp grey grass and filtering into the air. The tilled brown earth appeared, forming neat patterns against the soft summer green of grass and tree foliage. I looked to the north and caught a glimpse of the vlei. I could see the Mbumbuzi Forest, a solid chunk of green defying the green and brown of the village clearings. Half a dozen naked trees were etched on its horizon, waiting to be cut down by lightning or claimed by women for firewood.

Our compound area had been tilled and the mealies were sprouting. Next to the gate sweet-potato runners were inching across the path into the bush. The mango trees were big now, and drooping with green mangoes. The grass was dull green silver, the dew drying in the sun.

Simba was a fine dog, something between an Alsatian and a hound – tall and strong, with a shiny cream coat and sharp white canines. He bounced towards me, thrashing his tail, licking my knees and leaping up to lick my face. I struggled to keep him down.

'Hello Godi,' Mrs Pendi called from over the fence. I pushed Simba away and went to meet her. She laughed, hardly waiting for me to reach her.

'You are growing so tall,' she exclaimed. 'You've put on another two inches since the last holiday. Where do you think you are going? Do you want to touch the sky? You won't be able to pass through the doors without bending if you continue growing. And you've put on weight. Look at your cheeks, fat as tennis balls. What were they giving you to eat at boarding school?'

'Beans and porridge,' I laughed. I took the baby from her, lifting him high over the barbed wire. He was a strong little boy, with curly black hair and steady brown eyes. He scrutinised my face closely.

'Sam will be happy now he has a brother. Hurrah for the boys,' I said.

'The next one will be a girl, to spite you,' she laughed. She was darker now, and slimmer. Her skin had tanned gently. She no longer used skin-lightening creams as she had done when I first saw her. That was when she was fat and comfortable and decried everything. She still talked and laughed and scolded her children but she no longer chased them all over the compound. The countryside was taming her.

Her children came to say hello. Her daughter was growing into a young lady. Sam was not growing as fast as his sister. The two smaller girls could run and talk now. I remembered one of them had been a very tiresome infant but now she was growing into a little beauty.

I returned the little boy over the fence and took home the mangoes Mrs Pendi had given me.

Boyce had returned. He was younger than I had first thought, although he was still older than me.

'I went to see Mandlovu,' he said, rubbing his hands at the

fire. The dew had washed his ankles. 'She was just waking up. I told her I had come for your money. She said she didn't have anything because she had not brewed any beer for weeks. But she said she would brew next week, if she happens to get *mumera*.'

'Mandlovu is a crook,' said mother. 'I know all her tricks. If she sees me at the pump she runs quickly away because she knows I will ask for my money. Two dresses taken a year ago, and not a dollar paid. I will wait for two weeks and if she doesn't bring anything I will take every one of her chickens. If that doesn't satisfy me I will sell her goats to get my money.'

'You will grab her chickens, mother!' said Rita, evidently thrilled.

'Did she not throw a beer party last Sunday, Boyce?' asked mother.

'I think she did,' replied Boyce.

'And she says she did not have *mumera*. What happened to all her *mumera*?'

'You don't know her,' said Boyce. 'Mandlovu! She is the laziest woman in the village. She cannot even grow enough maize to feed her chickens. This year she reaped absolutely nothing. Her husband was ploughing *deruka* fields for money and tilled only one acre for her. But Mandlovu didn't even bother to weed that one acre. She drinks too much.'

'What do they eat then?'

'They rely on their cattle. Her husband inherited a huge herd from his father. Every year he sells about two cattle to get money to buy maize. But this year he bought only two bags of *mhunga* and spent the rest of the money on beer.'

'I should not have trusted her with those dresses,' said mother, biting her mango.

'Is one of the dresses blue with a white collar?' asked Boyce.

'Yes.'

'And is the other dress a brown one with a black belt?'

'Yes.'

'She wears those dresses alternatively, they are almost in shreds now and very dirty too. I bet the next time she washes them will be at Christmas.'

We roared with laughter.

'And did you see Mai Dori, your brother's wife?'

'Yes, I did, but she said she didn't . . .'

'I knew she would tell such stories,' cut in mother with a smile. 'Tell your brother I am coming for his chickens next. The only woman who pays her debts in this whole village is Ndoga's wife.'

'And Mrs Matudu,' I added.

'Mrs Matudu!' exclaimed mother. 'You don't know her. She takes two years to pay for a skirt. But wait till you see her pressing her own debtors. Now she is saying that if we don't hurry up and complete the payments for cattle we might have to leave a calf with her as interest. Whoever paid the full sum for cattle in this village in two months, let alone in two years?'

This reminded Jo of the cattle. He jumped up and said he was going to see them.

'Wait till you have had your breakfast,' mother told him.

We went with Boyce after breakfast.

'Where does your mother live, Boyce?' I asked as we went to Matudu's home.

'In Matuvi's compound. You pass two big compounds after leaving the headman's and you come to my mother's. There is only one small hut and one small grain hut. My father died when I was still young. At that time we lived in another village. Eventually my sisters got married and my brothers went away to work in the mines. My mother and I moved into this village; there was no need to build many huts because we are only two and I am away working most of the time.'

'Have you worked before, Boyce?'

'Yes, I first worked as a mill-operator. I spent all day grinding people's grain.'

'Did you enjoy working?'

'Very much. There were two of us, me and another boy. We lived in a room at the back of the mill. The owner lived in town and only came at weekends to bring the diesel and to collect the money. He was a nice man. Sometimes he brought us meat and bananas and gave us a few shillings above our pay. I worked for him for about three months, then the rains fell and I had to return home to help my mother. But I don't like to sit at home and ask for money, so after harvesting I got myself another job. It was with a *deruka* family in Goto's line. The man's name was Mugova. He was a very rich man. He owned two ploughs, two barrows and a tractor. He grew groundnuts, cotton and sunflowers in two huge fields. In the ploughing season we woke at two in the morning and went to plough the fields.'

'It must have been very hard work.'

'Yes. We worked hard all year round. In winter we carried manure to the fields. You know how heavy manure is. One day the oxen hit a tree and the full cart tilted backwards, lifting the smaller ox off its feet. Mugova's son Richard broke the yoke with his axe to free the oxen. The cart overturned and threw all the manure onto the grass. Mugova was really angry with me, although Richard and I had only done it to save the ox.'

Mugova was one of the illustrious agricultural demonstrators. He had built himself a fine white brick and zinc house and had fenced off his huge fields in the fertile land near the vlei. Here the soil was black and crumbly, so damp that worms burrowed it all year round. He kept his soil drugged with manure and fertilisers, so that even in bad years his mealies grew tall, and his acres went white with cotton balls. He was one of those *derukas* who enslaved the soil, overworked and underpaid their servants, and sent out huge herds of cattle to tax the humble meadows. In such homesteads milk, eggs, meat, vegetables, rice and green mealies were available at most times of the year but human sweat oozed all year round.

We approached Matudu's compound. It was a sprawling complex built on a steep slope. Of the five huts, only the kitchen was well built with a high wall and an even roof. Matudu built better huts for the *derukas* than he built for himself. A giant tree towered over the roofs, one of its branches struck off by lightning. The slope was so steep that the rain had torn the earth away, dragging fine white sand to the edge of forest. Coming down the slopes people found themselves running involuntarily. Two sides of the tilled clearing had been fenced off by two low strands of barbed wire, which had only succeeded in keeping out the cattle; goats had invaded the plot to nibble the mealies.

We proceeded along the path, where water from the girls' buckets had made cakes in the sand. Everywhere chickens were scratching in the green thorns and the lean brown hounds stared passively at us.

We crouched outside the big hut. There were nut-shells on the ground and flies buzzed everywhere. Matudu's daughter poked her face out of the doorway and greeted us. She was a dark girl, about sixteen, with a crop of plaited hair. There was sand on her knees. She had been kneeling near the door, grinding peanut butter on a huge flat stone.

'We have come to see the cattle,' said Boyce familiarly.

She went on grinding the butter.

'Are Jerome and Bvaku back from the maize mill?' asked Boyce, standing up.

'No,' replied the girl. 'They went late.'

'And where is everybody else?'

'Mother and the girls have gone to pick *mazhanje* and father is chopping logs near the kraal.'

'In that case I will see you some other time when your father is away,' said Boyce half seriously and the girl chuckled.

'Are the cattle still in?'

'Yes.'

We half walked, half ran down the slope to the kraal. It was a big one with thick white poles planted close together. There were forty or fifty cattle in the kraal, all stamping their feet and swishing their tails to keep the flies off. Matudu was felling a tree some distance away. The tree fell, squeaking like a giant mouse, and thrashed the ground with its branches. Suddenly there was a gap in the forest.

Matudu, victorious, threw his axe on his shoulder and came towards us, smiling.

'Wamambo!' he said, then added with a frown of mock anger, 'Why is it that you never come to see me? You only want to greet me when you meet me drunk on the paths, and then I don't remember afterwards.'

'But we only came yesterday,' I protested laughingly. 'And we have come to see you today. How are you?'

He clicked his tongue in a mock curse, half swung his fist at Boyce and put his axe down. He was a short man, thick-set, very dark and so red-eyed that children cried when he held them. His head was small and round, with short greying hair and a stubby white beard. His arms were rather too big and muscular for his small body, fingers shaped like clubs and nails black with dirt. Rivulets of sweat were trickling down his face, soaking his khaki shirt and even creeping to his brown shorts. He kept flicking his pink tongue over his lips.

'I am well, Wamambo,' he answered eventually. 'How was your father?'

'He was well.'

'Why didn't he send tobacco, even old newspapers for my cigarettes?'

'Headman Simon took all the newspapers we brought.'

'Oho! You give everything to Headman Simon, forgetting me. Did Simon build your huts? Did he till your fields? Or did he sell you your oxen?'

'We will remember you next time.'

'Next time! What if I die before next time? Don't you know I can become a ghost and torment you?'

Boyce burst out laughing and Matudu turned to him slowly, grinning, and said: 'Shut your cave, Boyce.'

'Oh, shut up, old man,' returned Boyce good-humouredly.

'We have come to see the cattle,' I said.

'Come to see the cattle. I see, and yet you never give me any tobacco. Your ox fell ill in spring. His foot swelled like a ball. He couldn't walk. I said to your mother, "Let us cut the swelling to let the pus out." She said, "No." But I knew the ox might die so I cut him on my own. I tied him by the horns to this tree. I roped his belly and pulled him to the ground, all alone. I squeezed his boil.'

'You did well.'

'For two weeks he couldn't go to the dip.'

'Which are the oxen?'

'They are not both oxen. You see that cow sitting in the mud near the white log?'

'The one with the white face and red tail?'

'And that strong brown ox with sharp horns, standing near the black bull?'

'Yes.'

'Those are your cattle.'

I threw a stick at the white-faced cow. She rose to her feet, stretching her dung-matted flanks and stiffening her tail.

She was a fairly old cow, and perhaps had calved half a dozen times. She looked at me with big tearful brown eyes and turned away, lumbering out of the corner. There was slight turmoil in the kraal. The sleek brown ox took his time. He tossed his sharp horns aggressively at the timid wrinkle-faced white cow, and the black bull stepped backwards, hardly blinking.

'How old is the cow?'

'She is old,' said Matudu, putting his arms on the white logs. 'She is old but she is still calving. She has had five calves, but any time now we expect her to have another one.'

'Milk,' said Jo happily.

Boyce smiled at Jo's happiness. Boyce had seen the birth of scores of calves. We looked at the cattle for a few more minutes and then went home.

There were tall green mealies and some yellow rice in the vlei gardens. Simba spotted a flock of goats nibbling green tendrils near a garden. He stood alert and his ears bristled, his half-forgotten hunting instincts roused. The foolish goats nibbled on, only sensing Simba when he was dangerously close. They scattered. Their movements excited him. He closed onto the scattering flock like a giant hound. We watched him breathlessly. Our desperate shouts could not stop the overpowering rush of his blood. He swung to the right, making for a pink-skinned kid at the end of the arc of fleeing goats. He gripped the poor scrambling creature, took it up by the legs and shook it like a cat shaking a mouse. He pushed his canines into the soft pink belly, thrashing the kid onto the ground, raising a cloud of dust around him.

I stopped for a stick as I ran and hit Simba once, twice, and he let go and ran off into the bushes, howling. I picked up the pink kid and shook it gently. There were deep bloodless tooth-marks in its belly. Its eyes were already half closed.

'What do we do now?' asked Boyce, his hands on his hips.

'Is it dead?' said a voice from behind me. He was a young man, as tall as Boyce, wearing a thin black tie.

'I don't know,' I said. He took the kid from me.

'Do you know who it belongs to?' I asked.

'Yes,' replied the young man. 'It belongs to my brother.'

I told Boyce and Jo to go home and tell mother about it. I followed the young man to his compound up to the slope. Outside the hut a woman was washing plates. She stood up when she saw us.

'What happened?'

'A dog bit it,' said the young man.

'Whose dog?' screamed the woman. The young man looked at me.

Another boy came out of the hut and examined the kid.

'My only goat,' he moaned.

'What kind of dog is that which hunts goats?' screamed the woman, looking straight at me. 'Did he think it was a buck? Why did you let him do it? You thought he was doing a fine job, didn't you, getting some meat?'

My heart sank. I couldn't talk. I sat down under the eaves of the hut and let them vent their anger. The young man went to call his father.

The father was a shrunken man, perhaps sixty or seventy, short, dark and almost toothless. His toes peeped out of his broken shoes. He greeted me politely and even asked after my health. His wife brought him pumpkins. He invited me to eat with him but I declined.

'What!' he exclaimed with surprise. 'You won't eat with me? Just because your dog killed my goat you refuse to eat with me. Don't you like pumpkins?'

I told him I did not feel like eating.

The woman overheard our conversation and came over with a wet pot in her hands.

'How can he eat pumpkins?' she shouted. 'He wanted meat. He is disappointed we caught him before he could carry the kill home to his mother.'

'Is your dog from the town?' the old man asked me.

'No,' replied the woman before I could open my mouth. 'The dog was born and bred in this very village. That boy deliberately sent it after the kid. The dog has been taught to hunt goats.'

'Couldn't you stop the dog?' asked the old man.

'How could he stop the dog?' screamed the old woman, throwing sand into her pot. 'He wanted meat. He must pay for the kid. We want our kid alive and walking this minute. You can take the meat to your mother and bring a live kid to us.'

I brushed off an angry tear. They had given me no time to explain.

'Where do you live?' the old man asked me.

He knew my father and mother, he said. He had known them in town, before he came to build his home in the country. He asked me more questions.

Mother shortly arrived. The old woman ran about finding her mats to sit on. The two women conversed about the weather and the crops and no mention of the goat was made while I was there. I later learnt that the old man had decided to let the matter pass as an unfortunate accident. He demanded no compensation.

After that we kept a keen eye on Simba. He knew his scarlet sin and whenever he saw a flock of goats he folded his tail, dropped his head and ran slowly on. But at home he was a fierce and efficient dog. Many people were scared of him. Mother warned us not to call him by name in public because if people knew his name and called him by it, he would soften towards them.

◆

Boyce turned out to be an expert with cattle as mother had said. He knew how to keep a yoked pair running with the plough. But he used his whip freely. Bellum's sleek brown skin seemed to absorb the blows, but Sigwe was less fortunate. The cracking whip slashed her hide, leaving red weals.

Bellum was younger than Sigwe, and being the ox he was more powerful than the cow. Sigwe often trudged slightly behind Bellum. Boyce whipped her mercilessly, till mother said rather uneasily, 'Let her rest for a while, Boyce. She is a pregnant woman.'

One day Sigwe stopped in the middle of a furrow. Boyce drove her with his whip, shouting, but she stood her ground. Then her belly heaved and her crying eyes bulged over her white face. Suddenly her knees folded and she slumped to the ground. The yoke tilted, the leather cords tightening on her throat. She grunted. I grabbed her horns and pressed the head down, trying to loosen the cord with my other hand. Bellum moved.

'Watch out!' shouted Boyce.

Bellum tossed off the yoke and surged past me. The plough came after him for a moment, its blade flying through the air. I felt the sharp glittering point stabbing my ankle. I fell. There was a snapping sound as the yoke broke. Bellum freed himself.

'Are you hurt?' asked Boyce and Jo at the same time.

'Not badly,' I said. I slapped Sigwe's back. 'Sigwe, Sigwe.' Her hide twitched and vibrated. Boyce took her stiff tail in his hands and twisted it like a woman wringing a towel. Sigwe moaned. Boyce did it again and again but Sigwe did not move.

'She must be dying.' Boyce gingerly released her tail. 'Go home and tell mother, Jo.'

Sigwe thrashed the dust. I suppose the darkness was clouding over her swollen eyes. Bellum saw her kick and he raised his head as if to catch a scent on the air. He came bounding towards us. Boyce and I jumped out of the way. Then Bellum jumped right over Sigwe's sprawling body. His massive dark form rushing must have totally alarmed Sigwe; she scrambled to her feet and raised her head.

'Is that what all animals do to their dying partners – jump over them?' I asked Boyce.

'It's the first time I have seen it happen,' said Boyce, patting Sigwe's back. 'Sigwe. You foolish cow. You wanted to die in my hands and get me into trouble.'

'What did mother say, Jo?'

'She said Sigwe would rise to her feet, if we let her rest. She said we should take her to Matudu's kraal as soon as we can get her to walk.'

'She didn't think it was serious?'

'She was alarmed but she pretended it didn't matter.'

'And you told her I was hurt?'

'I forgot . . .'

I threw sand onto the wound to stop the bleeding. I was not seriously hurt but I knew I would limp for weeks.

We took the cattle to Matudu's kraal. Bellum rushed ahead and we followed very slowly with Sigwe. Matudu's wife was waiting at the kraal when we got there.

'What are you doing bringing the cattle in after dark?' she snapped.

'Sigwe is not feeling well.'

'I told you not to take Sigwe. If you continue to drive her she will miscarry. Cattle are just like people, you know. Go and tell your mother that Matudu's wife says she should not yoke Sigwe.'

From the bushes came Matudu's hiccuping, drunken drawl.

'It's their fault if their cow miscarries. It's their fault . . . I bet them it is.'

Sigwe calved on Christmas Eve. The calf had a brown and white face like her mother. Sigwe would not let anyone come near her calf. Her meek eyes lost their humility and became dangerously alert. Boyce had trouble trying to milk her. Eventually he tied her by the horns to a tree and got hold of her teats. The sight of the frothing white milk excited me. I asked Boyce to let me try my hands on Sigwe. I washed my hands, crouched under Sigwe's belly with a jug between my thighs and pulled the teats determinedly. I must have managed two spurts, when Sigwe decided to refuse me her milk. The soft pink teats slipped out of my already numb fingers. The hungry, wet-nosed calf broke out of Jo's hands to claim her mother's teats. Sigwe decided that was enough. I ended up with milk all over my clothes and a big nasty kick on the chest for my Christmas morning present.

◆

For a whole week after Christmas the sky was overcast with storm clouds. It rained every day. The fat showers plummeted ceaselessly from the thick grey ceiling of heaven. God had forgotten to close his taps.

We pressed on with our work in spite of the rain. At five in the morning when the sun should have been rising, the air was still and warm under its grey cloud blanket. For two or three hours in the morning we weeded the rain-soaked acres. Boyce set the pace, cutting and hacking the earth with his hoe, his slim legs wide apart, his white shirt creeping up his back.

'Come on,' he laughed spiritedly. 'Let's do another lap.' He was a very hard worker, and even mother had trouble keeping up with him.

At around ten o'clock the sky broke and the rain fell. We took shelter in the trees, holding plastic sheets over our heads, but we always got wet. In the vlei the herdboys raced their tinkling herds home before the storm broke, but there was always a danger that one or two stray cattle would come for our mealies, so we never left the field until the vlei was clear of any cattle.

We returned home soaked to the skin and sat by the scalding fire while the rain splashed down outside. Sitting wet by a fire is nice. You suck the salty water from your nose and feel your flesh glowing to the bone. You put your fingers in the hot flames while your clothes steam. Eventually you drowse. You hate it when the rain stops and you have to go back into the wet sunny fields feeling hot, sleepy, damp; and full of biltong, and sadza with peanut-butter gravy.

Sometimes when it did not rain Boyce went to spend the evenings with his mother.

'My mother is getting married again,' he complained. He wasn't very happy.

His stepfather was Chinda, a southerner who had come to the village to work for the *deruka* families. After three jobs Chinda had decided to spend his energies on himself and build his own home. Exactly how he had gained his mother's affections Boyce did not know. But on the night of the Pendis' beer party and the subsequent fire, it was Chinda who had half carried and half dragged Boyce's drunken mother home.

'I know that as a son I am not supposed to make decisions for my mother,' said Boyce, ruefully. 'But I think it was a silly mistake on my mother's part to marry Chinda.'

'Why, Boyce?' enquired mother.

'He is a lazy man,' said Boyce. 'He hasn't ploughed a single furrow since the rains fell. What does he think my mother will eat? My maternal uncle gave Chinda full permission to use his oxen but he never bothered once. All he does is drink. You give him beer and he will drink like a fish until he forgets how to get home. I despise him!'

'Don't be too harsh on your stepfather, Boyce.'

'I will never call him father, not Chinda. He found shelter in my mother's compound when Headman Simon threatened to send him back south. And because he came to live with my mother, my brother and his wife have had to go and live elsewhere. My mother's huts are falling to pieces, her fields are reverting to bush. How can Chinda call himself a man when he doesn't even own a chicken? If I were a man . . .'

'Oh, Boyce.'

'If I were a man . . .'

'What would you do?'

'At least I would speak out against parasites like Chinda and protect my mother.'

'Perhaps she was a fool to marry him, Boyce, but it is not your duty to expose your objections. You should respect your mother.'

'Chinda drinks too much. I hate beer. It cripples a man. My brother drinks too. I won't ever drink. I will devote my energies to building myself a home that people will admire. I will grow nuts, maize and cotton.'

We met Chinda at the stream one day. He was fishing. He was a curious man, perhaps in his early fifties. You could not call him an old man because although his face and neck were beginning to crease, his body had the curious muscular energy of a teenager. He wore tattered blue overalls, through which his full-blooded hairless chest showed. Perhaps Boyce's mother loved him because he had a healthy young body. But he was squint-eyed, with a mouthful of misplaced yellow teeth and a crop of ashy grey hair. He chewed a wet, home-made cigarette. With his black fingers he handled his slimy fishing worms as if he would eat them.

We came upon him without warning, as he threw his fishing line into the river. His thin brown dog spotted us from the grass and growled.

'Shut your dog up, old man,' Boyce said to Chinda. The man barked twice at the dog and greeted us warmly. Boyce did not return his greetings. He started unwinding his fishing line. The fish did not bite well, but Boyce caught a big eel and several bream. Chinda sweated and coughed in the sun, catching nothing. There were only two little fish in his tin. After a few hours he stood up and Boyce asked scornfully, 'Have you caught enough fish for my mother?'

Chinda muttered something about the fish not liking the huge worms. Boyce gave him the two large bream.

'Make sure you deliver the fish to my mother,' warned Boyce. 'Don't trade the fish for a mug of beer.'

Chinda thanked him and left us his worms. He collected his tins and hooks and went home.

'You are very cheeky to your stepfather, Boyce,' I said.

'He deserves it. He married my mother just because he wanted a woman to share his hut. Some people never grow old.'

12

While we were walking home one evening we saw a girl ahead of us on the path and Boyce said, 'I had a funny experience with her one night last year. Her elder sisters kept nudging me into lying with her. The sisters both had illegitimate babies and were jealous of their young unspoilt sister, and they arranged for me to go into the grain hut with the girl. It was very dark in there and my head hit the roof. At first the girl refused to take her dress off but I tore it away from her body. The girl cried. But then I couldn't do anything. It was too dark, so dark that I couldn't even see my own nose.'

I had never imagined Boyce could do such things, let alone talk about his sexual blunderings.

'Have you ever fondled a girl?' he asked me. I had been anticipating the question, so I laughed.

113

'I can get you a girl if you want,' he continued without waiting for an answer.

'I do not want to be a father yet,' I laughed.

'It's not always dangerous,' said Boyce. 'I can get you a girl who is too young to have a baby.'

'A girl without any breasts and without a single curl of hair!' I laughed. 'You might as well get me a little baby. But you must be careful, Boyce. Even nine-year-olds can fall pregnant. This girl must have had breasts when you tried her?'

'She was only budding – things I could hold between finger and thumb. I know she wanted to, but she was afraid of the pain. And I did not like the atmosphere of her mother's grain hut. Something kept scratching the walls. I think there were little men there. I scrambled out and left the girl to find her own way out of that horrible hut.'

'How cruel of you.'

That night after Jo was asleep I decided to tell Boyce about Lulu.

'I fell in love once, Boyce.'

'Who was the girl?'

'Won't you laugh if I tell you?'

'No. Why should I laugh?'

'Lulu.'

'Lulu . . . Lucia?'

'Yes. Headman Jairos's daughter.'

'I know her. She is a beautiful girl. I almost proposed to her once, myself. Did she say yes?'

'I never told her. In fact we never talked about it. It all started when we went together to pick fruit in the forest. We swam in the river.'

'Did you do it?'

'No. We both fell asleep on the bank. Mind you, we were only eight years old at the time.'

'That was a chance wasted,' he chuckled. 'What happened afterwards?'

'We have always been friends. We went swimming again two years ago.'

'And did you do it then?' came the excited question.

'I put my arms around her breasts . . .'

'In the water, you fool! Did you think you were a fish?'

'I put my arms on her breasts and she screamed and said if I touched her again she would walk away and never talk to me again.'

'Girls are always screaming. That's their way of saying yes. I hope you did not give up.'

'I came out of the water, snatched her clothes and ran up the bank. She came after me crying.'

'Naked?'

'Yes. I felt sorry for her, so I gave her back her clothes.'

'You should never feel sorry for a girl when she cries. You shouldn't have given her back her clothes.'

'We have been friends ever since. But her father went mad and she ran away from home. I haven't seen her for a long time.'

'You love her still?'

'No.'

'So you want another girl?'

'No.'

'Then you still love Lulu. Just tell her you admire her and things will be all right for you.'

'You know where she is?'

'She is working in Goto township.'

'All right. I still like her a lot.'

'Good. We'll tell her this Sunday. You will have a good time.'

'But where will mother think I have gone?'

'To Goto village to see how good the crops are there. Come on, you are no longer a baby.'

◆

Sunday was a fine morning. Beyond the solid acres of dew-laden mealies the first boys were taking their herds to the vlei. It was still too early for the frogs to croak.

In the village smoke was rising from the grey-roofed huts. Girls chattered at the water pump, preparing for the day. On Sunday the village girls wash and oil their bodies, and put on their crisp Sunday dresses. The boys, too, scrub themselves, comb their hair and put on their baggy trousers. They go to the church to meet the girls. The Catholic service in the village church starts at eight o'clock, but eight is any time from sunrise to noon. There is never any hurry.

Jo knew that Boyce and I were planning to go to Goto, so he took the opportunity to take Boyce's much coveted fishing line and go off to the stream to catch fish. I knew he would enjoy it. He would make clay bulls for Rita, weave cattle whips, jostle the herdboys' bulls into fighting and bring back berries from the forest.

Goto township was half a morning's walk to the west of our village. Already the sun was hot and I could feel the heat of the sand through my thin canvas shoes. I knew it was going to be a long day.

'Do you think she will be in the church, Boyce?'

'I hope so. By the time we get there the service will be half finished.'

'The trouble with Catholics is that they kneel too much.'

We passed kraals where cattle stamped their feet and tossed their horns to keep off the flies. Here and there boys crouched in the mud, milking cows. Near some kraals we saw the familiar crumbling framework of grass and poles enclosing bulging mounds of earth. These were the homes of the dead, scattered all over the place, barely a stone's throw from the compound huts.

Some of the huts were elaborately built; roofs decorated by the alternating pattern of new grass interwoven with old grass, walls freshly painted and decorated. Others were square brick houses with zinc roofs. Scotch carts, water carts with drums and taps, ploughs, harrows, cotton-spraying equipment stood outside. Everyone was 'waking up'.

Not all the huts were elaborately built, of course. A significant proportion were clumsily built and had small grain huts. Here a few chickens scratched in the dirt and half-naked children loitered under the eaves. Thin dogs eyed us indifferently, too hungry to bark.

We came upon a very fresh grave and I asked Boyce who lay in it. It was a large one, with a wide path leading to it from the nearby compound. The wooden frame had been carefully erected. But in time the frame would crumble and animals would eat on its mound.

'Didn't you hear?' asked Boyce, surprised.

'We don't hear much,' I admitted.

'It is the grave of an old man who lived here. His wife poisoned him.'

'Why?'

'Because she wanted to inherit his wealth. The man owned a huge herd of cattle.'

'But how do you know she killed him? How do you know he did not die a natural death?'

'A natural death! You should have seen him. His stomach was swollen like a bull's and the dogs sneezed when they came near his body. He was only ill for two days, and then he died.'

'What proof do you have that she killed him?'

'Everyone knows about it. In a frenzy, she confessed that she

117

had poisoned him. People believe she has evil spirits. On the day they buried him she wanted to go into the grave with him. They struggled to pull her away from the edge. She had the strength of ten men.'

I looked at the grave, trying to imagine the dead man who lay in it. I could only smell the green of the grass, and the berries. I thought of the rain percolating the mound, dissolving first the flesh, then the framework of wood, leaving only dust and bones. Where would the spirit of the dead man go?

'Don't look at the grave too much,' smiled Boyce.

'Why?'

'People may be suspicious.'

'Who is the dead man's wife?'

'Mai Mapanga. She lives right here. Shhh . . .' cautioned Boyce, lowering his voice. 'She is coming.'

A woman came out of the hut and came down to the path.

'Walk slowly,' whispered Boyce.

The woman caught up with us.

'Good morning, Mai Mapanga,' said Boyce, stopping.

'Good morning, Boyce,' she replied. Her voice was thick, for a woman's.

'Are you going to church?'

'Yes.'

She wore a black mourning dress, a black headcloth, black beads and black bangles. She was lean, with long arms and bony legs. Her skin was light, set off against her black clothes. She was perhaps forty, with rusty yellow teeth, cracked lips and quick, brown, deep-set eyes.

'Are you Masiziva's son?' she asked me. I nodded.

'How are you, my son?' She held out her hand. Her palm was not hard as I had expected, and the fingernails were short. I wondered if I should console her for the death of her husband but I decided not to.

'How is your mother?' she asked, rubbing her breast vigorously as if something was moving in it. 'Does your mother still have maize to sell?'

'Yes.'

'Tell her Mai Mapanga wants three buckets. I will come on Thursday to get it. All my maize was finished at the burial of your old father here.' She motioned to the grave.

'I am sorry,' I said.

'Your father suffered, my son, and death only came as a relief. You had better go on your way. You might miss the service. Pray for us.'

'Goodbye.'

She went to the grave, stooped to clear some dry twigs from the path and when we last saw her she was leaning on the wooden framework of the grave, staring at the mound.

'Did you hear the way she spoke?' asked Boyce after she had passed out of hearing range. 'She thought death was a relief to her husband – as if she really wanted him to die. Don't be deceived by her voice.'

'She is a shrewish woman,' I said, but I wasn't so sure.

◆

In the village church the heat fell from the low zinc roof and pressed down on the people. The few windows in the whitewashed walls did not let in enough air. I could feel the heat pooling round me in waves. In the front of the congregation the priest was performing the last rites of the service. He was probably Portuguese, perhaps twenty-four years of age with a dishevelled head of brown hair falling across his forehead. He had sharp features – a long narrow face, thin lips and a straight nose barely separating the corners of his deep blue eyes. He had a starved look and an air of melancholy about him. Small and

119

lean, he wore dirty faded jeans under his robes. He spoke the local dialect fairly fluently.

I knelt, and moved my lips mechanically. My eyes searched the two halves of the congregation: the young men and the drummers on the right and the bright sea of yellow, pink and blue blouses on the left.

'Have you seen her?' I whispered to Boyce.

He winked, and gave a slight nod. A drop of sweat ran down my ribs. My armpits were damp already.

Suddenly the service was over and people were streaming into the passage between the flat benches, shaking hands and greeting one another. We were caught up in the slow, steady movement towards the door. Eventually we found ourselves standing in the piercing sunlight near the mango trees.

I saw her. She was coming out of the church with another girl, just in front of the priest. They were talking and laughing and when she saw me her laughter broke off slowly. She stopped.

'Hello,' we both said at the same time.

'How are you?' I held out my hand and she touched my fingers.

'You come to church often?' I ventured.

'If I can.'

'And this girl is your friend?'

'Yes, we work together in the store.'

The other girl had turned away and was talking to two boys. We walked slowly under the mango trees.

'Let's see your Bible,' I said.

She laughed and gave it to me. Her name was written in red capitals on the first blank page. I ran the pages under my thumb.

'From where was the reading taken today?' I asked.

'You weren't listening.'

'I came in late.'

'You don't often come. Today is your first time?'

'Yes. I still go to that church of ours under the tree, with my mother and brothers and sisters and the other women.'

I chewed a twig, and then a leaf and then a bitter blade of grass.

'So where are you going now?' I said, spitting.

'To the store where I work.'

'You work in a store. Which store?'

'That white one with a red roof. Chenge Store.'

'How long have you been working there?'

'Nearly a year now. I started last year in February.'

'I didn't know you were here.'

'How did you find out?'

I almost told her I had known by instinct.

'Boyce told me.'

'Boyce . . .?'

'Yes. He works for us now and he lives with us. We came to the church together and I think he has gone after some girls. Is it nice at the store?'

'It's not too bad, except on very busy days.'

'Like Christmas?'

'Yes. We spent the whole day behind the counter, serving the customers. I was so exhausted that I went to sleep without eating anything.'

'You don't come to the village to see your mother.'

'It's the work. I work every day of the week. The only time I am off is on Sunday when I have a half day.'

'Like today?'

'No, today I have to be back early. My workmate asked if she could go home to see her sick mother.'

'Where is your father?'

'I don't know. If he is not staying with my aunt in Matuvi's line then he must be somewhere else.'

'Does he ever come to see you?'

'He usually comes to ask for money.'

'Does he still drink a lot?'

'No. He doesn't drink any more. If he drinks he vomits so much that you think he might lose his guts.'

'Your poor father.'

'He will be all right. My Uncle Simon is preparing a family beer party to cure him.'

'You think it will work?'

'It might. And Mai Mapanga will address the family spirits.'

'Who is Mai Mapanga?'

'My aunt. My father's sister.'

'Mai Mapanga whose husband died a few days ago?'

'Yes.'

I tried to relate Jairos's madness and the death of Mai Mapanga's husband but it did not make sense.

'Are you in a hurry, Lulu?'

'Yes, I am. No, I am not.' She looked at me, her eyes half laughing. 'I can only spare a few minutes.'

'Can I come with you to the store?'

'You may.'

'Won't I be a nuisance, hanging around the counter and obstructing the customers?'

'Yes, you will.'

'In that case I will go home. Here is your Bible.'

She held out her hand but I did not give her the Bible. I did not go home either. Instead I touched her fingers.

'You haven't changed much,' I said.

'No. I have changed. I am a big girl now.'

'I don't believe it. You still look like the little girl I went fruit picking and swimming with.'

She creased her forehead in seeming puzzlement.

'Have you forgotten that day when I ran off with your clothes and you cried?' I asked.

'That was silly. I will never forgive you.'

'Then I will never be forgiven, because I came to take you for another swim.'

'Ah.'

'Why not?'

'I would drown. I can't swim. And besides, there is no river here for miles.'

'If there was a river would you come?'

'No, I wouldn't. I would drown.'

'I would save you from drowning.'

'You can't swim. You would drown too, and then there'd be two corpses.'

She was a big girl now, of course, and I knew why she would not come swimming with me again. But even if I had gone away for fifteen years I would still have remembered her calm brown eyes, her smooth light skin and slightly pouting lips shutting away her sharp even teeth. I had often taken a secret pleasure in imagining those teeth biting me. Perhaps if I had been more violent in the water she would have bitten me. I had not been violent enough, and now there was no way of telling what those two soft buds, which I had once touched, looked like. They were locked inside the bra whose pink strings I saw and envied under the shoulders of her dress.

She did not see my eyes. She was looking down at the path, swinging her free hand slightly. I saw a necklace at her breast.

'Let's see your necklace,' I said.

She pulled up the chain and put the stone in her palm. It was an opaque, bright-green oval stone, not expensive but very attractive. I stood in front of her and took it between my finger and thumb.

'Who gave you such a nice necklace?' I asked, stealing a secret glimpse into her dress.

'Someone.'

'He must be very kind.'

'Do necklaces always have to be given?'

'Usually.'

'Then you are wrong. I bought it myself.'

'You promised to knit me a white woollen hat, remember? You didn't, so I am keeping the necklace.'

She smiled uneasily and her hands grappled with mine for the necklace.

'I shall keep the necklace,' I said.

'No you shall not,' she insisted, half seriously.

'Then here it is.' I dangled the necklace in front of her. She dived for it but I snatched it back just in time and put it into my pocket.

'What is the good of keeping somebody's necklace without permission?' she said in the tone which always alarms ambitious lover-boys.

'At least I will enjoy keeping it.'

'You are behaving in a very strange manner today.'

'I want your permission to keep and wear the necklace.'

'But it's mine.'

'I know. I want us to share it.'

'You can buy your own. They are not very expensive.'

'No. I want yours.'

'But it's just like all the others.'

'I just want yours.'

'You are taking advantage of your strength. You wouldn't have snatched the necklace from a boy of your age. You took my necklace by force.'

'I didn't come to take your necklace by force.'

'Then why did you follow me?'

'I came to look for someone.'

'Then give me back my necklace and look for the person you want.'

'I will only give you back your necklace if you help me to find the person I want. She lives somewhere around here. You should know her.'

'What is her name?'

'It begins with a "J".'

'Joyce.'

'No.'

'Jenipher.'

'No.'

'Then who is she? What does she do?'

'She works somewhere here.'

'What does she look like?'

'Like you.'

'There is no one here who looks like me. Maybe she is somebody I have never met.'

'Never mind if we can't find her.'

'It must be unimportant if you are prepared to give up the search.'

'Suppose you are the person I really came to see?'

Lulu was silent.

'Suppose I really didn't come to see anyone . . .'

'Then what did you come to do?'

'Suppose you are really the person I came to see?'

'I don't understand you.'

'I came to see you,' I said. I stopped and looked into her face.

'You are seeing me now.'

'Don't be silly,' I said without a smile. 'You very well know I am looking at you, but that's not what I came to do.'

'I will be late at the store. I had better go.'

I let her take two steps and she stopped. She plucked a twig from a tree.

'You can't go before you hear what I came to say to you.'

She didn't say anything. She looked past me and chewed the twig.

'I came to say that I want us to be friends,' I said, my heart beating faster. I felt like an idiot so I continued, 'I know we have always been friends and have always liked each other. But liking is not enough. I more than like you. I want you to feel the same towards me.'

'I don't think that's possible,' she said daringly, staring past me.

'Why not? Is there somebody else? Am I late?'

'No. I just don't like to talk about it.'

'But just a little while ago, you were claiming that you are a big girl now.'

She rubbed her eyes.

'Won't you do something about it?' I asked hesitantly.

'Something like what?'

'Something to show me that you like me very much. Like letting me keep your necklace.'

'You still insist on keeping my necklace.'

'I am taking the necklace with me, with or without your permission.'

'Ah,' she said in a tone of resignation. 'You are a nuisance.'

'Promise me one thing,' I said.

'What?'

'To think about what I said to you.'

'You said so many things.'

'About us being friends.'

'There is nothing to think about.'

'Then you have made your decision already?'

'There is nothing to decide.'

'You don't have to keep me waiting if the answer is no. Think about it. I will ask you later.'

'Time won't change anything.'

In the store where she worked, boys leaned on the counters. Two of them were talking to Lulu's friend. The others looked inquisitively at us through the windows.

'Goodbye, Lulu.'

'But you said you were coming into the store.'

'I think I have to go now,' I said dubiously. Perhaps my going away would give her something to think about. 'Your customers are waiting for you.'

'They are just hanging around to talk. They probably won't buy anything. Yes,' she nodded, and added mischievously, 'and waiting for me.'

'So you had better go in.'

'When are you coming back?' she asked.

'Maybe next year.'

'Good riddance.'

'In that case I will come back this Thursday.'

She nodded very slightly and went into the store. I turned round to look for Boyce. I had seen him behind us in the mango trees but he seemed to have disappeared. I put Lulu's necklace into my palm to examine it. I stumbled onto the path, trying hard to decide if I was more worried than happy.

◆

Thursday was a hot day and Chenge store was full. Young men idled under the eaves, enjoying the free day. Inside boys stood leaning on the counters, gazing at the shelves and tapping their feet to the gramophone music. It was not a very big store. The whitewashed walls were cracking in places and at midday one could hear the zinc roof protesting. The unpolished cement floor was swept, but the swishing feet of the customers brought constant trails of fine sand that crunched underfoot.

Her hair was combed straight and I could just tell that she had applied something to it. She wore a bright-blue dress and as she darted from the counter to the shelves I caught a glimpse of her grey stockinged legs. Three fellows were talking to her across the counter. One of them, a short, dark, thick-set man in green shorts, was insisting that she should replay the record that had just finished. Lulu shook her head and smiled. The other girl at the counter was good-naturedly giving half an ear to the sweet tongue of another aspiring young man. She recognised me and gave me a knowing smile. She whispered something to Lulu, who afterwards came over to greet me.

'You are not very busy today,' I said.

'Not very,' she replied, drumming the coarse wooden counter with her fingers.

A small girl quietly put three cents on the counter. Lulu took the money and put six brightly coloured sweets in the child's palm.

'How did you know she wanted sweets?' I asked, exaggerating my surprise a little.

'She buys six sweets every day.'

The thick-set fellow had stepped to the window and was saying something to his friends. Together they laughed. Fat artificial laughter. I didn't listen.

'Four pounds of sugar, please,' I said to Lulu.

She ducked under the counter and put a packet of sugar on the table.

'I was joking,' I laughed, and she put the sugar back.

'So what did you decide?' I said at last, before a customer could claim her attention.

'Decide?'

'About us being friends.'

'Oh, that!' she smiled, shaking her head slowly. 'I didn't decide.'

'Why?'

'I couldn't decide. There was nothing to decide.'

'You probably need more time.'

'No.'

'Then what is it?'

'It's just that I don't feel like deciding.'

'I suspect you don't like me at all. Maybe I am boring you,' I said, lowering my voice uneasily. The fellows laughed again. I pushed my head forward as if to probe her. 'You don't like me.'

She nodded.

'Why did you not say so in the first place?'

'I had not made the decision.'

'But you said just now there was nothing to decide.'

The fellows went out of the store and there was a sudden silence. My voice seemed very loud and I wished they had stayed to drown it with their laughing.

'You are deliberately making things hard for me,' I protested, 'by being so evasive.'

'Am I?'

'Yes. I don't think it should take very long to make up your mind. If I had been in your position I would have said yes or no immediately after the proposal.'

She laughed and I liked that.

'It's difficult to decide . . .' she said, pretending to be helpless.

'No, it's not. You tell me now. I don't care if it's no.'

'Suppose it is no?'

'Then I will walk out of this store and hang myself in the nearest tree I can find.'

'The answer is no.'

'Is it?' I said, swallowing. She didn't smile.

'Will you tell me the reason why it is no?' I asked.

'There is no reason.'

'You write the reason on a small piece of paper.'

The other girl must have caught fragments of our conversation because I saw her trying hard not to laugh.

'Write the reason,' I said hoarsely, 'so that next time I approach a girl I will be aware of my disadvantages.'

'You really want the reason?' she asked, looking into my eyes. I nodded. She tore off a piece of white wrapping paper and, thinking again, crushed it and threw it away. She took a piece of coarse brown paper, laughed at her friend and wrote a few words, shielding the point of her pen with her left hand. It hurt me to see her putting me off so easily and lightly. She rolled the piece of paper up and bound it with sellotape. Then she bent over the counter and put it in my shirt pocket.

'I won't even read your piece of paper,' I said unhappily. 'I will throw it into the nearest dustbin I can find. Goodbye. Maybe I will see you next Christmas.'

'Next Christmas,' protested the other girl across the counter. 'Maybe Lulu will be dead by then?'

'It won't matter,' I said from the doorway.

My eyes blinked in the shimmering heat outside the store. I was thirsty but I did not want to drink anything. I just wanted to get away; away from the miserable shop, its laughing fellows and frivolous girls. I wanted to get away from the battering rhythm of the maize mill. I stumbled into a group of chattering girls entering the shop. I gave them a scornful look and walked slowly away into the trees.

She was a girl too and just because she didn't chatter it didn't mean that she was different from the others. It was very cruel of her to say no like that. I would never go back. To say no like that, after all I had done for her, after all our friendship. It was mean. At least she could have used a clean white piece of paper and a decent envelope. I took the slim roll out of my pocket and unrolled it. It was like a stubby cigarette. The paper was half soaked in oil and the ball-point pen had slipped. I deciphered the message slowly.

'It's all right, I love you too,' the message said.

I laughed aloud and creased my forehead in puzzled happiness. I read the message again and laughed. So she wanted me too. It was very cute of her to mislead me; to drive me to the brink of despair, only to crown me at the end. I fingered the coarse little piece of paper and laughed, talking to myself. It was not such a coarse little scrap after all. The sun was no longer hot. I suddenly didn't mind the noise of the mill, and if a group of chattering girls had passed me I would have embraced them. I couldn't contain my happiness. I wanted to shout Lulu's words to the trees. I plucked grass shoots out of the ground and threw them away to wilt. I drove the ants with twigs.

I suddenly remembered that she would be coming out for lunch so I hid behind a tree and waited for her. She came out after a long while. I sneaked up to her from behind and she gave a surprised start.

'I have come to punish you for saying no,' I said, hardly suppressing a smile.

'You punish people for saying no?'

'Yes.' I extended my hand awkwardly and smacked her face lightly with my fingers. She flinched slightly. It was a difficult joke.

'I didn't read your little message,' I said.

'Then you punished me for nothing.'

'I read it.' I laughed, and then asked needlessly, 'Where are you going now?'

'For lunch.'

'In your hut?'

'Yes.'

It was a small neat hut just behind the store. She pushed the door in and I hesitated in the doorway. One half of the room was occupied by a bed and the other by a small dressing table and two chairs. Her clothes hung from a rope above the bed. A small pot was frothing on a burning primus stove, and I could smell beans cooking. The hut had a curious lovable smell of soap, perfume, burning paraffin, coffee and cooking beans all blended together.

'You shouldn't come in,' she said, putting her hands on the doorpost.

'Just for a minute? I must come in.' I pushed the door and took a step inside. I put my arms on her waist and the door creaked loudly. I put my other foot into the hut and she fell forward, her breasts crushing against my ribs. I could smell her hair and my face was searching for hers. My mouth fell on hers and for one electric moment her tongue touched mine. I drew her lips into mine with a sucking sound but her tongue slipped back into her mouth out of reach. Her head pulled backwards and our wet mouths separated. We stood pressed against each other for five still minutes, till she said, 'You must go now.'

I released her and she patted her creased dress. I felt an intense passion. While I was holding her I had been too busy trying to capture the moment. We didn't talk as she took me half way down to the path, but the moment I turned my back on her I started reliving every minute of our embrace.

13

On the path behind the huts where the dew lay thick on the grass, Jairos made his morning rounds of the homesteads. He walked like a robot, very steadily, with a downcast face, arms slightly extended outwards like burning-hot rods. His dirty khaki clothes clung closely to the thin frame of his body, shielding his brown skin from the sun. There was a marked difference between his shielded and his exposed skin. His head and arms were black with sunburn and the dirt of months. The only sign of life on his face was his intensely fierce eyes and the pink inner folds of his lips. His tongue was grey.

The dew soaked his trousers to the knees and washed his cracked feet. He was past caring. Only his endless quest for food linked him to humankind. He was shut up in his own world. People shunned him. Children spat their insolence at him. He mauled his food like a hungry dog, hissing as if it burnt his mouth. He was as hungry as a tiger and as harmless as a puppy. We ran into him one cool April morning and he said abruptly, 'Please catch me an eel. A big eel.'

'We don't fish now,' I explained, wondering if he knew what month it was.

'Catch me an eel,' he insisted, his eyes desperate, globules of saliva oozing from his mouth. 'Catch me a big eel from Mbumbuzi stream.'

His plea faded to a whisper and he turned away. He'd already forgotten about the fish.

When the moon was full he was worse. He stood with an uplifted face, shouting strange requests and sometimes obscenities into the night.

'Ernest. Ernest. Put my water on the fire. I am going to buy milk for my tea.'

The address to the family spirit had perhaps failed to work.

◆

Simon tried his best as the new headman. He put duty before pleasure and he drank less. When people brought a case to him he paid close attention before passing judgment. He always tried to be fair. But like his brother, he suffered from too much passive optimism. His proposed projects to fence off the stream and build a dam and a new dip tank never came to anything. But perhaps it was not altogether his fault. The villagers paid no attention to the new council, being too busy with their own work. They were prepared to contribute funds but few people were willing to divert time and labour to a communal project whose benefits were not guaranteed. The newcomers were too busy growing crops, while the locals were waiting for the *derukas* to take the initiative.

From Jairos, Simon had inherited leadership of the village as well as its increasing problems. A decade of newcomers had put a strain on the land. There was a scramble for fields. Many families were fencing off their compound areas and building bigger kraals for their cattle. Worried farmers like Matudu were already putting pressure on Simon to guarantee the availability of land for their teenage sons.

The procedures of the headman's court were not strictly stipulated and perhaps that was why passing judgment was so difficult. The jury consisted of the men in the village who were neither complainants nor accused: prejudice was almost inevitable. The largest court case had centred on a *deruka* by the name of Madoo.

He was a tall slouching man with mischievous brown eyes. Perhaps he was thirty, but he looked older because he dressed carelessly in greasy shirts and trousers cut off at the knee. Boyce told us there were only three definite occasions on which Madoo bothered to wash himself, namely at New Year, Easter and Christmas.

Madoo was the son of a rich newcomer who had settled further north about a decade before our arrival. Having grown up in his father's compound, Madoo had decided to build his own home in Jairos's village. With his new wife and a small herd of cattle he settled in an old compound left by a trader. Perhaps Madoo was too lazy to build his own huts. The compound left by the trader had two smaller round huts and one large rectangular hut and there was a flourishing orchard of mango and peach trees. Madoo also acquired the trader's thirty acres.

I came to know Madoo one ploughing season. He was at once an industrious and a lazy man. With his pretty young wife he ploughed and sowed his fields from dawn to dusk. But he ploughed between sprouting tree stumps and unfelled bushes, and he never weeded his crops. His farming was not intensive enough to yield any profits. Rumour said that he even ploughed his fields on Thursday, a forbidden day for work. At one time Jairos had threatened to give one of Madoo's fields to a *deruka* – Madoo had successfully protested.

Madoo's huts were dilapidated. Grass was falling from the roofs and blocks of clay from the walls, exposing the wooden poles. The grass grew unweeded right to the walls of his huts. He had a fierce pack of lean dogs, which kept people away from his compound and from the orchard.

People said he had served a prison sentence for stealing a roll of wire from the local farmer's co-operative. Then news went round that the striking new blue door on his hut had been stolen. This was at a time when people's chickens and eggs were also mysteriously disappearing from their coops, while it was said that roast chicken and boiled eggs were prepared every night in Madoo's kitchen. Mrs Pendi was willing to swear that the new zinc tiles on Madoo's fowl run had been taken from her tool shed. But these were minor accusations and no one could actually prove Madoo's guilt.

Madoo had a pretty young wife but that did not satisfy his active sexual instincts. At village beer parties he was often seen in close conversation with the mother of the man who had married his sister. She was a portly older woman but pretty enough to attract much younger men. Her husband worked in town and was therefore away for months on end. When he was away she drank freely and jived to the gramophone at beer parties, and Madoo was her close companion. He bought her beer and accompanied her home. This meant that it was always very late when he returned to his own home. And he was often too drunk to notice that his wife was crying as she suckled the young baby. But she would be too tired to quarrel. She knew anyway that this would only raise his temper to dangerous levels.

But one night he did not come home. The cock crowed twice. She sat awake nestling her baby. Long after the last drumbeats of the beer party had faded away, Madoo had still not returned. She quietly put the baby down and opened the door. It was a dark night without a moon. Clouds had shut the stars from view. Only the tall grass and the dark crouching trees stared at her as she shut the door softly behind her. In the east the distant clouds cracked with a rumbling flash.

Wrapping her petticoat closely round her, she stepped into the path between the seas of grass, probing the night with her eyes. She heard a dog slink behind her and scolded the creature away. She glided into the path among the trees. She saw the two graves at the side of the road and shivered, her naked feet numb as they gripped the damp sand. But she pressed on past the gleaming pool near the water pump, down into the soft dark valley, full of a thousand fireflies and the muffled croaking of the frogs. She crossed the chilly stream and went up the sandy path.

Further along among the trees, two dark figures, a man and a woman, were staggering along the path. The man had his arm around the woman's large waist and her arms were thrown helplessly at her side. Somewhere a donkey brayed, breaking the silence. The woman started and he uttered a few words of reassurance. Close behind them the young woman darted among the bushes, hiding the whiteness of her petticoat.

The portly woman suddenly seemed to crumble. He held her by the shoulders. She started vomiting; the stuff gushed out of her as if something was pumping it out from below. Some of the vomit must have slapped his arms but he let her vomit for a while. Afterwards she walked more steadily and even mumbled a few words to him. She collapsed again at the next bend of the path and this time he let her fall onto the soft, deep sand. Then he knelt down beside her, put her arms on his shoulders and tried to lift her up. He failed and she laughed, thin cackling laughter barely floating above the beer frothing inside her. He tried again and failed. Then he laughed too and fell onto her bulging stomach. She squealed like a puppy. He laughed drunkenly as he undid his trousers. A moment later she had stopped squealing and was hissing and gurgling like a choking child as he crushed her huge, plump body.

He was up on his feet first, fastening his trousers.

'Get up,' he said, kicking her hips. She grunted and lay still. He pulled her arm and kicked her again. She cried out in protest. He dragged her, so that her feet ploughed the ground. Then she pulled her hand from him, cursing mildly, and staggered to her feet.

The young woman wept in the bushes, and had the staggering pair been less drunk they would have heard her. The man helped the woman to the door of the square hut looming before them. He pushed the door and eased her in. She fell to the floor, like a bundle of wood, and he came out. He did not go away but stood near the door, making himself a cigarette. He was no longer as drunk as he had seemed and with a sly cough he went into the hut again. A moment later he came out carrying something wide and heavy on his shoulders. He struggled through the narrow doorway. The figure in the bushes let him pass. He was panting

137

under the weight. His wife darted behind him long enough to see what he was carrying and then let him go on ahead. She took another path through the forest and ran home crying like a girl.

By the time he had pushed the bed into his grain hut the east was tinged with purple, and when he entered his own hut he found his wife asleep from fatigue and crying.

They went to work in the fields the next morning as usual; and as usual, she returned at midday to fetch their lunch. But he was surprised when she did not return. He was hungry. After a while, he set his oxen loose and went to find her. On reaching his homestead, he found four men lifting the bed out of the grain hut.

'What is happening here?' he asked, bewildered.

'You are in trouble, Madoo,' said Simon laconically.

His young wife had shown the men the vomit on the path and the marks where Madoo had defiled her marriage.

'Why did you do this to me, my wife?' he asked gently. She did not reply. She just stared at the ground.

He did not beat her. He was not even harsh to her. Instead, he begged her not to testify against him in court, promising to reform.

People talked. Many were delighted by the irony: the betrayal of an erroneous husband by his own wife. The less malicious sympathised with the disillusioned couple. Madoo promised to buy his wife a cow if she did not betray him. But he had wronged her in front of her own eyes. He was her husband. He was the father of her child. She did not know what to do.

On the day of the trial she initially sat, composed, in the middle of the gathering but when she was questioned she broke down. She was young and easily confused. They could not get a single word out of her and two old women almost slapped her for humiliating the court. But it was useless to question her. She had given the four men more than enough evidence with which to prosecute Madoo. The court broke with grumbles from the men and loud protests from the women.

The elderly woman's husband, the man whose bed had been stolen, through the licentiousness of his own wife, had been surprisingly calm during the whole procedure. He never rebuked Madoo. He divorced his wife, sold his cattle, packed his bags and left the village. His son followed suit by divorcing Madoo's sister, his wife. Madoo's marriage somehow survived the wreck.

◆

But the court case was a watershed; life had changed in the village. Jairos had had an easy time as headman: the village was young, the forests wild, human wounds healed as easily as new foliage grew on trees.

Now the forests were gone and people had become restless. The owls did not hoot any more. The huge trees where they had perched had been cut down for firewood. Ten years previously, owls had been part of the village, but now when an owl hooted people woke up, with throbbing hearts, to listen. Snakes no longer came slithering across compound clearings attracted by firelight. They kept away from the tread of human feet.

Village children shook the once-respected fruit trees, battering their trunks with rocks to make them shed their fruit. Some children even collected green fruit to ripen at home and sell to the bus passengers on the road. Gone were the days when children believed that shaking fruit trees would get them lost in the forest and that walking with upturned axe blades would anger the Gods into withholding the rain. It was the reign of the axe and the goats; the axe which opened the forests to the ravishing plough, and the goats, which mushroomed in number and were rarely killed for meat, but served only to create hatred between neighbours as they ate everything in sight.

14

And sadly, somewhere on the fringes of this decay, I remembered my father, who for many years had forsaken our home. Somewhere between his teens and late twenties the history of my father had got lost. He had been a bright and eager scholar, walking miles to school in the winter cold or in summer rain, often hungry, to get an education. In his mid-twenties he had found a job as a salesman in town. But in between these two stages of his life lay a gap that I could never fill.

I knew him as my mother's devoted husband and my determined father who had worked for two decades without a holiday in order to give us an education. He had been born and raised in the country, among smoky huts, cattle and millet. Later, his rural memories had pulled him back and he had built his own rural home, but he had been too busy working for our education to participate in its pleasures or its fruition.

Each time we arrived in town from the country, after our school holidays, I felt a pang of alarm on seeing him emerging from the bedroom to meet us – in his vest, red-eyed with sleep. There was something sad about the way he blew the wood in the stove to make tea for us, something cold about his dusty, wifeless house. He would always first ask questions about mother, the girls and the crops, before discussing the details of our school fees. Our education was his burning obsession, and we spurred him on because we were good scholars and potential graduates.

I knew that by the time he went to work in the morning, mother, a hundred miles away, would already be out in the fields in the early morning dew. Father spent the day on his feet, his workshirts slightly torn under the armpits, selling clothes. Mother spent the day weeding, and pacing the fields in her tattered gumboots, defending her precious crops from cattle and goats. In blazing sunshine or drenching rain, she was the human fence to our fields.

When I weighed up my parents' work, I found myself sympathising with my mother. I could imagine the trial of standing on one's feet all day, selling clothes; but I knew the greater trial of weeding under a blazing sky, or standing under dripping trees trying dismally to shelter from the driving rain, without a raincoat. But when I returned to town and saw the lean, solitary figure of father stretched out alone on the double bed, I always found myself questioning the justice of my sympathies.

It was by no means a question of my father's obsession with education versus my mother's farming instincts. Mother was equally concerned about our education but she thought our country home might reduce our expenses and help father to save money for our school fees. Later father disagreed, saying that it cost more to run two homes.

They never quarrelled openly but I knew the issue was a slow-burning fuse between them that must be put out. I knew from the moment mother received his letter saying that he would not be home for Christmas that a silent battle of principles had begun. That was why she had decided to run our rural home on her own, growing groundnuts, selling home-made clothes and buying two cattle. We were proud of her. I knew that secretly father also applauded her imaginative industry, but he was too consumed by his own principles to display his admiration. I dreaded what would happen if the war went on. We all wanted him back.

◆

He came back very suddenly, like a prodigal, one January afternoon. He crept stealthily upon us while we were weeding. Rita saw him first, cried out and ran to him. He put his umbrella under his armpit, then took her in his arms and came to greet us. His great big black gumboots laid flat the ridges of earth erected by the plough.

'You are doing a fine job,' he said, smiling, while pacing the acres of groundnuts we had just finished weeding.

'How long did it take you?' he asked. A month, mother told him. He paced the field again and again, only returning after dark. He sat with us in the kitchen.

'Your firewood is wet,' he said, screwing up his soft town eyes against the smoke. We ate sadza and fish and he asked if we had caught the fish ourselves.

'Not this catch,' I explained. 'We bought it from the women who sew nets.'

'There are a lot of fish in the stream,' he said. His mood was exultant, as it always was when he talked about fat cattle, fertile soils and good crops.

'But we don't catch big fish any more,' I said. 'The women clean the stream of all the large fish with their nets and sacks.'

'So what do you do for relish?' he asked hesitantly.

Vegetables from the garden, *madora* from the forest, milk from the cow, *nyovi* and mushrooms from the fields and fish, when we can get it, we told him. Mother did not answer any of his questions. Then we sang a chorus and he prayed. Afterwards we went to sleep. He went off with mother, swinging the flickering paraffin lamp at the mango trees to examine the fruit.

He was up early next morning, out in the dew to see the cattle his wife had bought, and to have a look at the garden. Before the sun was up he was in the fields, before us, hacking at the weeds with his huge hoe. He refused to sit down to drink *maheu*, and worked twice as hard as Boyce, sweating freely in the sun.

'You are leaving the weeds behind you,' mother said jokingly, pointing out a single blade of grass that had survived his huge hoe. 'You don't know how to weed.'

We all laughed.

At noon we took a break and the girls went home to fetch lunch. Father went out in the bright midday heat, emerging from the forest an hour or so later carrying something in his shirt, which he had taken off.

'What did you bring us?' mother asked inquisitively as he put the makeshift parcel down. 'Are these not poisonous mushrooms?' she teased.

'These,' he protested good-humouredly, fingering his small treasures, 'these are *nhedzi*, the best and most nutritious mushrooms. You cook them with the lid off the pot so they can boil freely.'

'That will boil out their taste and smell,' said mother critically.

'But that is the way they should be cooked,' he insisted. 'I will cook them for you tonight. I used to cook them for myself when I was a schoolboy. I almost lived on mushrooms then.'

I loved these morsels of childhood memory.

Immediately after lunch he was up on his feet, attacking the weeds with his hoe.

'You don't have to work in this heat,' mother rebuked him. 'You won't get very far.'

'I will,' he boasted, hoeing even harder.

'It's up to you,' said mother, 'but we don't want you fainting and unable to work tomorrow.'

At sunset he allowed mother and the girls to return home while he showed us the land he wanted earmarked for our fields when we grew up. The area was about thirty acres square, and he cut down the bushes along each border and laid them out in a rough line.

'Tell Headman Simon that I propose this area for your fields,'

143

he said in an imposing tone that made Boyce smile. He cut the bushes fiercely, his feet wide apart. We could hardly suppress our laughter.

'What's wrong?' he gasped, stretching his back. 'Don't you want fields?'

We laughed at the way he kept extending the boundary, at his pathetic little bushes, which would serve very poorly as markers. We laughed at his determination, which was blind to the gathering dusk and the fact that he was assuming the role of the headman.

'Don't you want fields?' he rebuked us with a smile. 'Can't you see that soon there will be a shortage of farming land in the village and that the snails will get nothing? It doesn't matter if we claim your fields now. We can fence the area off and chop the trees down later. It doesn't matter if you are all going to be graduates and live in nice big town houses. Then you can buy a tractor and have someone plough your fields for you. You will be able to use fertilisers and manure and plough five acres. You will grow hundreds of bags this way. You can never make a final break from the country.'

His words sobered us.

We brushed our way through the bushes on our way home in the dark. Then we came to the edge of an open field and stopped. There was a big gap in the forest, as if someone had cut a rectangular patch of hair from a man's head, leaving a gaping section of scalp. It was a field of about twenty acres. I saw the dark open sky and the stars above it. On the field dying tree-trunks lay stretched, their wilting grey branches reaching out lamely to the sky as if begging for life. Only the stumps of the trees stood out like still sentinels watching over their own decay in a large open mortuary.

'It's a beautiful field,' said father, surveying the darkness.

'Yes, it's a very big one,' agreed Boyce. 'Marufu chopped

down all the trees alone in two weeks. He is a monster of a man.'

'Marufu?' said father, puzzled.

'The man whose cattle destroyed our mealies last year,' I explained.

'I remember now. A tall man with a grey beard. He has worked very hard,' said father, 'but he hasn't done a very good job. He has chopped the trees too high up. The stumps are too tall for the oxen and plough. And he should have cut the branches up to allow them to dry quickly for burning.'

He led the way through the sad dark maze of stumps, tree-trunks and branches. I saw the glow of a fire through the trees.

'Which route are we taking?' I asked.

'The shorter one, behind the village line,' said father.

'Behind people's huts?' said Boyce resentfully. 'It's not good to walk behind people's compounds at night.'

'Why not?' asked father, amused.

'It's not safe,' said Boyce.

'Why?'

'We can get bitten by dogs on the back path.'

'But we can also get bitten on the front path.'

'It's not wise to walk near the kraals at night.'

'And the graves,' I added.

'Are you afraid of ghosts?' asked father, coming to the point.

'I would rather not take any risks,' I said.

'What would you do if you found out that you had married the daughter of a witch? Never pay your mother-in-law a visit because you would be afraid of meeting her ghosts?'

I laughed.

'Do you believe in ghosts?' said father, suddenly turning serious, 'Don't you believe in God?'

I stopped laughing and felt my cheeks twitching uneasily. I had not expected the question, nor did I know how to answer it.

145

'I believe,' I replied hesitantly, 'but I would rather not take risks.'

My uneasiness grew in the long silence that followed.

'But don't you believe in ghosts, father?' I asked, suddenly remembering a fragment from his youthful past. One night he had had to lie flat on his stomach on the side of a path to let a strange phantom pass. A tall dark form like a man standing on high stilts. An unearthly creature that took long stiff strides. Fear froze his senses. It would simply remain a phantom for the rest of his life.

'Ghosts,' said father loudly, 'do sometimes exist. They are the spirits of the dead, people who have led evil lives who are left to roam the earth. Sometimes they are simply evil spirits conjured up and given shape by witches. But a ghost will not hurt an innocent soul.'

'But there are ghosts which beat innocent people,' said Boyce.

'Believe me,' father responded firmly, 'ghosts won't ever hurt an innocent soul. Have you met anyone who was beaten by them?'

'A man was beaten here once, in this village,' said Boyce. It had happened two years after our arrival, but we had never paid much attention to the story. The victim was a tough, hard-working man and people said the injuries had been inflicted by a jealous neighbour in order to cripple him. He had stumbled home with a broken jaw and his mother had screamed on seeing him.

'Let us walk along your dangerous path and see what happens,' said father, and we had to follow him.

In the vlei the frogs were croaking and the fireflies were shining in the reeds. Already the chilly air was creeping into the forest and I knew there would be buckets of dew in the morning, buckets – useless beautiful dew scattered over hundreds of acres of grass, sparkling in the sunshine. One could not drink the dew,

146

or collect it, but it nourished the crops and kept them cool through the hot mid-morning hours. And dew was good for the milk cows that were up early enough to catch it.

But now was not the time to think about foaming milk and sparkling dew. Village huts, cattle pens and graves loomed before us in silhouette.

The darkness itself seems to have its own particular smell. Sometimes it is warm like baking earth, sometimes murky like the mud in the streams. There are distinct pockets of smell and as you come up from the valley you can distinguish them. You can even pick out the scents of the individual fruit trees and flowers. And as you leave the forest and approach the village, you are suddenly confronted by the strong smell of humanity. You feel half reluctant to walk into the warm earthy smell of the mud huts, the smoke, the heavy damp stink of cowdung and beneath it all the smell of the rubbish heaps.

As you pass each compound you can tell what is cooking, and what the relish will be – mushrooms, fish, *nyovi*, peanut butter and, maybe, chicken. The smell of food is reassuring. You pass your eyes over the cow pens and quickly over the frames of the graves. You can smell the dogs too.

They dashed at us from the bushes, but Simba stood his ground and growled, so that the cowardly creatures turned back and fled, yelping.

'I see Simba is a formidable dog,' said father, laughing. Then he observed, 'People are fencing off and ploughing their compound areas.'

'There is a very big scramble for land but unfortunately Jairos is no longer sane enough to answer for it,' I said. 'He packed this village with *derukas*.'

'How can you say that?' said father, alarmed. 'Where would we be if Jairos had not "packed" this village, as you decide to call his hospitality? You haven't seen a really crowded village.

You have never been to the south. The pressure on land there is three times what it is here. No one owns more than six acres. We are still quite well off here. I am surprised you are blaming Jairos, as if it is he who commanded the human race to multiply.'

I felt so hurt and confused that I barely heard father announce triumphantly that we had arrived home unscathed by the proclaimed evils of the back paths.

15

After reaping the crops he had sown in April, Boyce announced that he wanted to go home to his mother. He had already left when we came home for the December holidays.

'It was only an excuse,' mother explained. 'He really wanted to find a job in town.' We were going to miss Boyce and we wished him well.

'I don't know what I will do without someone to help me with the ploughing in October,' lamented mother. 'Boyce was a nice boy, so industrious and cheerful. He thought he would hurt me by saying that he was going to town – that's why he said he was going to his mother.'

'You will find another boy before the rains, mother.'

'It will be difficult. The young men are tired of the countryside and flocking to the towns. And besides, people are reluctant to part with their sons.'

'Why, mother? Do they think they are underpaid?'

'There is more money in the towns. And people are realising that it pays to work for themselves. Things are not the same any more.'

I would miss Boyce because he had been the listener and judge of my adventures each time I went to see Lulu. She was still the girl of my dreams and I tried to see her every school holiday.

'We must beat last year's sales,' said mother. 'We must work hard this summer.'

In an industrious spirit, Jo and I woke up in the crisp early hours of dawn to yoke the oxen in Matudu's kraal. All morning we ploughed the green acres. Then came the weeding, the sunstroke, the pouring rain and the nibbling goats. And dew in the morning on the green grass when we went to guard the crops.

As if to add our problems, Matudu decided that he had looked after our cattle long enough. So he drove them to our compound and left them unceremoniously inside our fence. Jo and I spent two days building a kraal for them, and Jo had to look after the cattle until we found a small boy to do this for us.

'So Matudu simply decided to dump the cattle here without warning,' said Mrs Pendi at the fence, clutching her ailing baby. 'My little boy has been coughing all night,' our neighbour continued, soothing the baby. 'What a night we had! There was an owl hooting on the roof of my bedroom. We couldn't sleep. And this very morning a snake slithered into my fowl run and swallowed a live chicken. You haven't seen a snake like that, Masiziva.'

'It's very strange,' smiled mother.

'This village is not safe any more. And what are the people coming to? How can Matudu just dump your cattle like that? Who will look after them when your boys go back to school?'

'Godi will be here for a few weeks longer. You know fifth-formers start a bit later. But I suppose I should try to find a boy.'

'Herdboys are so difficult to find these days, Masiziva. And apart from that they disappoint you even if you can get them to work. Take this boy Midu, who has been looking after my cattle. I cannot understand him.'

'Why?'

'Doesn't he seem strange to you? His eyes, his voice.'

'Well . . .?'

'Don't be deceived by his boyish looks. He is quite old, that boy. Yet he behaves just like a toddler. He has been working for me for over a year now but hasn't bought himself a single shirt. He prefers to spend all his earnings on sweets and biscuits.'

'But you ought to buy clothes for him. He needs your guidance. He is only a boy.'

'No, Masiziva, Midu is an exception. You can't persuade him to do anything constructive.'

'But he is only a boy,' said mother. 'You should never put all the cash in his hands. He doesn't know what to do with it. Give him enough to buy sweets and keep him happy. Save the rest of his money to buy him clothes, or send the money off to his father.'

'You don't know his parents, Masiziva. If you buy clothes they will complain that they are not worth what you should pay the boy.'

'But what can we do? When we take a boy to live with us, we must make sure that he is at least properly dressed. We can rest with an easy conscience that way.'

'You are right there, Masiziva. I could buy clothes for Midu or send his wages to his father. But when Midu's father entrusted the boy to us, he said we should give all the money to the boy.'

'Maybe that was just talk. He might be happy if he hears that you are buying clothes for his boy. If he comes now and finds his son half naked, he won't believe you are paying him anything.'

'You are right there again.' Mrs Pendi nodded, the way people nod when they think they have had more than enough advice. 'But Midu is a queer boy. Each time he goes to the dip he buys himself a loaf of bread and a can of bully beef and he packs his stomach as if it's the end of the world . . .'

150

'All young boys are gluttons at some stage of their lives,' laughed mother.

While they were talking, Mai Mapanga and Jo came hurrying along the path. Mai Mapanga proceeded to the Pendis' gate and Jo came through ours.

'What's happened, Jo?' Mrs Pendi demanded apprehensively, clutching her baby. 'I thought you had gone to the mill with Midu.'

'Something's happened,' said Jo hesitantly. 'Midu had some kind of shock and he fainted.'

'Shock! Fainted! How and where?'

'We had gone to Mai Mapanga's homestead to ask for a pump.'

'Mai Mapanga's compound! To ask for a pump . . .'

'One tyre was almost flat . . .'

'What *is* wrong with Midu? Asking for things from a stranger's homestead? As if we had no pump here . . .'

'And then what happened?' interrupted mother.

'We sat on a log and Midu just fell flat on his face. He was breathing, but he had lost consciousness.'

Mai Mapanga drew up beside mother and Mrs Pendi. She was visibly panicking. One could almost see her knees knocking together.

'What is this I hear about Midu fainting in your homestead?' snapped Mrs Pendi. Mai Mapanga's lips opened soundlessly. I suddenly remembered the day I had seen her standing at her husband's grave. I remembered her dry lips, her cracked teeth and her soft palm. She still wore black mourning clothes.

'It just happened,' she explained shakily. 'Midu and this boy came to my homestead to ask for a pump. They sat down on a log and before I had even returned their greeting, your boy fell forward on his face and did not move.'

'Was he bitten by a snake or a scorpion?' demanded Mrs Pendi.

'I do not know, my daughter,' replied Mai Mapanga. I half expected Mrs Pendi would reject the salutation. 'He just fell forward. Maybe it was from heat and fatigue.'

'From heat and fatigue!' said Mrs Pendi angrily. 'Since when did boys start fainting from heat and fatigue at six o'clock in the morning? And in other people's homesteads? You know what you did to my boy and you will tell me.'

'But I did not do anything to him,' protested Mai Mapanga.

'You will explain to my husband and the boy's father when they come this weekend.' Mrs Pendi put the baby down and hurried away with Mai Mapanga. We followed.

Quite a crowd had assembled at Mai Mapanga's homestead. As we drew nearer I observed that the crowd had formed a ring round the outstretched figure of Midu. Headman Simon was shaking something over his body.

'He was lucky,' said Simon quietly. 'They didn't really beat him. They just blew their chilly breaths over him and clouded his mind for a moment.'

Mrs Pendi pushed her way through the ring.

'Mai Mapanga will tell us what she did to my boy,' she said as if she was going to cry.

'He will be all right,' said Simon.

'Is he breathing?' asked Mrs Pendi.

'Do not touch him before the powder settles,' cautioned Simon. 'The powder will drive them away.'

For about five minutes there was silence, in which only Midu's belly seemed to move. He lay on his back with his face turned to the sun. His mouth and eyes were open but there was a vacant look in his eyes.

Men brought medicine in small bottles, liquids thick and yellow as cooking oil or brown as chocolate, powders like cocoa and jellies like mucus. Each brand of medicine was administered to Midu's body by its owner. Men muttered advice.

'We can put him by the fire now,' said Simon. 'It will drive the chill out of him.'

A man pointed to a fire roaring in the middle of Mai Mapanga's homestead.

'I would rather take him home and put him near my own fire,' said Mrs Pendi, and people muttered in agreement.

Simon took Midu on his back like a baby, and someone held the dangling head in place to prevent it from straining his neck. The procession went slowly to Mrs Pendi's compound in a silence that was broken only by the hushed whispers exchanged by members of the crowd.

They laid him by the fire in Mrs Pendi's kitchen. Jairos staggered into the doorway of the crowded hut and stared at Midu and the medicines. There was alarm on his face as he whispered, 'The little men beat him . . .' He turned and went away, muttering to himself.

Midu lay by the fire for a while. At last he moved his legs, opened his eyes and sat up like a boy waking from sleep. He sneezed twice into the fire. They took him out behind the hut to empty his bladder. The sneezing and the passing of urine were good signs of recovery, said Simon. Midu sat blank-faced at the fire all day, long after the hut was empty. But the next day he was up and about, herding cattle as if nothing had happened.

Three days afterwards Mrs Pendi accompanied her children to school. My family also packed and left, leaving only Midu and myself in the two compounds. We were to share each other's company in the evenings and sleep together.

◆

I felt very lonely after they had left. I opened the kraal to let out the cattle. Bellum eyed me eagerly. Sigwe rose lazily from the ground and the calf came to sniff my hands and lick the tips of my fingers with her small rasping tongue. I whipped the cattle grudgingly as I drove them to the pastures, punishing them in advance for the trouble I thought they would give me.

It was still very early when I reached the fields and there were no cattle in the vlei. It was very still and I wondered how long the dew would last before the cattle arrived and scattered it with their hooves.

I left my cattle to browse in the lush grass near the edge of the field. I sat in a commanding position from which I could keep an eye on them as well as on the fields. I opened my novel and was absorbed in it until the tinkling bells warned me that the other herdboys were coming. I had been happy to be first there, but now as the herds of cattle thronged the vlei, I felt unhappy. Bellum lowed and went on browsing. All round me I could hear the cattle pulling grass out of the ground and munching it.

Towards noon two girls walked past the field and went down to the gardens. They came back later carrying baskets of vegetables on their heads. I stood up to greet them.

'How are you?' said the older of the two. She was not so much a girl as a woman and I realised that she was possibly married. 'Has your mother gone to town yet? I wanted to pay for the dress she sold me.'

'You can leave the money with me if you like,' I told her.

'I did not bring the money with me,' she said, chewing a blade of grass, 'but I can bring it tomorrow. So you remained behind to look after the cattle?'

'Yes,' I replied. 'And guard the crops.'

'Guard your mother's crops well,' she said. 'She works very hard.'

'Could you sell me a cabbage?' I asked, just as they were turning to go. I put my book down and went towards them. I realised that the other girl was much younger than I had supposed. Perhaps sixteen, with dark plaited hair. Her breasts were showing like little horns inside her dress. Her knees were soiled from kneeling in the mud. There was something sad in her wide face and slow, brown, widely spaced eyes.

'You can have the cabbage for nothing,' said the older woman, 'because your mother is kind to us.' She handed me a cabbage and said to the girl, 'Give him two mealies, Jeni.'

I took the mealies from the girl and thanked her. She made an effort to smile. They went down the path and disappeared into the grass. I turned to my book again.

It had been hot all day and the storm built up suddenly. A sudden chill swept in from the east. I stood contemplating the rain, shivering in my shirt, waiting for the last herds to leave the vlei. Then I rounded up my three cattle and quickly drove them home, but we were enveloped in the downpour. I shut the cattle in the kraal and went into the kitchen. Simba lay under the grain hut. He whined when he saw me, apologising for not joining me in the rain. I realised with surprise that he had not been with me to the vlei in the morning.

I lit a fire and sat sleepily over the flames knowing that I was safe. By the time the storm abated, the sun was setting. It was too late to take the cattle out again, so I went to check the field for stray cattle.

I had finished feeding Simba and bathing myself when Midu arrived. It was dark. He loomed in the doorway, the lamplight vaguely defining his body against the dark night.

'Hello, Midu,' I said.

'Hello,' he muttered.

'I didn't think you were around. There was no sound from your place. Did you come back late?'

'No.'

'Just after sunset?'

'Yes.'

'Have you had supper?'

'No.'

'I am sorry. I have just finished mine. I gave all the leftovers to Simba.'

He sat on the floor near the fire, his chin on his knees, surveying the hut slowly, blankly.

'So where were you herding your cattle today, Midu?'

'In Mbumbuzi Forest.'

'You don't like the vlei?'

'I went with Matudu's sons to Mbumbuzi Forest.'

'Is there a lot of grass there?'

'Yes.'

'I was just about to go to bed. I wish I could get you something to eat. You haven't eaten anything?'

'No.'

'So you are going to bed hungry?'

'I ate mangoes.'

'I see. But you ought to have a proper supper.'

'I will cook something tomorrow.'

'Shall we go to sleep then?' I asked. I lifted the lamp, went out of the kitchen and bolted the door. When I turned round I was surprised to see Midu's figure disappearing in the shadows.

'Where are you going, Midu?' I half shouted.

'To get my blankets,' he said without stopping.

'We can share mine tonight,' I volunteered, but he didn't stop. I wondered if I should follow with him with a lamp. Somewhere a baby cried. I heard Midu kicking open the door of his hut in the Pendis' compound. He did not even strike a match. I heard him close the door again and make his way back.

'You are not afraid of the dark?' I asked, and in the lamplight he looked as if he might smile.

He spread his blankets out next to mine and took off his clothes. He lay on his back, staring at the roof.

'Won't you go to sleep?' he asked me.

'I want to read for a while,' I told him, flipping the pages of my book. 'Do you want something to look at?'

I gave him a magazine full of pictures and he turned it over to examine it, moistening his thumb.

'Is this a train?' he asked me, pointing at a picture. I nodded.

'And is this the head of the train?'

'Yes.'

'Does the head push or pull the train?'

'It pulls.'

'I think I would enjoy a ride on a train.'

'Have you never been on a train?'

'I haven't ever seen a train. Maybe I will see one when father takes me to town next month.'

'Is your father coming?'

'He might. Here is a girl with a big packet of sweets.'

'A very big packet.'

'They almost look like real sweets. I could tear them out of the page and eat them. They make me feel hungry. Who draws all these pictures?'

'A person. But a machine prints them on the paper.'

'Oh, a machine.'

The lamp burned between us. I could smell his thick, curly, uncombed hair. His skin was very smooth and light, but his eyes were too large and his eyelids were swollen. His lips were moist and thick and stayed open all the time. There was something both old and young about his features. The smoothness of his skin put him at eleven or twelve but his thick, gaping lips and his slow dark-brown eyes suggested he was fifteen or sixteen. There was something stern, even aggressive about his eyes, even when he smiled. He had a clean body and slept naked like a baby. His arms were small and boyish, but his knuckles and fingers looked swollen. There was black earth under his fingernails. I wondered if he had been digging for mudworms. Perhaps he had been fishing.

'I have finished my book,' he said, gathering the tattered pages into place. 'You haven't finished yours yet.'

'Mine is a novel. I have to read all the words.'

'All the words? Every single word?'

'Yes, or I will not understand the story.'

'But it's more interesting to read pictures.'

'You think so,' I said, and put my book away. 'When are they dipping this week?'

'On Friday.'

'I have never been to the dip.'

'We get up very early.'

'Are you going to the dip?'

'Yes. Why do you ask?'

'I thought perhaps you wouldn't, after the day when you fainted.'

He lay on his back and stared at the roof. Outside in the dark the Pendis' gate clicked. Midu jerked his head.

'It's that sick old man Jairos coming to mess the toilet,' Midu said loudly. 'I wish I was there to scold him.'

'What really happened, Midu?' I asked, brushing talk of Jairos aside.

'When?'

'That day you fainted in Mai Mapanga's compound.'

'They hit me.'

'Who hit you?'

'Mai Mapanga's little men.'

'You saw them?'

'I saw a bit of them.'

'What were they like?'

'I can't easily describe them.'

'You can try.'

'I only saw them for a very short time. They were two very little, black men, black as soot, and with backs bent like wire. They had very small feet.'

'Did they make any sound?'

'They seemed to mutter and hiss.'

'And they raised their hands and slapped you?'

'They did not slap me. I just saw them and fainted.'

'You fainted just from seeing them?'

'Yes. They blew their cold breath over me. I saw them, felt cold and fainted.'

'You don't remember anything else?'

'No. I only remember waking up lying near the fire and going out to pass urine.'

'You are not afraid they will beat you again?'

'Again?' he seemed puzzled. He had never thought about it.

'Why do you think they beat you?'

'Maybe because I sat on their log.'

I blew the light out and went to sleep. In the middle of the night I woke up and saw Midu's dark, upturned face. His mouth was open, but he did not make a sound. He slept very quietly like a baby. The blankets had rolled off his body and he lay on his back with his knees in the air. I covered him with blankets and felt a vague sensation on touching his dark, naked body. He did not stir. Outside in the dark Simba was growling ferociously.

When I woke up Midu had already left. He had left his blankets carelessly on the floor. The door was half open and I could see that the sun was rising. I stretched my arms and yawned lazily, reluctant to get out of bed. I hated rising early.

Midu was picking mangoes.

'You are up early,' I said to him.

'You are up late,' he replied across the fence. 'The sun is up. The chickens came out ages ago.'

Simba jumped up at me and put his paws on my chest. I patted his head and pushed him away.

'Have you milked your cows?' I asked Midu.

'I shall. Have you milked Sigwe?'

'I shall.' I laughed. I went to the pump to get water, washed the dishes and made a fire.

'You are cooking something sweet,' said Midu across the fence. 'Something fat and oily.'

'Oil buns,' I told him.

'Come and get some mangoes,' said Midu. I went to the fence and he handed me a plate of mangoes.

'Thank you,' I said. 'They are so ripe.'

'There was one very big one in this tree. It was almost ripe, but now I can't find it. I think Joki came and stole it.'

'Who is Joki?'

'Munyu's last boy. He herds the cattle. He is a nuisance. He comes to play here and he steals things. He pays most of his visits at meal-times too.'

'You should discourage your friends from coming to play here, Midu,' I advised him. 'Otherwise Mrs Pendi won't be very pleased to learn that you were bringing people here during her absence.'

I went into the kitchen with the mangoes and saw Jairos coming. He came into the kitchen after me and dashed for a chair, his eyes all over the place.

'Please let me have a bun,' he said desperately, his eyes glued to the pan on the fire.

'But they are not ready yet,' I told him. 'Will you have a mango?'

'I don't like mangoes. They make my teeth ache. I want a bun. A bun please, that brown one in the middle of the pan.' He went to the fire to point at it.

I eventually forked the dripping bun out of the pan and put it on the table. Jairos took it with unsteady hands, took one bite and put it down again.

'Can I have some tea?'

'The water is only warm.'

'It doesn't matter.'

I poured the warm water into a cup and stirred tea-leaves and sugar into it.

'What about milk?'

'There is no milk. I haven't milked the cow yet.'

'You haven't milked the cow. Does the cow have no milk today?'

He took the tea, however.

'Where is your mother?' he demanded, munching the bun.

'She is away in town.'

'And your father?'

'He is in town, too.'

'Tell him to send me tobacco and gin. He doesn't like me any more. He wants me to die.'

He finished eating and picked up his dirty woollen hat.

'Do you have a shilling?' he asked, stopping in the doorway.

'No.'

'Can I have a shilling?'

'No, you cannot. What do you want it for?'

'I want to give it at the funeral.'

'At the funeral? Who died?'

'Jeni died. You didn't hear?'

'No.'

'You don't have a shilling?'

'No.'

'All right, I will ask next door.'

He went out humbly, holding his hat in his hands. He put his hat on, coughed and shuffled away. Midu arrived just after Jairos had left. He found me having my tea. He sat on the stoep of the hut.

'I am having breakfast,' I told him.

'Yes.'

'Would you like a cup of tea?'

'Yes.'

I gave him a cup of tea and a bun.

'You fry well,' he remarked, eating the bun.

'You still haven't milked your cows?'

'No.'

'But you should. They say if a calf has too much milk, it will have a running stomach.'

'I will milk them.'

'I have to take my cattle out now,' I told him, picking up the cups.

'But it's still very early in the morning.'

'I have to guard our field,' I told him. 'There could be stray cattle eating the crops even now as we talk.'

'But no one takes cattle to the vlei this early.'

'There might be stray cattle.'

'And there is the dew.'

'It doesn't matter.'

'So you graze your cattle near the field.'

'Yes.'

'All day?'

'Yes.'

'I may see you in the afternoon.'

I took the cattle to the vlei. I felt more tolerant towards them. They were only cattle, I told myself, and all they could do was munch grass. They all ended up in the cooking pot. I looked at them and tried to imagine myself eating their meat. Sigwe was too thin and there was an air of melancholy about her slow sad eyes. Bellum was fat and sleek. I knew every inch of his body. I would prefer his meat because he was fat and there was an aggressive defiance about him.

I sat reading under a tree. From somewhere in the village I heard voices but I could not tell whether they were singing or not. At noon I put my book down and ate sadza with sour milk. I stood up and looked out across the vlei.

The grass stood tall, still and as level as a crop. It obscured the stream at the bottom of the vlei so that all I could see was a portion of the steep bank, which the water had poured through in the heavy rainy season. Across the stream I could see a narrow plain of grass and the thick forest beyond.

There were no cattle in the vlei. It was quiet. I could not even hear the grass rustling. In the morning when the grass was glossy with dew I would stare out at the plain, wondering when the dew would dry up. Did I like the dew, I wondered. It was so beautiful, but it made you wet and could give you a cold. But once the dew had dried, I was still entranced by the grass. I swept my eyes from one end of the vlei to the other, wondering what to do with it.

I could bring paints, brushes and paper out to the fields but I had never been a good painter. I would never reproduce the glossiness of the grass. The view was too wide. I would make too much fuss over individual features. The forest looked thick from far away, but I knew that as you drew near and started seeing individual trees and sunlight spilling in between their crowns, you realised how isolated, how denuded, they were.

I could write about it, but words alone were not enough. Perhaps I wanted to take off my clothes, kick off my boots and wade down through the grass to the shimmering stream. To be drunk with sunshine and sensation – a sentimental consummation of some kind. And then what? Exhilaration? Shame?

Two figures, Midu and another boy, came into the field, parting the tall grass with their hands, and my dream fell in fragments.

'Hello,' I said, as they sat near me under the tree, scrutinising my empty lunchbox.

'You graze your cattle so near the crops,' said Midu loudly. 'One day they will eat your mealies.'

'I keep a sharp eye on them,' I said.

Joki, Midu's companion, dug in the dust with his toes.

He was a skinny boy with a face like a knife and dirty oversized clothes.

'What is the box for?' asked Midu, pointing.

'For putting things in,' I replied.

'You bring your lunch out to the fields?'

'Yes. I can't go home and cook in the afternoon. What do you do for lunch?'

'I don't cook in the afternoon.'

'But you don't cook in the morning either. You only eat mangoes. You never cook. That's probably why you fainted.'

'I just do not feel like eating.'

'If I gave you something to eat would you refuse?'

'Do you want to give me anything? Is there anything in the box?'

'No, I ate everything. Are you fishing today?'

'I did not bring a fishing line.'

'I don't have a hook,' said Joki.

'Who is singing?' I asked, listening. 'I have been hearing the voices all morning.'

'Didn't you know?' said Joki with surprise. 'There is a funeral. Someone died.'

'Jeni died,' said Midu.

'Jeni?' I said incredulously.

'Majuru's daughter,' said Midu.

'What does she look like? I mean what did she look like?'

'She was a big girl,' said Joki.

'With dark plaited hair?'

'Yes.'

'And long slim legs.'

'Yes.'

'Where did she live?'

'In Matuvi's line.'

'Does she go down to the garden to get vegetables and mealies?'

'Yes,' said Joki. 'She usually went with her brother's wife.'

'I saw a girl like that yesterday. It must have been her. She was with an older woman who addressed her as Jeni. They were coming up from the gardens . . .'

'That was her,' said Joki.

'But she did not look ill yesterday.'

'She died suddenly,' said Midu, 'of witchcraft.'

'Mai Mapanga bewitched her,' interjected Joki.

'Her little men tortured her for many nights.'

'Mai Mapanga and Jeni were enemies. Mai Mapanga hated Jeni because she worked hard . . .'

'Because Jeni worked so hard in the fields . . .'

'Mai Mapanga said, "Let me kill her and see who will work for her parents. She thinks she is a tractor and yet she is only a girl." '

'And so Mai Mapanga started torturing her . . .'

'Jeni couldn't sleep at night. She woke up every morning complaining that someone had been sitting on her back all night.'

'And yesterday when she came from the garden her foot started swelling . . .'

'Mai Mapanga had set a medicine trap on the path . . .'

'She felt pins moving in her breast . . .'

'Last night she did not sleep . . .'

'Early this morning she was dead.'

'I thought I heard singing,' I said. 'And Headman Jairos asking me for a shilling, to offer at a funeral. I thought he was confused.'

'She was such a nice girl,' said Midu.

'She gave me two cobs yesterday,' I said. 'I can't believe she has died.'

'She was an industrious girl,' said Midu. 'I wonder why Mai Mapanga killed her.'

'She was jealous of her. She will kill us all.'

'She wants to raise her spirit and turn it into one of her little men.'

'When are they burying her?' I asked.

'On Monday.'

'Why so late?'

'They want her body to decompose first, to make sure that the witches don't dig up her grave and eat her flesh.'

I looked out over the grass and saw the girl offering me two mealies. The tall grass floated with the wind over her body. Her breasts looked like two little horns under her blouse. The mealies had fallen out of her hands and rolled in the grass and I was afraid to take them. Her whole body seemed to crumble like hard clay until only the eyes were left: large, dark, widely spaced eyes. Now her body lay rolled in a blanket inside a hut. There were flies all round it. Outside people wept and Mai Mapanga wept among them. She still wore her black mourning clothes. There was a strong stench in the air. A deep narrow stickhole in the grave suggested that someone had tried to release the dead man's spirit. There were tall weeds on the grave mound and Mai Mapanga stood knee-deep in the grass plucking the grass seeds into her basket in the rain.

No, it wasn't raining and there was no one in the grass. The sun was still shining. I asked Midu to stand up to see if my cattle were still grazing in the tall grass near the edge of the field.

◆

On Sunday morning the sky was overcast. I woke up late. The village was soaked. Grey roofs were dripping rain. Mud fell from the walls, exposing wooden poles like lipless teeth. I hated the ground when it was green with moss. I knew that if the rain came again, it would come later.

I asked Midu to take my cattle out to the pastures, promising to return early in the afternoon. I took my umbrella and raincoat and set off for Goto township to see Lulu. People were going into the church when I got there but I hung around in a nearby thicket idly stripping the bushes of their leaflets and feeding them to the wind.

I saw her after the service. She came out with her books and said hello to me. I stood with my back to a tree, digging into the dust with my heels.

'You didn't come in for the service,' she said.

'No. I didn't feel like coming in.'

'You are a heathen,' she laughed.

'Satan will have a nice big fork for me and a bag of coal in Hell.'

'You make fun of the Devil?'

'Sometimes I can't help it.'

She wore a knee-length dress and she had stretched her hair and combed it backwards. I could see the skin on her head under her hair. Just above her breast I could see her neck bones. She wore no necklace. I still wore hers and felt guilty at not having provided a substitute.

'So how is work at the store?' I asked.

'As usual.'

'Boring?'

'Not boring. Just hard.'

'I am living alone these days.'

'How alone?'

'All the others went to town, including mother. And would you believe it – I am looking after the cattle.'

'So how come you are here?'

'Instinct.'

'Go back and take your cattle out to the pastures. They are starving.'

'Midu is taking care of them today. I came to take you out to the pastures. Hiya Lucia! Hey, come! You cow.'

'I am not a cow and I am not coming to the pastures. I don't eat grass anyway.'

'You can come over to our place now that I am living alone.'

'To do what?'

'To see me. So where are you going now?'

'Where else? To my hut.'

'Can I come with you?'

'No, you cannot.'

She unbolted the door of her hut and ducked in, shutting the door in my face.

'But I want to come in,' I protested.

'There is no place for you in here.'

'I shall bang the door down.'

'It will be your fault if people see you and think you are crazy.'

She opened the door slightly and peeped out. I pushed in and the door gave way. I knew as soon as I had done that, that she did not want me to go away because she put her arms around me. She put her palms on my cheeks and kissed me.

'I want to sit down,' she said, pulling away from me and patting her dress. She sat on the bed and put her head on the pillow.

'You are ill?' I asked.

'Yes.'

'What ails you?'

'Headache.'

'Can I help you?' I bent forward.

'No you cannot.'

'Why not?' I asked, sitting on her bed.

'There is no place for you on my bed.'

'In that case I am going away,' I said, going to the door.

She kicked her shoes off and stretched her legs out on the bed. Somehow she seemed to chide my boyish fantasy in the vlei.

I closed the door, came back to the bed and put my nose on the pillow.

'Is that all you want?' she said like a pail of cold water. I had nothing to say.

'You know the state my father is in. Our affair can never go anywhere.'

I looked blankly at the pillow.

'You don't have to say anything,' she said, 'and you know you don't live in this village all the time.'

'What has come over you, Lulu?'

'I am no longer a child. I know it's hopeless. I can never dream of belonging to you. There is too much competition.'

'What makes you say that?'

'You wouldn't marry me. A girl who works in a shop? You, with your education.'

'But . . .'

'And there's my father.'

'What has your father got to do with this?'

'Since he became ill I have been thinking . . . thinking of my family. You know how poor we are. I should be helping them. I shouldn't be having affairs.'

'But this is not an ordinary affair.'

'It wouldn't be right for me to enter too deeply into this.'

'Who has been talking to you, Lulu?'

'I didn't have to be told, although my mother warned me. No.

I am sorry. I would have loved us to be together. But I have been working for a long time now and I have been growing up.'

'And you want me simply to break it off and leave you?'

'Yes. Not because I want you to go. But I just want to be alone to think out my problems and to be responsible.'

'You can't imagine how hard it is for me . . .'

'Do you think your mother would be happy to have me in your home? If I had another father perhaps . . . or if I was educated . . . Your mother likes me but do you really think she would accept me? Don't answer.'

There was nothing I could say. She lay there quietly while I tried to absorb the shock and the truth of what she had said. Later she handed me my raincoat and umbrella and took me to the path. She couldn't take me far because she said her head was aching and the storm was coming in on us. I put on my raincoat and turned blindly away.

◆

After shutting up the cattle that evening I went morosely to the kitchen and prepared myself a meal. I ate a little, and then took the paraffin lamp and went out to feed Simba. He was barking furiously in the dark near the trees, just beyond the fence. I called out twice and whistled before he stopped growling. He approached me very slowly, his ears bristling; he was growling even as I fed him.

Afterwards I bathed on the grass in the lamplight. Midu had still not arrived. I stood in the doorway of the kitchen looking at the Pendis' compound. The big compound lay in silence. Not a hen clucked in the fowl-run. Only the huge zinc roof of the big house gleamed timidly in the darkness. Midu had still not come when I went to bed. I did not read. I just lay in the darkness, unthinking, vainly courting sleep.

In the morning I staggered into the sunshine. The light and the dew did not thrill me. Simba ran up to greet me. He seemed glad that the night was over. I saw Midu just when I was going to take the cattle out.

'You did not come last night,' I said.

'I could not.'

'You didn't sleep in your hut either.'

'I went to sleep with Joki at their place.'

'I knew you were away because it was so quiet. I was the only soul here.'

'Were you afraid?'

'Not very. Except when Simba barked.'

'He barked a lot?'

'Yes. At the fence near the trees over there.'

'What was he barking at?'

'I don't know. It was so dark. So why did you not come home last night?'

'I can't tell you. I might scare you.'

'Come on. I am not a baby.'

'There was a strange light near our lavatory.'

'A fire?'

'No. A light.'

'Torchlight or lamplight?'

'A strange light. It seemed to hang in the air.'

'Near the lavatory?'

'In the doorway.'

'You are sure it was not Jairos's cigarette?'

'No, the fire was too big.'

'So you saw the light and you ran?'

'I saw the light and I ran back to Joki's place. I slept there.'

'Did the light go on and off?'

'No. It was on all the time.'

'Was it big? Did it throw any shadows?'

'I can't remember very well. But it didn't throw any shadows. It just shone and its light obscured everything else.'

'Are you sure it was not my lamp? I came out to feed Simba.'

'No, it wouldn't have been you. The light was right in the doorway of the lavatory. It made it look as if it was on fire. And I think you were asleep when I came. There was no light in your huts.'

'I went to sleep early. So you think it was a – ghost?'

'I don't see what else it could have been. There certainly wasn't a fire burning near the toilet.'

'What would a ghost do in the lavatory? Wait for people?'

'Or maybe for Jairos.'

'But this is strange. Why should a ghost choose to appear now when we are the only two people left in the compounds? Why now, of all times?'

'That I don't know.'

'You think maybe someone sent it?'

'It could be.'

'But are you sure you were not imagining it? I was within view of the lavatory and I never saw a thing.'

'You don't believe me, Godi. Why should I lie? I swear I saw it with my eyes.' He raked his tongue with his index finger and made a cross on his forehead. He was not lying. He had seen something. He was a brave boy and not easily scared by the darkness.

He opened the kraal to take the cattle out. I knew he had not eaten anything. He did not even take any mangoes with him. He was away before me and later I realised that Simba had gone with him too.

He came back in the evening, exhausted by hunger. I knew now why he was so skinny. But his flesh had a glow that seemed to withstand his sustained, self-created bouts of starvation. Simba came back with him, limping.

172

'You took Simba with you,' I said.

'I couldn't get him to return.'

'He is limping. What happened?'

'Is he limping? I didn't notice. Where?'

'The hind leg. The right leg, as if something hit him.'

'Maybe it's a sprain.'

'Where did you graze the cattle today?'

'In the Mbumbuzi Forest.'

'He did not chase anything?'

'No, I didn't see him chase anything.'

'At least you ought to have noticed he was limping.'

I took Simba's leg in my hands. He whined. There was no bruise – nothing to indicate how he had hurt himself. Afterwards I prepared my evening meal. Midu and I ate together and went to sleep.

In the morning Simba limped heavily. I took his leg up and was surprised to find a huge circle of pink flesh showing just beneath his stomach, as if his fur had been neatly plucked off. The skin had not been cut. I did not know what to do.

'Give him wild melon juice,' Midu advised. 'Bathe the sore with the juice and make him drink some of the juice.'

I followed Midu's advice. I had heard of the cure before. That day Simba lay in the shade near me, not running about as he used to do.

In the evening Midu did not come. I spent the night alone. In the morning Simba's voice was hoarse. He limped very heavily. I wished I could help him. I only hoped that he would hang on till mother returned, then I could attend to him. He did not come with me to the fields.

I came back at sunset and found him dead. He lay on his side under the grain hut. I stood near the hut looking at him and felt angry and remorseful. I wanted to force Midu into saying how Simba had received the injury. I felt remorseful because I had not loved Simba as Jo had done and because I had watched him die.

He was a huge dog and in death he was even bigger. His brown belly was swollen. I wondered if it was the air inside him, and why the air did not rush out through his open mouth. His tongue was already stiff and ran out of his mouth at the side. His eyes were open, staring at me. There was no smell. I guessed he had died in the afternoon. As I watched him a big green fly entered his mouth and buzzed inside.

I knew he would smell soon. I would have to bury him up the slope in front of the village line. If I put him behind the village line the wind might blow the smell up the compounds, and the rain might expose his bones.

Grimly I tied his uninjured hind leg with a rope and tugged him up the slope, weaving through the crops of mealies. He was heavy and his body swept the sand like a bag, leaving a fine white trail on the ground. Twice I ran him over wooden stumps. Some of his fur remained twisted on the stumps. I pulled him under the fence of barbed wire and into the trees where he had been barking and growling a few days before. Already the darkness was falling.

I started digging with a shovel and felt my anger rising again. The ground was hard. I wished I had a pick. I cut the roots with the edge of the shovel and scooped the earth out with my fingers. There wasn't enough earth to fill the shovel. I fumbled on in the pressing darkness. I felt the dark trees looming over me, staring at the strange company I was bringing into their midst.

I pulled Simba into his grave. His body slumped in clumsily, his hind feet out of the cavity. I enlarged the hole and pressed his feet into it. It did not take me long to replace the earth. I was glad of the darkness because had it been daylight, I would have seen his brown fur turning a dirty grey as the earth hit him. I picked up the shovel and noticed that the rope was still tied to his leg. I did not want to uncover his legs to untie the rope so I just chopped it off with the shovel. Perhaps later someone might spot the tattered rope shreds locked round a piece of bone but they would never bother to dig the bone up.

I hurried out of the trees in the darkness. I felt angry and miserable. I could not eat. I did not want meat. I went to bed and lay staring at the roof, knowing that outside there was the darkness but Simba was not there to bark any more. He couldn't bark because there were clods of earth in his mouth.

'Where is Simba?' Midu asked the next morning.

I did not answer.

'What happened to Simba?'

'I don't know,' I replied angrily.

Midu did not believe me. He saw the fine trail weaving through the mealies and I knew the whole village would know by sunset that Simba was dead.

◆

Mother and Rita returned after three weeks. They arrived without warning. It had been raining and I stood drying myself in the sunshine, whistling, when I heard their shouts. Rita ran up to me, laughing. I swept her up from the ground.

'You did well to come,' I said.

'How are you? How was your long stay alone?'

'Not too bad, but I was beginning to feel lonely. Did Tendai start well?'

'Very well. They put her in the "A" stream. You guarded the crops very well. Not a nibbled plant in sight. Your cattle look fat. You gained weight too.'

I grinned.

'Anything happened while we were away?'

'Two women brought money.'

'And how is everyone?'

'A girl died.'

'What girl?'

'Jeni.'

'How sad. And Midu kept you company at night?'

'Only the first few nights.'

'It must have been lonely for you. But you had Simba.'

'Simba died too.'

16

Remoni was a local young man with a good record. He had worked for two or three *deruka* families who all reported on his industry. So I was very happy when mother wrote to say that Remoni had agreed to work for us. I looked forward to seeing him.

But he was not the person I had expected him to be. He was very short, very dark and lean. His eyes gleamed and he had a sly look. He wore a dirty yellow shirt and tight white shorts, and went about without shoes, leaving the unmistakably small prints of his feet on the ground. There was something imposing about him because when we asked after his health he did not reply but instead tersely asked after ours, as if his health was a concern of his alone.

At table he was neat and well-mannered, but he always threw his first morsel of sadza into the fire. Later I learnt that he believed that by doing this he was rendering himself immune to any possible poisoning by the food. If his first piece of sadza fell to the floor before it reached the fire, he would not eat, believing that the accident was a warning from his guardian spirits not to do so.

He kept one small suitcase, his mat and blankets in his hut, hanging his two or three items of clothing on a line. I smelt oxhide ropes in his sleeping hut and the vision of an iron chain and the cattle yokes sent a shudder through my body. I had heard that he was a great night worker.

He woke up at three in the morning. The moon was shining brightly through the doorway, and I felt very tired after the journey. Remoni was gathering the chains and the yokes for the oxen. Jo was already up and dressing. I rose hesitantly and put my clothes on, too.

'Wake mother up,' said Remoni. But there was no need to. We went to yoke the cattle in the dark. Remoni did not even shout. He just slapped the cattle's faces and they moved into their positions. We took the path behind the village. Everywhere there was moonlight. It could have been just after sunset, except there were no children playing under the eaves of the huts. Instead there was silence, except when a cock flapped his wings and crowed, and others echoed his cry.

We reached the fields and started ploughing. The grass was so tall that at first I could not see the furrows. Remoni held the plough and barked short orders to the cattle. He seemed to know by heart where every tree-stump was. Once I tried my hands on the plough, and narrowly missed knocking my teeth out with the handles when the plough hit a tree-stump. Remoni laughed softly and took over, leaving Jo and me to drive the cattle. Mother came behind us dropping maize seeds into the furrows.

The moon sank just before sunrise and the day broke slowly on us. In the vlei the haze melted like wax till I could make out the waves in the grass and the individual trees. The sun slowly flooded the vlei with an orange light. The forest did not look so dark and forbidding. I chided myself for having felt fearful. What was it about darkness that made people afraid? Just because the sun left the earth for a while – but the landscape did not change; each tree remained in the same place. The same reeds bore the fireflies, the same frogs croaked, the same footmarks remained on the paths. It was only the expectant imagination which saw distorted figures in tree-stumps and heard the tread of feet in the movement of leaves.

Or perhaps it wasn't?

By the time the sun had risen to the crowns of the trees and the other ploughboys had arrived we had ploughed two acres. People stared at us as we went home, wondering how we could return again so early in the morning.

'That is the trick,' said Remoni, smiling. 'Plough at night and play during the day. Surprise the lazy loafers. They see you leaving the fields in the morning when the dew is still on the grass and they laugh. But when they spy on your fields and find the mealies tasselling, we will have the last laugh.'

After breakfast I lay on a mat and tried to make up for the sleep I had lost, but Remoni would not let me rest.

'Won't you come and see what I have done in the garden?' he asked in a tone which mocked my exhaustion. I put on my boots and went with him. I felt tall beside him so I let him walk slightly ahead. He took short, quick steps. His muscles were so hard that the flesh of his thighs did not tremble.

He had done wonders in the garden. The cabbages, choumoulier, onions, spinach, tomatoes, rice and budding mealies were all flourishing.

'Your mother planted too many mealies,' he said.

'But it's a fine crop,' I said, 'and it's ripening too.'

'It would have been even better if the plants had been more spaced out.'

'You used fertiliser?'

'No. Manure. Cowdung.'

'You did a fine job.'

He grinned.

'You repaired the fence as well. There was a big gap here which the goats broke through to eat the vegetables.'

I stood admiring the garden.

'Won't you take some vegetables home?' he asked.

'Mother didn't say anything, but we can take a cabbage just in case . . .'

He chose a large cabbage, gave it to me, closed the gate and we went home. At the side of the path we came upon a *nhengeni* bush laden with berries. I put the cabbage down and ate the berries, holding the thorny branches up with my fingers.

'You eat those bitter berries?' enquired Remoni.

'I like them,' I said, sucking. 'Won't you have some yourself?'

'No. They are for kids. I only eat them when I am drunk, then they seem to taste like curry.'

'Do you drink?'

'A little,' he said, smiling quickly.

'Yesterday I was in trouble,' he resumed shortly.

'What trouble?'

'The two sons of Munyu were after me with axes and knob-kerries. That is why I am staying at home all day today.'

'Why were they after you?'

'They caught me in their sister's hut on Sunday night.'

'What were you doing in a girl's hut at night?'

'What does a fellow do in a girl's hut at night?'

'So they caught you and beat you?'

'No, I was too fast for them. The younger brother swung his axe at me but I was already out of the way. The axe hit the doorway and broke it into two.'

'Why take such risks?'

'I enjoy it. I can't spend two nights without entering a girl's hut. There is not a single girl's hut in this village whose interior I do not know. I want to know all the girls, too. Every one of them. I want to know how they hold a man and how they cry.'

'You are not afraid?'

'Of getting caught and beaten?'

'Besides that . . . of making the girls pregnant.'

'It's up to the girl,' he laughed, shaking his small head. 'I usually deal with the wide-awake ones who know how to go about it.'

'But it's still dangerous.'

'Not these days. There is not a girl who doesn't know about pills.'

'Pills from the hospital?'

'No. From Mai Joki. She has got a whole basket full of them and she sells them by the cup.'

'Mai Joki! Where on earth would she get the pills?'

'Her brother works in a clinic. He gets them for her.'

'But she could get into trouble. It's illegal.'

'Why should she get into trouble? She is helping young girls not to fall pregnant.'

'She is helping to corrupt them too.'

'I don't think so. Pills do not drive a girl into trading with her body.'

'But there are those who refrain out of fear of pregnancy. The availability of pills will drive them into doing it.'

'Maybe.'

'So what do you give your girls?'

'Me!' He put his hands on his hips and stopped laughing. 'Me! Give a girl anything! Not me! I am too smart for them. I flatter them into doing it. I don't spend my earnings on those girls. I don't work for them.'

'But there are always other dangers. The girls who sting.'

'Oh that! I am too smart for those too.'

'You keep away from them? But how do you know if they sting or not?'

'I don't have to keep away from them.'

'You go to the clinic afterwards?'

'I don't waste my time going to the clinic. I know the simple remedy for the girl who stings. The moment I finish with her I go out of her hut and urinate. It washes everything out. And I wash immediately afterwards, of course.'

I looked at his tense, dark-skinned thighs, his bulging, tight-fitting shorts and his moist, dark, laughing lips. There was a bold aching sensuousness in his diminutive features, which many girls would no doubt find attractive. A sudden thought struck me: perhaps disease was eating him away very slowly.

'The only trouble with me,' he said with a sudden, surprising frankness, 'is I can't have children.'

'You have a wife?'

'Yes. I have been married for nine months now, and my wife has failed to conceive.'

'Where is your wife now?'

'In Goto village.'

'With her parents?'

'No, in my compound.'

'You have your own place?'

'Two huts and a ten-acre field. If I was not working, I would have built myself a big zinc and brick house. The trouble with me is I have worked too long for other people. Had I stayed in my own compound, I would have produced fine crops, and raised cattle and sent my children to school. I don't want them to look for other people to read and write their letters for them when they grow up.'

'I didn't know that you were married.'

'You are not the only one,' he laughed. 'I know I am a pleasure-boy but when I decide to work hard and do something

I can really do it. My wife doesn't go about naked. We never buy maize. We never beg. We can look after ourselves.'

'So when do you see her?'

'During the weekends.'

'I'll tell her you plan to enter every girl's hut in the village,' I threatened.

'She knows I do.'

'How does she take it?'

'Sometimes she fumes. But she is only a woman.'

'I hope you don't beat her.'

'Double-crossing, yes. Wife-beating, no. I think it's below a man's dignity to beat his wife.'

When we arrived home, Remoni went over to our hut. I entered the kitchen with the cabbage and saw a man sitting there, waiting, his bicycle against the wall. 'Call Remoni,' mother told Jo. 'Tell him there is someone to see him.'

Jo returned saying Remoni wanted to know why the man wanted to see him.

'It's about the money I lent him,' said the man.

Remoni said he had nothing whatsoever to do with the man, but on mother's insistence he came to the kitchen.

'I want my money, Remoni,' said the man.

'I told you I don't have it, old man.'

'You have been saying that for the past eighteen months. It's month-end now and I want my money this minute, Remoni.'

'But I told you I don't have it,' said Remoni angrily. 'What do you expect me to do, old man? Tear myself into dollars?'

'Eighteen months is a long time, Remoni.'

'Come next month.'

'I don't trust you, Remoni. You don't care. I think your employers should hold back your wages till you pay me.' He looked at mother appealingly.

'I don't think I should become part of this dispute,' said mother.

'But I don't trust Remoni,' the man protested. 'He is a cheat.'

'Come next month,' insisted Remoni.

'All right. I will come next month. But if you don't give me my money, then . . .'

'What?' interjected Remoni, smirking. 'You will go to the *n'anga*?'

'No.'

'You will hack me to pieces with an axe?'

'No.'

'You can do anything you want, old man. If you go to a *n'anga* the poison he gives you will turn on you and destroy you. I am immune to witchcraft. My grandfather was a great medicine man.' He bared his chest to show razor slashes. 'This medicine will protect me. Even the little men of the night flee from me. Your axe will bounce lightly from me and hack you, its owner, to pieces.'

'I will leave you to your own imagination,' said the man with a dignified air. He rose to go, proud and solemn. He mounted his bicycle and rode off without another word.

'Give him his money, Remoni,' said mother.

'He is an idiot!' laughed Remoni. 'To spend eighteen months pressing me for a miserable shilling or two he lent me while we were playing cards.'

'You should pay him all the same,' said mother, seriously.

'No, I won't,' grinned Remoni. 'I will teach him to be clever next time. Let him go to the *n'anga*, let him send his little men. Or let him go to the devil. Like I said, I am immune to witchcraft. And besides, he won't dare do anything.'

◆

After breakfast Remoni usually went away, sometimes to drink. When he drank he came back in the afternoon, full to the nose. But he controlled himself amazingly and only the slow twinkle of his eyes told me he was drunk. At sunset he would yoke the cattle, even when he was drunk.

'But it's going to rain,' I would protest. I hated going to the fields at night.

'It might not rain,' mother would say.

'It will not rain,' said Remoni.

The rain did not come and Remoni drove the cattle into a neat gallop, so that whoever handled the plough had to hold fast and keep a keen eye for tree-stumps. Then he would build a roaring fire in the middle of the field and the flames threw long red rays over the vlei. I knew somebody would catch a glimpse of the fire through the trees and think it was something else.

'The fire will drive the ghosts away,' explained Remoni.

At one point Jo whistled loudly at the cattle and Remoni chided him laughingly.

'Don't whistle at night.'

'Why?'

'They will take your voice.'

We ploughed on into the late hours, leaving after midnight, tired to the bones.

On Sundays Remoni put on his best suit – or rather his faded grey trousers and a jacket that was too big for him. He wore a white shirt, red tie and thick khaki stockings. One day a boy came to fetch *his* tie from Remoni and so we concluded that most of his clothes were borrowed from his friends. His own belongings were not numerous enough to fill a very small suit-case, although he evidently enjoyed referring to his things specifically as his 'property'.

He always claimed he was broke, although he could afford to get drunk three or four times a week. Then he came and sat on a chair at the fire and opened the pots to see if there was meat cooking. He hated vegetables.

He was one of those people who go through a dozen different jobs in a few years. He had been on the roads, in the dips, and in the tsetse-fly teams. He talked enthusiastically about the road and dip-building as if he were one of the shareholders in the building companies. You could pity him for expending his personal energies on projects that were so vastly remote from his personal comfort. Yet you could admire him for his selfless devotion to work that did not directly improve his way of life. He enjoyed work. The benefits of his industry were not even enough to foot the expense of his licentious life but somehow he kept himself alive and breathing.

You could believe most of his personal accounts but it was easy to see through his exaggerations and self-glamorisations. He was always the hero who fought the lion, hauled stuck lorries out of the mud and killed the pythons in the forest. It was he who always escaped from the jaws of the hippopotamus and the tusks of the elephant. You could listen to his accounts with curious enthusiasm, delighting in his imaginative originality but secretly rebuking him for his exaggeration.

He had had his first job at the early age of ten. That was a herdboy to a huge herd of cattle. The herd was so large that three boys in all looked after it, but even then a few cattle managed to stray away every day. There were always buckets of milk from the cows. The boys got tired of drinking milk and longed for meat. They eventually conspired to kill a calf once in a while and keep the meat, drying it in a tree. Remoni and his mates ate meat till their teeth ached. The owner of the cattle assumed that the missing calves were dead or lost, till the day he caught the boys roasting meat in the forest. There followed much thrashing and weeping and all the boys lost their jobs.

At fourteen Remoni found his second job as a labourer to an

agricultural demonstrator. That was when he got the opportunity to learn about fertilisers and gardening. He was held in high esteem by his employer, until the day he was caught with his employer's daughter. It was a very dark night. The two were in the mealies. They had taken off their clothes. The demonstrator saw a white shirt and pink blouse hanging on a mealie stalk. He could hear the mealies rustling and the sounds of his own daughter. He crept in dazed anger towards them. He stood like a statue, watching them. The girl did not get pregnant, but within minutes of the discovery Remoni was out of the compound with his small suitcase. The demonstrator had not even gathered enough strength to strike him.

Remoni spent the night in the bushes near the kraals. Early in the morning he was on the road to town to seek his fortune. He trudged at the roadside with his suitcase. Towards sunset when the heat and hunger had exhausted him, a car stopped to pick him up.

The car dropped him on the outskirts of the town. He clutched his suitcase and stared around him. He loitered on the pavements for a while, till hunger drove him into a café where he bought a bun. The café closed early in the evening and he had to go out. There was only one other place where he could go and that was the beerhall. But there he sat feeling very lonely in the midst of all the noise and the shouting. No one offered him a mug. The beer was expensive. Even the girls did not excite him. They threw their painted dark eyes at him, mini skirts dancing over stockinged legs, busts shaking under see-through blouses. Lipstick and wigs and high-heeled shoes scared him. He preferred the village girls. They were much less sophisticated.

Later the beerhall closed and he went out to sleep under a hedge. He woke up early the next morning to the bell of the milkman. The sun was shining and he was very unhappy.

The glare of glass and metal hurt his eyes and the smell of

petrol fumes upset him. While he was wandering in the market-place he ran into a man who was recruiting volunteers for the tsetse teams. He volunteered and after two days he was on the back of a crowded tractor, snaking along the thin track of road going further north to the villages where he had worked as a boy.

The roads and dips and wild elephants were still to come.

◆

Sometimes he came home very late in the night. Frequently he whistled. He banged the door when he entered, and simply fell on top of his blankets, leaving the door slightly ajar. Sometimes he stripped himself so that in the morning he was completely naked on top of his blankets.

One night he arrived very late. It was after midnight. I woke up to the tread of his feet. Something thrashed in the bushes and moments later he burst in, breathlessly. I could almost hear the beating of his heart.

'They chased me all the way from the stream,' he gasped. In the starlight coming through the doorway his face had a strange expression.

'What?' I said, rubbing my eyes.

'The things of the night chased me. The water in the stream was red as blood. I saw my image in it. Then I heard them coming at me from the reeds. I ran like a rat. They chased me right up to the water pump and only turned back at the gate.'

'You saw them?'

'They looked like flying black rags. They squeaked like giant mice.'

'You haven't bolted the door,' I said.

'It won't make a difference. They won't come in.'

'What are you doing?'

'Putting my charm in the hut. It will keep them away.'

He lay on his back with his clothes on. He did not snore.

The incident did not stop him roving about at night. But from then he always wore his charm. It was a charcoal block, heavy, chipped and oily. He wore it on his breast. Nothing would hurt him as long as he wore it, he boasted.

After the ploughing came the weeding. Remoni hated weeding and openly indicated his feelings. It was woman's work, he said. Men worked with oxen and ploughs, not with hoes.

'So what work will you do in place of weeding?' mother asked him in a tone of resentment. In the ploughing weeks he had been her superior but now she was his.

Father did not receive Remoni's decision not to participate in the weeding with pleasure. Employees never decided which types of work pleased them and which did not, he complained.

'You will clear the field of the thorn trees and the bushes and the stumps,' father told him sternly, when he visited us at Christmas. 'And you will repair the compound and the garden fence. You will also fetch cartloads of firewood from Mbumbuzi Forest.'

Remoni listened quietly, staring into the fire. There was the suggestion of a smirk on his lips. Later he stood with his axe on his shoulder, contemplating the girth of the trees he was to fell. There were four thorn trees with very thick trunks and thorny branches.

'But the trees will crush the mealies,' he protested lamely.

'It doesn't matter,' said mother. 'It will only be a few mealies.'

He chopped slowly at the smallest of the trees. Every now and then he stopped to rest and to pick the chips out of the wedge with his fingers. The tree fell slowly, its trunk groaning as the fibres at its heart snapped. It lay in the dust on a small patch of mealies.

'I am going to sharpen my axe,' said Remoni, going down to

the village. It was about nine o'clock in the morning. He did not return. He did not come home in the evening either.

We found him in the field the following morning, chopping the second tree. He did not talk to us. He left again after felling the tree.

He yoked the cattle at sunset and fetched home a cartload of firewood. The wood was not dry. The lichen was still green on it and you could strip ropes out of its bark. He was very silent and polite in the evening.

'So when are you going to repair the fences?' mother asked him quietly.

'As soon as I finish felling the trees,' he replied.

'But you can't ever hope to do much if you take one whole day to fell a tree, and work only half the morning.'

'But after chopping the trees, I go to chop firewood.'

'Damp firewood.'

'What can I do? Have you not heard that people are no longer allowed to chop firewood in Mbumbuzi Forest? Matudu had his axes confiscated by the forest-keeper last week. And besides that the cart couldn't stand the trips into Mbumbuzi. The wheels need new axles and bolts.'

'But we have got to do the best we can with what we have, Remoni. I sent for spanners. Why did you not repair it?'

'I couldn't find the time.'

'You obviously can't find time if you decide to spend half the working day on holiday.'

'I will repair the garden fence tomorrow,' he announced, and left. He came home in the morning to say that his cousin had died in Goto village.

'So when are you coming back?' mother asked him.

'It depends,' he replied calmly. 'Many of our relatives are coming from distant places to attend the funeral and it's difficult to expect an early return.'

He put on his suit and went away whistling. He came back ten days later, wearing different clothes.

'How was it?' asked mother.

'It was a big funeral.'

'What did he die of?'

'A swollen belly. Someone poisoned him. He died in two days. There will be trouble in the family sharing out his property. There will be trouble from the deceased. They did not bury him the right way. They put his head facing east.'

'How could they make such a mistake?'

'They were careless. They only realised the mistake after they had covered his grave up.'

'They are courting trouble.'

He sat at the table eating a mealie.

'How is the weeding going?' he asked.

'We finished with the groundnuts. You took so long to come back.'

'It was a big funeral.'

'Ten days?'

'But I couldn't leave before it was over.'

'If we had to spend the rest of our lives attending to our dead, life would come to a standstill, wouldn't it?'

'I didn't spend a lifetime. I only spent ten days mourning my cousin.'

'The rituals were over in three days.'

'Three days! Maybe you *derukas* can forget your dead after three days. We locals mourn for as long as we feel like. We think funerals are important.'

'No wonder a lot of your people starve half their lifetimes. Never mind what your customs are, or what you claim they are, I have got full evidence that you spent the past week in various places, and not at the funeral.'

'Who told you?'

'Never mind who told me.'

'Why shouldn't I travel about? Am I chained to one place like an animal?'

'No, you are not chained. And you are not an animal. But we all have to observe regulations of work. If my husband had to go away from his work, as you did, without giving good reason, we'd all be starving and there would not be a cent for your wages. My husband also works, you know.'

'But I had a sound reason. A funeral . . .'

'The funeral took three days, Remoni. You spent this past week on an unauthorised holiday. And besides, you had been doing nothing before you left for the funeral.'

'Doing nothing?'

'Yes.'

'I chopped down the thorn trees.'

'If someone asked you to give an account of the work you had done since Christmas you would be ashamed of yourself.'

'I chopped the trees and the firewood.'

'Two trees and one cartload of firewood. Nothing more. And you only worked half days. You worked two hours in the morning and then went off for the rest of the day without telling anyone. Can you deny it?'

'But if I can do a day's work in two hours, there is nothing to stop me spending the rest of the day in whatever way I like.'

'You call chopping down a tree a day's work! My son Jo would do that in an hour.'

'Then why did you not let him do it?'

'You refused to do the weeding, didn't you? You can't refuse the alternative. And you can't work half days. You can't do as you like.'

He put down the mealie he was eating and stared into the fire. I could see the veins sticking out in his neck. There were drops of perspiration on his forehead. Mother looked away from him, out into the night.

'You have a grudge against me, haven't you?' he said eventually.

'What!' exclaimed mother, her eyes darting back to him.

'You heard me,' he replied loudly. 'I said you have a grudge against me.'

'Why on earth should I have a grudge against you?'

'Since I started working here, you have not left me alone for a single day.'

'I must be deaf or you are speaking a different language,' said mother, her nostrils flaring. 'Talking about a grudge! And not having left you alone for a single day! What exactly do you mean, Remoni?'

'Exactly what I say. You have been pushing me about. You have treated me like an ox.'

'You ungrateful boy!' shouted mother, angrily. 'Your ingratitude shocks me! I have treated you like an equal, barely knowing you could harbour such ill feelings towards me. And for no reason! I never knew you would be such a snake in the grass, Remoni.'

'I have reason enough.'

'What reason? Tell me.'

'I don't have to tell you, you know.'

'You have got to tell me. My conscience demands it.'

'You and your husband. You piled lots of work on me. Useless work. Just to keep me working like a machine, to make sure I earned every little cent you paid me.'

'What do you mean by useless work?'

'Do you want me to tell you? What do you call chopping down thorn trees? Why did you not call back the man who cleared the field to complete his work? The trees had been standing in the field for years, waiting for Remoni, I suppose.'

'You refused to do the weeding and we had no option but to give you other work. And the trees had to be chopped down some time or another. And you had refused to weed. *Refused!* Did I say a word against your refusal? Did I complain that you refused to do the weeding? Tell me honestly.'

'But thorn trees . . .'

'I know they hurt. But you know their roots harm the crops. Are you satisfied?'

'I have other reasons,' he said, trying hard not to budge.

'What reasons?'

'You don't respect me.'

'What do you mean?'

'You called me a boy just now.'

'How many times have I called you "boy" before? Think honestly and tell me. I called you boy just now because you were reasoning like a boy. You showed an ingratitude that only boys can show.'

'You are treating me like a boy even now.'

'Because you choose to behave like a boy, Remoni. You want to pick a quarrel with me but you can't find sound excuses. I decided from the first day you came to live here that I could be nice to you and treat you like my own son. I speak from the conscience of my heart. It only hurts me to see you hurling my kindness back into my face.'

'You make yourself out to be a very kind person.'

'What do you want from me, Remoni? I can't stand your insults any more.'

'Nor can I yours.'

'In what way was I unkind to you? Haven't I paid you twice as much as what you would normally be earning? Haven't I lent you money, never to claim it when I realised you were always in debt? Didn't I pay your wife's medical fees when she was in hospital? Didn't my husband give you clothes? Have I ever quarrelled with you before, Remoni?'

He stared into the fire, battling not to let his anger melt.

'You are always praising yourself.'

'You are a fool, Remoni,' shouted mother, losing patience entirely. 'A stupid fool. I wasted my time on you. Had I known what an ungrateful boy you are I would never have taken you on.'

He stared blankly into the fire. He had never imagined she could be so bold. 'I wasted my time too,' he said eventually. 'I should never have come to work for you. I will leave you and see what your little compound will come to.'

'Do you think your leaving will cause an earthquake? That is why I said you are a boy, though you have beard on your face. Were you here to help when I built the huts? Did you till my first field? Did you contribute a cent to buy my cattle? How long have you been working for me? Is it not only three months? Yet you seem to think your going away will unroof my huts, crumble my walls and send the clay back to the claypits, and the poles back to the forest. No, Remoni. Ten men like you would not wreck me.'

I expected him to spring from his chair and strike her. I wondered what would happen then. Jo and I might try to stop him, or even fight him. He was short and small. But he did not rise. He sat staring into the fire, hardly comprehending her attack. She attacked him relentlessly, with a lack of mercy that surprised me. 'You were nothing when you came here, Remoni. And you are still nothing. People like you are born to own nothing of their own.'

'I have my own property,' he bleated lamely, falling for the trap.

'What property? You call that little suitcase property? Have you got a cow, or a goat, or a chicken, or even a rat to call your own?'

'I have got my compound and my wife.'

'Talk about your compound and your wife! Isn't it your wife who built the huts before you married her? Even the soot on the roof of the huts belongs to her, and her alone. And is it not your father-in-law who supports your wife, while you spend your time filling yourself with beer and wasting yourself on the scum of the village girls? I pity your wife. She is a bold and resolute girl. A beautiful girl. Sometimes I am happy you couldn't give her a child.'

'My affairs are none of your concern,' he blurted angrily.

'You are right. Your affairs are none of my concern. I made them my concern to show you what a poor little creature you are. I was soft with you and then I realised I was wasting my patience on you. I replied to your verbal insults accordingly.'

'I stop working for you tonight,' he announced unceremoniously. 'On Monday I am going to town to look for work.'

'I wish you good luck in your quest. I hope you will keep your job if you find one . . .'

'Tomorrow I am coming to get my wages.'

'You are coming to get what?'

'My wages.'

'You got your wages for December.'

'I mean, for the days I worked this month.'

'But you were away on your ten-day leave. You are not getting anything for those days.'

'Why?'

'Because you spent the days on an unauthorised holiday.'

He grinned suddenly, and waved his hands at his ears.

'I will get that money from you. Even if it means going to Hell.'

'In that case you can get your wages from the Devil himself. You can go to the grave of your grandfather to get the strongest medicine he can give you and I shall not part with a cent you don't deserve. After all witchcraft has never worked on innocent people.'

'You will give me my money,' he said, rising. He went out into the dark and moments later we heard him digging behind our sleeping hut.

'What is he doing?'

'Probably digging up the medicine he put behind the hut,' said mother.

'He believed the things of the night were after him,' I explained.

We didn't hear him pack. There was very little to pack. We only heard the squeak of his small suitcase and the click of the gate. And the quiet shuffle of his feet as he left.

17

I stood at the side of the path hesitating. The thin brown dogs eyed me apprehensively. I decided they would not bite me. I proceeded slowly along the path. Behind the huts the smell of urine met my nostrils. A girl stood in front of the hut stamping mealies in a wooden mortar. Her dress kept moving up her thighs as she raised the pestle, shaking her breasts. She only saw me when I was within a few paces of her.

'Good morning,' I said. There were balls of blanket wool on her plaited hair and white smudges on her mouth. I caught the scent of her body as I passed. It was the smell of sleep – of blankets, perspiration and virginity, I decided.

She returned my greeting briefly, her pestle still poised in mid-air. There were peanut shells and dry mealie leaves on the ground. The girl was still observing me when I turned to look back. She pounded away at her mortar uneasily.

I went into the next homestead, already regretting that I had taken a path that went right between the huts. A woman in black came out of a square, decorated mud hut escorting a little boy who had just emerged from his blankets. I recognised her as Mai Mapanga.

'Good morning,' I said, squatting down. It is rude to stand while talking to elders.

'Oh, it's you. Good morning, my son,' she replied. 'I had almost forgotten you. How is your mother, Masiziva?'

'She is fine.'

'Have you finished harvesting your mealies?'

'Not yet. We only arrived last week.'

'You are still at school?' she said, astonished. 'In what grade are you now?'

'I've finished with grades,' I said, smiling.

'Work hard and become a teacher. The fathers in the mission school want teachers.'

She wiped the boy's nose with a cloth. He was a strong stout fellow – her grandson, I thought.

'I am looking for Gandanga's huts,' I said, inviting her to direct me.

'Did your mother send you to collect money from him? He took two dresses for his wife.'

'Yes.'

'How much does he owe your mother?'

'I am not sure.'

'He sold a cow two weeks ago. He should still have some money on him. That's his hut there,' she said, pointing. 'The one with the red door. He should be awake now.'

There were five huts in a rough circle. In the centre a group of

197

men sat round a huge fire, talking. A few cobs sizzled in the red-hot coals. I crouched near the assembly, waiting to be noticed.

'Her little grandson says he saw Jeni in her hut this morning,' a man was saying. 'The boy also says he saw a child's hand in one of her cooking pots.'

'This village is turning into a nasty place,' said another man, turning his cob in the fire.

'Women have to throw away the water and any leftover food at night . . .'

'She walks at night. They say she rides on the backs of men. They caught her at the graves once . . .'

'She didn't have a thread on her skin.'

'She claims she is only a sleep-walker.'

'She is the worm that has corrupted this village.'

'Old Jairos refused to have her sent away . . .'

'She being his sister of course.'

'No headman can really have the power to expel villagers . . .'

'Many people are witches to some degree but witchcraft is her profession.'

'There is also that old lady living on the slope who uses medicine to steal the green from people's crops.'

'And the little men at night who are beating people. No one knows who sends them.'

'They might be just the evil spirits of long dead . . .'

'They are the spirits of our own relatives, raised and enslaved by witches, to torment us. Haven't you seen the stick holes in the fresh graves?'

'And the plastic bags of blood and medicine which seemed to fall from the sky . . .'

'Only the witchfinder can sniff them out and beat the witch-craft out of them.'

'Yes, only Chikanga, the witchfinder.'

'Yes, Chikanga.'

'But even witchfinders can be overcome by the power of some witches . . .'

'And they can be bribed.'

'Not Chikanga! He lived with the maids of the river, eating mud and fish for three years. He sniffed out every hut and he beat the witches till they howled for mercy.'

'At least he frightened them for a while.'

'He burnt all their herbs and potions.'

'But witchfinders demand money.'

'A goat from each man . . .'

'Better to give away a goat than die. Let's call the witchfinder.'

'Yes – Chikanga.'

'Chikanga from the south.'

Gandanga came out of his hut. He was a huge muscular man. I recognised him instantly, although I had never seen him before. He glanced disinterestedly at me and went to join the men by the fire.

'This young man has come to see you, Gandanga,' a man said.

'Which young man?' said Gandanga. He raised his head and this time he saw me. He walked towards me, his hands in his pockets.

'My mother sent me to . . .' I began.

'Collect her money?' he interrupted. 'I don't have it.'

'She . . .'

'I don't have it,' he reiterated firmly. 'I sold a cow last week but I lent the money to someone going on a long journey. I don't expect to be repaid for a long while.'

I knew it was useless to say anything else.

'Tell her I don't have it,' he said with finality, returning to the fire.

I got up and went home.

◆

That night Jo and I sat waiting for our bath water to get hot. We had made a big fire in the centre of the compound clearing. Jo lay on his back, half asleep, while I sat staring into the fire.

It was a dark night. There were no clouds and the stars seemed remote. I looked to the north where the land sloped downwards to the stream and up again on the tree-denuded slopes. In the south I could see the dark crust of Mbumbuzi Forest, in the west the line of trees bordering the fields. That was where I had buried Simba.

The fire threw faint beams on the hut walls. There was silence everywhere, the kind of silence you could actually hear; the low-toned shrill of the night itself.

I stirred the fire restlessly and the logs blazed. The bucket of water cried in the heat.

I took my eyes away from the flames. For a moment the landscape was one exploding blanket of darkness. I looked up at the twinkling stars. The milky way fell away to the south. A star seemed to fall from the sky and plunge into the trees.

The Pendis' gate clicked.

Jairos ploughed his way in the darkness, making his usual hissing noises. He stopped in the middle of the clearing, turned, and came towards the fence. I recognised him because it was only he who moved like that.

'Godi!' he shouted, his voice strangely sane in the night. 'Give me a stick of fire, please. I want to light my cigarette.'

I took a burning stick and went over to the fence. I could see his eyes gleaming. He snatched the stick over the fence and put it to his mouth, as I turned to go back to our fire.

He steadied his hand but the red point of fire shook visibly. He cursed, put the stick down and rolled his cigarette again. He was about to pick the stick up when he stopped, looked to the west and gasped.

I followed his gaze. A man was walking with a paraffin lamp.

The light was very orange and concentrated to a small ball. It seemed to cut right across the tree-trunks, as if they and the dark air were made of one substance. It moved very steadily, from one direction to the next, now fast, now slow. It came down from the fields, cutting through the darkness as if making towards Simba's grave. Somewhere near the fence it went out.

Jairos gasped again, threw the stick down, turned and left. Jo woke up. I put my fingers gingerly into the water.

'Is it hot now?' he asked.

'Obviously,' I replied cuttingly.

He raised his head and saw the light. I followed his eyes. The light was shining again, this time moving steadily into the forest till it seemed to sink into the solid black horizon. I was not afraid as long as I could see it, but after it went out, I peered uneasily through the darkness, searching for it, expecting it to burst into view somewhere without warning.

I saw Jo looking into the darkness too. We did not talk about it. I fumbled for the soap and the towels.

I knew now that the light was not a paraffin lamp.

◆

We did not tell mother about it. We did not even talk about it ourselves. On several nights I stood in the doorway of our hut staring into the fields, searching for the light among the trees. If the moon was shining the light seldom showed. Sometimes for days I saw nothing and sometimes there were two or three lights moving about at random.

Mother never confessed to having seen anything, although I suspected she probably kept her observations to herself, fearing to scare us. But whenever we talked about witchcraft she repeated her unshakeable belief that witchcraft never worked on those who did not believe in it.

'Only those people with charms to keep off spirits will indeed see the spirits. I have never used charms to keep spirits away from my homestead and I have never seen anything unusual. Other people talk about owls on rooftops, unfamiliar footsteps on the sand, strange residue on plates and pots in the morning, things I have yet to see. Ghosts and spirits exist but they do not work at random. They work on people who believe in them.'

I listened to her, wondering if I should let her beliefs reassure me. Perhaps she too had her secret fears. Why should such things hit Midu if they only attacked superstitious people? He was only a boy.

How naive I had been to think there were no ghosts or witches in the village! Perhaps once they had not been there. Perhaps there had been fewer sightings when the village population had been small. It took years for the true personalities of the villagers to emerge.

It did not matter who caused the nocturnal disturbances. Witchcraft did not choose between the locals and the *derukas*. The hard fact was that something was happening in the village. One could not disbelieve everything.

◆

The news that the witchfinder was coming to 'sniff out' the village steadily gained ground. He was well known throughout the country. I wondered if I should take his coming as a consolation.

'I saw him once,' mother explained, 'but it was only for a short time. You would never believe that he is a witchfinder. He is a very affluent man. He wears expensive suits, drives his own Combi and employs several girls to help him. People say he lived with the mermaids under the great river. They taught him everything from rainmaking to witchfinding.'

Headman Simon went round the village collecting contributions to hire Chikanga to clean the village.

'Are children supposed to come too?' mother asked.

'Only the older children,' said Simon. That included me and excluded Jo.

There was a varied response to Simon's call for contributions.

'Chikanga is charging too much.'

'Chikanga could be bribed.'

'Chikanga will create hatred between families.'

But Chikanga was coming.

18

The chief's compound was a big one, as polygamists' compounds usually are. There were twelve huts and twelve granaries for his twelve wives. By mid-morning, when we arrived, tired from the twelve-mile walk in the heat, the place was already swarming with people. Men and women sat together, the former on stools, the latter on mats. There was a buzz of chatter that increased in volume with the passage of time and the growing anticipation of Chikanga's arrival.

At around noon a sudden hush descended on the gathering. All heads turned to the road as a battered Combi squeaked to a halt. A wiry brown man in a black suit jumped energetically out of the driver's cabin and walked towards the crowd. Six young girls climbed out of the back of the van and followed him.

Among the gathering, faces grinned and others wilted. People sprang up to see more clearly; they were shouted down. A woman ululated. Slowly the wavering crowd gathered itself into one movement, a loud clapping of hands.

Chikanga picked his way through the seated people like a master-farmer walking through a crop of mealies. Turning his snake-like head from side to side, he assessed the assembly like a farmer making a preliminary survey of his crops and assessing the weeds.

The crowd edged outwards to open up a space for him at the centre. He sat like a king with his pretty teenage girls flanking him. He looked very ordinary – and sly. The only hints of his profession were the inches of red and black bangles on his wrists and his long necklace, which was brown and shiny.

He sat on his high stool arranging his gourds and calabashes. He took off his shirt, rubbed his chest with oil; took off his shoes, rolled his trousers to the knees and oiled his legs. His girls rubbed oil on their faces and arms. When they had finished they rose and, making their way through the seated crowd, disappeared into a clump of trees, emerging later with thick green sticks. The crowd gasped and whistled, guessing their purpose.

'You brought building poles, not whips, girls,' said a woman.

'Your poles will kill people, not discipline them,' added a man, and the crowd laughed.

'Witches!' burst out Chikanga, gesticulating violently as he jumped from his stool, instantly stilling the crowds. 'Sorcerers! Magicians! Eaters of human flesh! Today we will beat your witchcraft out of you. We will burn your herbs and poisons but not before we have made you eat some of them. We will beat every inch of your skin till the whips are in shreds. Today we will teach you to live without the smell of human blood. We will teach you to shun your craft. Girls, my tools.'

The girls took his tools out of his suitcase – among them a huge looking-glass, a bottle of water and a calabash with a black cork. The crowd started murmuring again.

'Do I hear voices?' said Chikanga authoritatively, scanning the people around him. 'Do I hear murmurings of fear? You don't have to display your fear now.'

The crowd shut up. Faces gazed fearfully at him, lips half open with frozen words.

'This is the mirror through which I will observe people's characters,' he explained, raising his instruments. 'This is my water. Each one of you will touch the bottle. Whoever touches my bottle and turns this water red is a deadly killer, an eater of human flesh. Whoever turns the water brown or grey is a mild offender, but a dangerous person all the same. Whoever touches the bottle and leaves my water as it is, is as innocent as a baby. Before I start, let me make it clear to those of you with black hearts that any attempts to injure me or my girls will only harm the offenders themselves. I shall sniff out all the twists of poison, all the roots hidden even in the remotest corners of the village. The offenders themselves will be beaten thoroughly before they are sent to the witches' hut for cleansing. Anyone who tries to use medicines again will die of a strange sickness. The chief has given me the names of all the villagers so no one can escape. I shall begin.'

The first woman to be called was from Goto village. She rose slowly and stood beside Chikanga.

'Touch my water,' he told her. She put her finger on the bottle. 'Touch it with all your fingers,' shouted Chikanga. 'What is it that you have under your fingernails that makes them shun the bottle?' The woman put all her fingers on the bottle. I could see her hand shaking. Her eyes were glued to the bottle.

'I can see into your character,' said Chikanga, looking into his mirror. 'You are not an evil person. You are not a witch and you have never tasted human flesh. You don't walk at night and you don't spin stickholes in fresh graves. You are not evil. But your spirit is weak before the forces of evil.'

The woman trembled. The water had not changed its colour.

'Your spirit is weak. Strengthen it. My calabash tells me you don't have a child. Is that true or not? Answer me.'

'It is true, my king. I have no child,' replied the woman, trembling.

'You don't have a child because you refused to inherit the witchcraft of your dead grandmother. You disappointed her. She punished you by shutting your womb for ever. For years now you have been visiting village doctors to ask why you have no child. Is that true or not?'

'It is true, my lord.'

'You were unwise to refuse to bring home your grandmother from the grave. But you were wise to refuse her witchcraft. Your wisdom is greater than your folly.' He raised the bottle up to the sun and looked through it. 'You did not change the colour of my water. I dismiss you.'

There was a split second of silence before the crowds burst into ululation and congratulatory grunts. The woman's face broke into a disbelieving smile. She cupped her hands and ululated, sketching a short, impromptu dance with her legs. The crowd laughed at her joy.

The next person was a young man, newly married. He put his fingers on the bottle before Chikanga told him to do so.

'What!' exclaimed Chikanga, flaring his nostrils. 'Have I told you to touch my water yet? You want to elude me with speed. My mirror tells me you steal other people's crops by magic. You are young, yet you are lazy. You never make use of the first rains. You prefer to transfer the greenness of other people's crops to your own poor ones. Fortunately your herbs have never worked. But had you found the effective herbs you would have ruined your neighbours. You are guilty of the will to swindle your neighbours by magic. Look! You changed the colour of my water.'

There were gasps of surprise when Chikanga raised his bottle. We did not have to strain our eyes to see the muddy grey tint in the water.

'Grey water. Where do you keep your herbs?'

'I know no herbs,' replied the young man.

'You lie too. You lie to Chikanga. You keep your herb in your sleeping hut, don't you? Brown powder in a piece of cloth. Your wife thinks it's the herb for pneumonia. Have I lied?'

The young man lowered his eyes and crushed his knuckles uneasily. He mumbled something.

'Tell the gathering where you keep your herbs. Loudly,' said Chikanga.

'In my sleeping hut,' shouted the young man, only looking up long enough to say so.

'And you spray the powder over your neighbours' green fields?'

'Yes.'

There was a loud clicking of angry tongues.

'When do you work?' pursued Chikanga.

'At night,' replied the young man, shamelessly.

'You are a lazy fool. Go home and eat every grain of your herb. Every grain, I say. It's your fault if it cuts your bowels. And tell the crowd you will never do it again.'

'I will never do it again,' shouted the young man, not daring to look up. He took a step backwards as if he wanted to return to his place in the crowd.

'Ah! Ah!' shouted Chikanga. 'Where are you going? Who said it's over? Have I dismissed you? You haven't received your punishment yet. Teach him, my girls.'

The pretty young girls rose from the mats with their green sticks. They surrounded the young man. He inched backwards uneasily, his fingers twitching at his side, face torn between a grin and a grimace. The girls thrashed him quickly. I could hear the crunching sound of thick green sticks against his bones. They beat him till he screamed like a child, and left him moaning on the dust.

'Up!' commanded Chikanga.

He scrambled unsteadily to his feet, fingering his badly bruised face.

'To the hut of the guilty,' Chikanga beckoned.

The young man limped away painfully. No one helped him. Chikanga put fresh water in his bottle.

Two other people from Goto village were found guilty and were beaten and sent to the hut of the guilty.

Mother came fifth in our village.

'My mirror tells me many things about you,' Chikanga told her. I looked at my mother. My mind ran unconsciously to her folk-story of the belated hunter with the black and white dogs. For the first time in my life I felt really anxious for her.

'You are an unusual woman,' Chikanga told her. 'Have you ever wondered why the little men never hit any of your children? They came very close to your compound on several occasions. Once they even beat a next-door boy, did they not? They chased a man who worked for you right up to your gates. Have you ever wondered why none of your children were bitten by snakes, or poisoned by mushrooms, or died of strange diseases? I see a deadly snake that came to your homestead years ago. An ugly black snake with a mane and scales. It smells. The snake was meant to bite one of your children. I also see two cursed birds that lodged in a tree near your fence. Did the rain-maker not send for them and order them to be destroyed? You were lucky. Had the matter been pursued, you would have been accused of stopping the rain from falling because the birds lodged next to your compound. You could have been sent away from the village. But you were not banished. You lived among enemies, some of whom have been working, since you planted the first pole of your hut, to bring harm to you. Yet you are safe. You have reaped fair crops in lean years. You even sell maize to your fellow villagers. Do you believe it's your wisdom, which has kept you safe and well off? Answer me.'

'No,' replied mother.

'Then what is it? Do you own little men to weed your fields and ward off strangers at night?'

'No.'

'Do you use herbs to steal other people's crops?'

'No.'

'Then what do you use?'

'Nothing.'

'Yes. You use nothing. There is not a twist of herbs in your huts, no nails in your trees to keep the lightning away, not even a single root to protect your homestead. Perhaps you do not know it but the spirit of your father protects you. Tell me. What was your father's death wish? Did he not ask you to do something for him?'

'He asked me to remove a speck in his eye.'

'You did not find that speck. But that was an indication of the favour he bore for you. Never fool yourself that your own wisdom has kept you safe. No one is safe from witchcraft and medicine, even the innocent. You may go to church but you must never forsake your deceased father. Never, never, ever. I don't have to hold my bottle of water up to see if you have changed its colour. My mirror alone has spoken for you. I congratulate you and dismiss you.'

She smiled, turned and went back to her place. There was loud ululation for her. I stood up and waved my fists in the air.

Munyu came next and was beaten and sent away for plotting to cripple Madoo by magic. Madoo himself narrowly escaped the whips but was very sharply rebuked for being a bad neighbour and a loose-tongued brawler. Charamba and his wife were both thrashed and sent away for first-rate witchcraft. Both of them admitted to having mutually poisoned to death their neighbour's son.

Makepesi came after them. He took off his cap and put it under his arm. Chikanga uttered a long whistle and shook his head reflectively over his mirror.

'Who taught you to love the smell of human blood, my son?' he asked him. 'You still have your mother's milk on your nose, yet you are the son of the Devil himself. Have you ever spent a single full night in your sleeping hut? I doubt. Even the owls of the night know you. You are the living cousin of the ghosts whose lights shine in the night and blind the eyes of the innocent. How many stickholes have you spun in the graves? How much hair have you cut from the heads of people while they slept? Tell me, son, where do you keep the horn of your witchcraft?'

Makepesi stared at the ground, his fist on his chin.

'You cut the hair from the head of your own sister's son, to use for your potions. What did you do to Jairos? Did you set a trap for him on the path or did you send your little men to beat him? Did you poison his mug of beer? Tell us what you did to Jairos.'

'He gave my field to a newcomer,' said Makepesi, momentarily raising his head.

'And you thought that was enough reason to turn him insane? You turned him into an animal. Have you ever listened to his hiss and his mutterings? Why did you not kill him, instead of turning him into an animal?'

Makepesi did not waver. He clasped his cap, waiting for the girls to beat him. The girls cut him down with their sticks. He did not utter a sound. He lay still on the ground, taking their blows without any protest, like someone who knew well why he was being punished.

Mai Mapanga came towards sunset, after dozens of people

had been sent to the hut to bath in Chikanga's water. She still wore a black mourning dress. She approached Chikanga very slowly, her eyes encircling him desperately. Chikanga's mirror fell from his hand. A bright beam of sunlight shot from it like an exploding bullet. There was dead silence and the black figure of Mai Mapanga stood trembling, staring at the mirror in the dust.

'Her evil overpowers my mirror,' said Chikanga, stooping to pick the mirror up. 'Even I am afraid of your powers. If you touch my water you will turn it to blood. Put your fingers on my bottle.'

'I will not,' whispered Mai Mapanga. Those who heard her laughed.

'Why will you not touch my bottle? You very well know that you will turn the water into blood.'

'No, I will not.'

'Then touch my bottle like everybody else.'

'I won't be made a fool in front of everyone,' she said boldly, loudly.

'You are too evil to be regarded as a mere fool. Touch my bottle.'

He took her fingers and touched the bottle with them. She tried to pull away but the water had already turned red. An opaque, flowing mass of red. Everyone saw it. Mai Mapanga threw her head back and cried. Chikanga dropped her hand and she stumbled backwards. She put her face in her palms, covering her eyes and cried.

'You ate human flesh.'

'I didn't know it was human flesh,' she protested in a hoarse, sobbing voice. 'One side of it was goat's meat and the other was a meat I didn't know.'

'Then why did you eat the flesh?'

'I didn't know.'

'You knew. It was the flesh of your own sister's son. He didn't have his tongue when they buried him. You had eaten it.'

'No.'

'You woke up in the night to dig him up. You ate his heart and his liver.'

'No, I didn't.'

'Yes, you did. Your hunger for human flesh did not subside. You killed your husband too. You poisoned him. You fed your little men on human flesh and they grew fat on it. As long as you kept them fed there was no trouble. But there were never enough corpses, and then the trouble started. They refused to do your errands and threatened to eat you. You had to act fast. So you poisoned your husband. He died after only two days. When he died you wanted to eat his flesh too. But your little men beat you to his corpse. You found only bare bones when you dug him up . . .'

'He died a natural death . . .'

'A natural death you call it? With his stomach swollen like that. After only two days. The stinging hunger drove you to despair. You did worse things. You chose poor Jeni, that pretty, hard-working daughter of your neighbour. Her flesh was young and soft. You drove worms into her breasts; it did not take her long to die. But they let her body decompose before they buried it. For days they lived with the stench of her body. For three days after they buried her, they guarded her grave. They starved you. Your little men pressed you for meat but you could not give them anything. You had failed.'

She cried.

'I pity you,' pursued Chikanga. 'I pity you very much. Your own little men you raised from the graves are driving you insane, and threatening to kill your grandson. You taught them to eat human flesh. They loved it, but now you can't supply them with flesh any more. I pity you because you are your little men's next victim. They will tear you like cats tearing at a bird and people won't even find your skull. Your bones will be scattered all over the forest . . .'

'No!' cried Mai Mapanga, her eyes wild with fear.

'Where do you keep your little men, Mai Mapanga?' he asked softly. 'Bring them out and we will thrash them like we thrash corn. Where do you keep them? In your grain hut? In your sleeping hut?'

She cried and people did not laugh. They clicked their tongues softly and shook their heads.

'Tell us, Mai Mapanga,' said Chikanga.

'In a sack in my grain hut,' she sobbed, and then cried even more loudly, wringing her hands.

'We will destroy them, Mai Mapanga. I am glad you now realise that witchcraft does not pay. Witchcraft is the cub that grows up to tear the limbs of his master. I will help you to destroy them forever.'

She screamed when she saw the girls coming for her with the green sticks. She darted this way and that with her arms spread out like a bat. They closed on her, cutting her down mercilessly, tearing her black dress to expose her withered black breasts. She howled like a dog and yet fell down lightly like a bat. People thought she was dead.

'People like her don't die,' said Chikanga. 'She has just fainted. Take her away.'

The girls took her by the limbs and carried her to the hut of the witches. Her eyes were open and solid as brown marble. There was white froth on her lips.

19

Six months after Chikanga had passed his judgment on the village and gathered and burnt all the herbs, potions and sacks in a bonfire, the rains came.

People came out to till their fields again. They bought fertiliser and seed from the Grain Marketing Board and turned the crisp green weeds into the brown earth.

The sky seemed to promise the village a fresh start, but with the rains came lightning, and several trees were struck. And with the rain came overcast days and mouldy earth.

Jairos was caught many times on the paths by the storm, and drenched. In his terrible quest, he never stayed indoors long enough to dry his clothes at the fire. Even at night we could hear his sandals swooshing on the wet sand. His weather-beaten body could not take it any more. Skin started peeling off his face and legs, and he grew surprisingly silent, so that when he came to our hut he sat quietly at the fire, not even asking for food. There was a strange new sobriety in his eyes.

Two weeks before Christmas he fell violently ill. They took him to the hospital, but the doctors were baffled. They knew that the rain had sparked off the illness, but what it was, they never understood. His body had been breaking down over the years, was all they could say. After only a week in hospital he died, and there was no one to bring him home. For a week he lay in the mortuary. Eventually an ambulance brought his body home.

There was loud weeping in the village. I could hear Lulu's voice weeping above that of her aunt, Mai Mapanga. 'The *derukas* have killed our father. He died giving them land. Now they can have his body as well.'

Makepesi cried with the others. 'You have come, Jairos. I was expecting you.'

They buried him in the pouring rain on the day before Christmas. He had delayed the Christmas preparations. They did not even have a coffin for him. They just wrapped his body, small and bony as an unfeathered chick, in a blanket and laid him down to rest.

When they put him in the grave Lulu rolled on the wet sand. Her mother and Mai Mapanga pulled her up and struggled with her. She wore a black dress, and her head was shaven in sorrow. There were deep shadows beneath her eyes but her face had a haunting beauty that frightened me. As they led her away, I thought of the day when I had made Jairos a cup of cold tea and forked a bun out of the pan and told him I had no shilling for him to give at the funeral. With a shudder I realised that all along Lulu had been deeply caught up in this web of sorrow.

As they shovelled the glistening wet sand over him, the rain intensified. Everywhere the trees and the grass dripped. A drop of water snaked down my back and I tried to curl my sandalled toes away from the wet earth. One more shovel of sand, and Jairos was gone. He had come and gone like Cheru and Boyce and Remoni and Lulu. No one, nothing, came and stayed. Each had promised a fresh start but the many callings of life had torn them away. All that remained were memories, and now anxiety and fear.

The gathering had just begun to disperse when people stood half frozen in their steps, staring at the newly erected mound of the grave. A strange silence had descended on them. I edged backwards. Men and women hunched their shoulders against the rain, lips open, pink tongues softly sucking in droplets of rain.

There was something on the mound, a plastic bag with something red in it that no one dared to touch or describe. One by one they turned to go home to prepare for Christmas.

And I too turned and went home in the rain.

Glossary

biltong   salted dried meat, originally a way of preserving and storing meat, now eaten as a delicacy

calabash   a gourd or similar large fruit that can be used as a container for liquid

choumoulier   leafy green vegetable similar to a cabbage

deruka   newcomer

groundnuts   peanuts

Kisimisi   Christmas

kraal   pen for cattle

Iobola   bridewealth, dowry

madora   caterpillar of the emperor moth

maheu   a thick, nutritious, non-alcoholic drink prepared from cooked mealie meal

Mai   Mother; term of respect for an older woman; it is followed by the name of her oldest child

mazhanje   wild loquat

Mazoe   brand name for concentrated orange juice which is drunk diluted with water

mealies   maize or maize cobs

mhunga   sorghum (cereal similar to maize)

muhacha   mobola plum tree; fruit of this tree

mumera   indigenous grain also known as *rapoko*

n'anga   herbalist, traditional healer

nhedzi   edible mushroom

nhengeni   sour plum

nyovi   wild vegetable, the leaves of which are eaten

sadza   stiff porridge made of maize meal, eaten with vegetable
   relish or meat stew
stoep   small unenclosed verandah
tsetse flies   large flies that feed on cattle and cause sleeping
   sickness in humans
veld   open, thinly forested, unfarmed land
vlei   wetlands, marshy ground